$\mathcal{A}$ngels
in the
Architecture

Mary-Rose MacColl has worked as a corporate writer, university administrator, cadet journalist, nursing assistant, photocopier operator and supervisor in a boarding school. Her first novel, *No Safe Place*, was runner-up in the *Australian* Vogel Literary Award and was published in 1996. *Angels in the Architecture* is her second novel.

Angels

in the

Architecture

MARY-ROSE MacCOLL

To dear Kelley

with warmest wishes.

come, visit us some time

Mary-Rose MacColl

October 1999

ALLEN & UNWIN

AUTHOR'S NOTE

There is no Archangels University or Archangels School that I know of. I made them up. There is a Catholic girls' school in a place like the place I've imagined Archangels in Brisbane, it does have a wall and I did go there for a while. But all the characters and buildings in this book are imagined. On history, I made up some events to suit my narrative, but I attempted to retain a sense of Brisbane and the local Catholic presence as they've been narrated by history books.

Queensland

First published in 1999 by
Allen & Unwin
9 Atchison Street, St Leonards NSW 1590 Australia
Phone: (61 2) 8425 0100
Fax: (61 2) 9906 2218
E-mail: frontdesk@allen-unwin.com.au
Web: http://www.allen-unwin.com.au

National Library of Australia
Cataloguing-in-Publication entry:

MacColl, Mary-Rose, 1961– .
  Angel in the architecture.

  ISBN 1 86508 061 6.

  I. Title.

A823.3

Set in 10.5/12 pt Goudy by DOCUPRO, Sydney
Printed and bound by Australian Print Group, Maryborough, Victoria

10 9 8 7 6 5 4 3 2 1

ACKNOWLEDGEMENTS

It takes many hands to fashion a book and I thank all those who've touched this one. To the many people who supported me in my new career including Lenore Cooper, Cherrell Hirst, Wayne McLeod, Cathy Sinclair and Theanne Walters. To Carol Davidson, Nick Earls, Rebecca Lamoin, Catherine Sheedy and Adam Shoemaker for sound advice. To Arts Queensland for money that bought time to write. To the experts, with the caveat that the mistakes are all mine—on trees one-time forester Peter Forster, on buildings Queensland Department of Environment and Heritage Officer Fiona Gardiner, on bones UQ Forensic Osteologist Walter Wood, on crimes Public Prosecutor Paul Rutelage and lawyer Eddie Scuderi. To Pat Cunningham from St Stephens Cathedral for a tour of works and to All Hallows' Principal Sister Anne O'Farrell for some space in which to work. To the thoughtful readers of many drafts: Jo Fleming, Sasha Marin and Belinda Ogden. And to the Allen & Unwin team, especially Annette Barlow and the mighty Sophie Cunningham, who believed this book would be good.

For David, who made things possible

CHAPTER ONE

Harriet Darling ran to the trellis at the top of the drive, dropped her bags, pushed back her sunglasses, and peered down the terraces towards Old Archangels. At first, it looked as if the chapel was just as she'd left it on Friday. Its twin bell towers still led her eye to the tower on Archangels House and from there to the peaks of the Story Bridge. Beyond the bridge, the gold cliffs of the far bank gave way to the grand blue sky. Harriet turned to the alabaster Virgin who watched the scene through the arch of the trellis, and smiled.

The young architect closed her eyes. Perhaps she'd walk down the hill and nothing would have changed. After the interview, she'd stopped here, smelled the burned-coffee hops of the nearby brewery and felt the warm sun on her scalp and hands. They were an odd pair, a fairytale villa with a whimsical timber belvedere beside an austere gothic church with bristling twin turrets. But they'd sat together on the grass for over a century. They'd entertained viceroys and convicts and watched the Story Bridge stretch across the water for the first time. They shouldn't be disturbed, her preliminary report told the university on the Friday just gone.

It was the firm's first Brisbane job. Archangels University wanted to develop the chapel and house at the river end of their campus. They'd invited tenders from heritage architects who could guide them through the mire of government and church regulation. Harriet couldn't say why she'd tendered. She had no love of her own Catholic heritage, and Brisbane was a long way from Corsair Maple's Melbourne base. Her partners were against it from the start. Richard Corsair called anyone from Queensland a white-shoe developer and the university owners were developers made dangerous by intelligence. After the interview, Harriet was inclined to agree with him. The deputy vice-chancellor, Professor Max Palethorpe, spoke sharply about the need for her to be flexible in a way that suggested he wouldn't be. When Harriet told the panel that some buildings were too important to develop, he closed his eyes and shook his head slowly. Harriet was amazed when the chair, a woman from the University Board, called her back into the room after they'd deliberated to make an offer. She was even more surprised she didn't refuse straightaway. She said she'd get back to them. On her way out, she wandered down the hill for a closer look.

Inside the chapel, she was struck first by the quiet— ferries, trucks and hammering construction sashayed to silence with the inner door—and then by the light. The bright sun bled through clerestory stained-glass windows and onto shifting particles in air, creating soft streamers that crossed the church and spilled onto the marble floor. Harriet reached up and touched one of these streamers of light; it coloured her hand. In the apse, a large window framed an altar cross and looked to a Moreton Bay fig and the green river. Originally of stained glass and traceried stone, the window had long ago been replaced with clear glass and timber. Harriet knew the replacement was less than authentic, but it gave the whole chapel an ethereal glow. She preferred it, although she'd never have admitted as much to some of her more fundamentalist colleagues.

It was a straightforward cruciform design, but surprisingly balanced and elegant given the blockishness of the building's exterior. Harriet walked the giltframed stations of the cross that lined the nave. They told a happy crucifixion story, of a stylised Jesus who strolled up Calgary with a matchstick crossbar. Other icons were similarly naïve—a statue of Joseph, little Christ the King, a brass stand of long-finished offering candles, and to the right of the altar the red sanctuary lamp that once burned strong and constant. Behind the lamp was the tabernacle with a chalice mosaic on its doors. The lamp was extinguished and the tabernacle emptied when the Church moved out.

Harriet sat with her back against the cool marble altar for over an hour and watched the river slide beneath the shifting leaves of the fig. She had a *déjà-vu*-like feeling she couldn't quite shake, vaguely alarming and reassuring at the same time. It was almost as if the place—the chapel and altar, the view of the fig and water—had been waiting for her to finish a picture. If she'd kept her schoolgirl faith, she might have said it was a sacred place and she was moved by some holy spirit to act against advice and her own better judgement, because she took the job and left Archangels feeling ebullient. She was going to help Max Palethorpe learn about heritage and what it meant. That couldn't be too hard. She was going to save the chapel and house. She was sure nothing could go wrong.

This morning just a month later, she smelled woodsmoke along with the hops on the river breeze, from burned mahogany and maple she knew they could never replace. She heard the gaggle of emergency workers and their slamming cars and trucks. And when she opened her eyes, she saw the fat orange jackets of fire workers matching the orange plastic fencing like an open wound around the chapel site. Men scaled the towers in harnesses and crawled the perimeter of the slate roof where glass from burst louvres glittered. She looked closely at the white walls of the rest of the building, now greyed with soot, dark around the empty nave windows.

Harriet slumped onto the green garden chair under the arch of the trellis and took her time changing into steel-toes and hardhat. She'd rushed from Melbourne on the first flight when Neal French called. Not that there was much she could do, but she had to see for herself. The fire was so hot it had melted the gold altar cross, Neal had told her. Harriet might have said the cross was bronze, but Neal was the firm's researcher, always better on detail. He'd pulled her out of a deep sleep and, at first, she'd thought her father must be dead. He'd made no sense. 'An act of God HD,' he'd screamed down the line. Her muscles had frozen round the news as if she'd been thrown into icy water, and it had taken time to start breathing again. But after he'd hung up and she'd woken properly and booked a flight and made coffee, she decided that while an act had taken place in the chapel that night, it didn't necessarily have anything to do with God.

Harriet was joined by a butcher bird that ruffled its grubby plumage and waddled its tail to settle itself on the other end of the garden chair. The bird was nothing much to look at, lacking the slick definition of a magpie or the shock of azure of a kookaburra. But it made a long skewed shadow in the morning sun like a winged angel with outstretched arms. And when it started singing, it sang high and sweet. Harriet looked at the messy bird stretching itself with its song, and was surprised to find tears coming. She narrowed her eyes and sucked in air to stop them.

The butcher bird flew up to the bougainvillea lining the trellis where it was joined by a mate. The first bird let out a long joyous call. The second tilted its head but otherwise didn't respond. Harriet took a large handkerchief from her pocket, blew her nose and stood up to walk down the hill to Old Archangels.

CHAPTER TWO

Neal was waiting outside the chapel. 'We're clear and the team's in,' he said. 'The engineers we used last week, like you said. They've started in the nave but Tim reckons it will take days to sort through. I stopped them blasting. Here's a muffin.' He looked at her face carefully.

The paper bag was warm. 'What blasting?'

'A demolition team, last night. They say the site's a safety risk. I found something.'

Harriet took a large bite. 'This is good, red bits. On whose authority?'

'It's raspberry. Kevin McAnelly. I stopped them this morning. They hadn't started, and we're stable as far as we can tell. They're over there, family business I'd say.' Three men lounged under the fig tree. 'They want to finish the job.'

'I want the engineer's report on structural damage today. Get a photographer to cover all this, including them. We need a record in case they try again. Safety risk?' She looked up towards the roof of the church. 'Upon this rock. My neck's killing me. What's it like inside?'

'Probably looks worse than it is, but it's not pretty. Most of the outer structure survived. Some areas you'd hardly know. I've been up all night.' Neal took off his glasses and wiped his eyes. 'I found something.'

'Later. We'll talk, Neal. I wish I'd been here, too.' She handed back his brief and the empty muffin bag. 'How'd you know I missed breakfast?' He smiled and said she always missed breakfast.

Two of the men rose slowly when they saw Harriet approaching. The third stayed lying on his side, pulling at the grass. They were dressed in stained flannel shirts over sweaty shearers' singlets and black shorts that concertinaed at the front from squatting.

'You can go,' she said, looking at each of them in turn. 'You're finished.'

'Yeah, and who're you?' The man on the grass looked up lazily.

'I'm the architect.'

'And I'm dynamite.' He laughed asthmatically, and was joined by his two brothers. 'Wen't bin paid.'

'What?'

'We're done some digging. Had a deal. Wen't bin paid.'

'That's not my problem. I don't want you in there again. This is a precious building. It's Brisbane's oldest Catholic church. Don't you know what that means? Out of here.' The man stood up. Harriet faced him, gripping the first two fingers of her left hand tightly in her right fist.

'Listen, girlie, you din't put us on, you don't put us off.' He poked a finger at her. She walked closer to him. He wasn't tall but Harriet was so tiny she had to look up a long way to meet the average eye, always a disadvantage when she wanted command. She was wearing a white business shirt over light khaki dungarees with a wide belt. In her big brown boots and hardhat she was like a miniature explorer whose shock of red curly hair hadn't been cut during the trek. The blaster smelled of sweat.

'Fine, you can stay here all day if you like. I'm bringing in the press. They might want to talk to you, put your face on TV. That's what I'd do. I know you, you hear? I know you. You're the fellows who destroyed the Odeon Theatre in the middle of the night. You got children? They'll never see the Odeon because of you.'

'We just take the job. None of our business why or what.'

'For godsake.' Harriet turned to walk away.

'We were told to knock it down,' he called after her. 'It's not safe.'

'You'll be paid whatever was agreed. Just get off the site.'

He turned to his brothers. 'Told ya we'd get paid.'

Harriet was still shaking when she strode through what was left of the front door of the chapel, and it took a moment for her mind to register what her eyes were telling her. She let out a gasp that made the workers around her stare. It was the light. The light was wrong. She walked slowly up the aisle like a bride, looking around with a dumb grin, gripping two fingers of her left hand with her right.

Most of the high stained-glass windows had cracked or burst, and light flooded the nave. Water dripped softly from the walls and ceilings onto the delicately patterned marble floor, which was now a mess of grubby foam and what was left of the pews. Halfway up the aisle, Harriet was met by the fire investigation officer, who said something she didn't hear. The loss. Most of the rich dark wood of the ceiling under the choir was gone, although the choir itself, a mezzanine at the back of the chapel, looked stable. The high vaulted ceiling along the rest of the nave had survived, too. The altar was intact and the window behind still led the eye to the old fig. The stations of the cross were destroyed, as were most of the icons. Neal was right about the cross. Bronze or gold, the blaze had melted it, and Jesus was nothing but a shiny

8

teardrop on the altar. What statues were left were black—
Joseph, John the Baptist, Christ the King, even the Virgin
Mary. Harriet leaned heavily on the altar. Neal was beside
her. 'It's not as bad as it looks. We've still got the structure.
And it's uncovered something.'

'Those bastards, Neal. We should have known they'd do
something like this.'

'We don't know if anyone did anything yet. Maybe it was
an accident.'

She glared. 'They never wanted us here. They took us on
to give themselves credibility, and as soon as we said no
development, they did this. Richard was right. What do they
say caused it?'

'Electrical. The security system.'

'Not Kevin McAnelly?'

He nodded. 'They have a sensor system, like the Melbourne office, uses a bit of power. Why on earth would you
secure a church? Anyway, it blew up. I've asked our chap to
look over it. He's waiting for a sparky. By the way, Kevin tried
to lock me out on Saturday, after they got our report. He told
me we weren't authorised.'

'Authorised. Who does he think he is? This is a church,
for godsake. I could wring his bloody neck.' She bit her
bottom lip. 'It's nearly gutted.'

'You okay?'

Harriet realised she was sitting on the blackened floor and
Neal, whose solid frame didn't fold easily, was on his haunches
to talk to her. She made herself look at Neal's spectacles
instead of the chapel, and at the kindly grey eyes behind the
frameless lenses. She was about to compliment him on the
glasses when she realised this wouldn't return his confidence
in her. 'You're right. I need to get a grip, don't I? Take control
of the situation, that's what Martin would do. Martin would
say we have the advantage of time and right on our side.
Don't we, Neal?' Neal was nodding but she had an impression

he was humouring her. He couldn't stand Martin and usually took every opportunity to say so.

'I know I don't sound quite all here. It's been a shock.' She blew her nose noisily and took several deep breaths, which made her realise she hadn't been breathing for quite some time. 'Right now, we need some action.' She focused on the collar of Neal's checked shirt. 'You let head office know what's happened. Tell Richard I'll call him later.' She was thinking as she spoke. 'I want to meet with the National Trust and the Heritage Council.' As the words came, she started to feel them. 'If they want to play dirty, we can play dirty.' Neal started to interrupt. 'I don't care, Neal. If they're willing to destroy this building rather than look after it properly, they should be exposed for what they are, and bugger the consultancy. We don't need their money.' She chanced a ginger look back around the nave. I can do this, she thought. 'Yes, national support. And press, let's get on to the press. We'll fix these bastards. We need a storm, and fast, Neal, before they get a chance to start blasting.' She walked towards the door.

'Harriet!' Neal called sharply. She turned around. Then, more quietly, 'I'm trying to tell you. I found a chamber under the sacristy.'

'We know there's a burial crypt, Neal. It's in the report you helped write.' Harriet was thinking about the press, maybe television, the church would look good on television.

'No, that's on the other side. I'm talking about the sacristy side. This is different, Harriet, it's a trapdoor. It's really something.'

'Show me.' Harriet had got to know the Archangels Chapel like the house in which she'd grown up. There wasn't an inch she hadn't crawled into, stared at, assessed, categorised or valued. If there was a trapdoor, it was a well-kept secret.

But Neal's arms were crossed, which usually meant he was right. 'Blessed is he who has not seen and yet believes.' A non-Catholic leaning into atheism, Neal had taken to quoting

10

scripture since they'd started at Archangels. When Harriet asked him, he said he found the Bible soothing. 'You don't have to believe in the next life to want one,' he'd said.

He led her to the small sacristy which formed the western arm of the transept. Originally, this was the whole chapel, designed by Carlo Canali and constructed in 1850 as Brisbane's first Catholic cathedral. Canali was invited to design a larger church on the site forty years later, but he couldn't bear to lose his original building, so he incorporated it in the new building. According to early drawings and Harriet's research, the burial crypt was under the boarders' chapel, which was on the other side of the transept. Neal cleared a pile of debris, which before the fire had been a cedar wardrobe for the priest's vestments, to reveal a metal trapdoor with a round rusted iron handle. He smiled like a proud father. He was right. This trapdoor was in the wrong place to lead to the burial crypt. 'Oh ye of little faith.'

'You been down there?' The colour in Harriet's face was returning.

'All I did was camouflage it and wait for you.'

'Why didn't you tell me about this when I arrived?'

'I tried, HD, but you were otherwise occupied. Your bum's black by the way.'

'Got a torch?' Harriet did her best to dust the two round patches of soot from her dungarees.

'A good scout.' Neal produced a penknife torch and checked that no one was watching before he pulled the trapdoor up easily. 'That's funny, I'd have thought it would have rusted tight.'

'You call this a torch?' Harriet peered into the hole, making out rough stairs down a level. She looked back to Neal. 'What are we waiting for?' She stumbled down the uneven steps.

At the bottom, they came to a short passageway. Harriet smelled oysters, more likely mangroves, and something else, sharp and acrid, that reminded her of lemons. 'It's a place for the little people.' Neal was only five nine but had to bend to fit the space through which Harriet moved comfortably. She noticed his voice had taken on an echo, suggesting they'd moved from the first tunnel to a larger chamber. The floor was tiled but earth had leeched through. The chapel above them settled and let out a cracking sound on their ceiling. 'I'm not sure this is stable.' He pushed at the wall. 'What do you think?'

'I just draw buildings, Neal, I don't check whether they fall over afterwards.' He squinted when she shone the light in his face. 'Yeah, we're safe,' she said, 'I think.' She pushed against a wall herself as if making sure. She noticed tiny indentations in the rock wall, too deep for convict picking. 'There are drill holes in these walls. Shelves?'

The floor above them shifted again. 'Maybe we should come back with a team when we're sure about the structure.'

'In a minute. So what do you think?' She ran the torch around the perimeter of the room.

'If it's part of the original chapel, it was built by convicts. Maybe this was a place for them to hide. Maybe it was even supported by the Catholic Church.' He was following Harriet's torch beam round the line of the low ceiling. 'But I think we ought to come back later.'

'Good theory, Neal. I like it. We know the Irish were anti the English Government. Maybe Canali was in on the whole thing and secretly designed the chamber. By the time he came back to do the new church, he'd forgotten about it or it wasn't needed any longer so he sealed it off. I mean, he must have put it in here for something, and, as you say, the burial crypt's on the other side. You've got to admit it would enhance the building's significance if we could prove it. They'd have to stop their blasting if there's a convict past here. I reckon we could just about call what we have proof, don't you?'

'Call me pedantic, but I'd prefer one or two facts to the simple absence of fact, Harriet.' Then more loudly, 'Why are we whispering?'

Harriet raised her voice, too. 'I bet this is at the same level as the crypt.'

'Meaning what?'

'Maybe they're connected under the chancel.' Harriet was running the torch over the tiles. She stopped suddenly. 'Neal!' Face up on the wet floor, in the narrow beam of the torch, inches from their feet, was a human skull. Instinctively, Harriet grabbed for Neal's arm. At the same time, he grabbed for her, so they nearly pushed one another over into the skull. They stumbled back and recovered their balance, but held on to each other. 'My God, Neal, this is the burial crypt, we got it wrong.' The eye sockets appeared to move in the skull as Harriet shifted the torch.

'No, it's on the other side,' he said softly. 'We'd better call someone.'

She let go of his arm. 'Yeah,' but she didn't move. She was trying to orient herself, which was impossible in the dark chamber. She might still be under the sacristy but she might as easily be under the chancel or even on the other side of the transept under the boarders' chapel. She heard Neal telling her that they should leave, but she kept the beam of light on the skull as if she wasn't sure what it might do. It was dull grey and porous with eye sockets and nasal chambers that twitched in the flickering light. The jaw was locked in an eternal grimace with overemphasised teeth since there was no flesh to flesh them out. It was asking for something. She couldn't stop looking at it. 'But let's look around first,' she said. 'Maybe there's a connection to the crypt. Can you smell something sweet?'

'Nasturtiums? Something like that. I just want out. I feel as if we're being watched.'

Harriet gestured towards the skull. 'Maybe there are some clues. Who's supposed to be in the crypt?'

'It goes back to the school period and before. The bishop, Gerard O'Hare, I think, and maybe a couple of the important nuns, Damian, Bernadette. They sealed the crypt in 1950. Sister Mary Cecilia said they want to move the remains to their Stanthorpe convent now that the university's talking about developing the site. You think it's one of them?'

'How do I know? You're the historian.'

A shoe scraped on stone and a light flashed behind them. Harriet grabbed Neal's arm. Neal yelled as he swung a punch into the air. Harriet stumbled and dropped the torch. There was a scramble to pick it up, Neal yelling, Harriet yelling, and the man in the entrance to the chamber calling over the top of them. 'Miss Darling, is that you? It's me, Kevin McAnelly. It's all right, I'm here, you're safe.'

Harriet crouched on the floor next to the skull where she'd managed to recover the torch and shone it into Kevin McAnelly's eyes. They were powder blue in the tiny beam of light and he squinted and held out a hand. Kevin was in charge of security at Archangels, and he was strange enough in the light of day. Harriet felt anything but safe with him here, his face illuminated from below.

'Gee, Kevin, don't sneak up like that,' Neal said. 'I nearly decked you.'

Harriet looked over the floor near the skull while Neal explained how they'd found the chamber. She saw the remains of clothes, perhaps a brown cassock or habit, covered in earth. She ran the torch around a fragile shoulder and along an arm, wrist and hand to two long fingers. They pointed towards the stairs and might have been forming a blessing if they hadn't been the bones of some poor soul locked in a secret chamber. Harriet ran the beam from where the fingers pointed out towards the wall. She saw something glinting on the floor. She moved closer. It was the silver clip of a small black leather purse. She'd have missed it entirely except that the finger bones pointed straight to it.

'You have to clear the scene, Miss Darling,' Kevin said. 'I'll need to call the police.'

'He's right, Neal. We have to get out of here.' Neal shook his head and muttered.

Harriet looked at Kevin, who was pointing his torch back towards the exit. Before she turned to leave the chamber, she reached down, picked up the purse and shoved it deep in the pocket of her dungarees.

CHAPTER THREE

'I didn't even hear you, Kev,' Neal said when they were back in the bright sacristy.

'Training.' Kevin was waiting on his mobile. 'I know how to be quiet when the need arises, Neal. I wouldn't be so confident about you decking me, either.' Harriet looked over to her researcher. Neal had been a wrestler in his university days. It might have been twenty years ago, but he was solidly built and his arms were powerful. He'd have decked Kevin if he'd had a mind to. As it was, he smiled amiably and agreed that the younger man had a point.

Kevin was lean and tough in his cheap grey pinstripe and dusty black shoes, and a pager added to the middle-aged look he worked hard to cultivate. But his bright eyes, cherry cheeks and full red lips told a different story, and an angry red birthmark over his left eye gave him a vulnerability that made him seem even younger than his twenty-eight years.

Harriet hadn't felt she'd got to the real Kevin yet and for this reason alone she wouldn't have trusted him. But he also ran the university security system. From the beginning, he'd made life difficult, refusing to let them into Archangels House because the vice-chancellor was abroad, and creating obstacles to their access to the chapel crypt.

He smiled as he spoke confidently to the police operator. 'No, I don't think we'll require an ambulance. It's a skull, I'd estimate it's been there a hundred years.' When Kevin finished, Harriet asked him about the demolition team. 'Prof Dawes said the church was unstable.'

'And how could he tell the Archangels Chapel was unstable from Europe?'

'Seoul, he's on the way back. He said we should finish it off in case someone gets hurt.'

'I've sent them away, Kevin. It's not on. I don't know how this fire started, but I intend to find out. And I'm going to do everything I can to save what's left.'

Kevin smiled in a small, satisfied way. 'This?' He gestured round the sad interior of the church. 'You shouldn't have acted without my authority.'

'And you shouldn't have acted without mine. This is a monumental loss for Brisbane. And you tell Professor Ted Dawes from me,' emphasising the professorial title like an accusation, 'I'm looking forward to giving him my report in person when he gets back. This church belongs to the faithful, and it always will.'

Two shorn constables answered Kevin's call. Neal introduced himself with a hearty handshake and led them down the stairs. Kevin took up the rear, chattering all the while in an excited, boyish voice about his speedy action to clear the crime scene.

A powerful flashlight gave Harriet a better view of the chamber. The walls were stone, probably Brisbane tuff, so it was constructed as part of the first chapel or before. It would be hard to imagine how it could have been put in later at any rate. The space was as she imagined, a narrow passage giving way to a rectangular chamber. They could now see other bones scattered around the skull that might be pieced together to form a whole skeleton. The brown material Harriet had seen earlier looked like a wool suit, which supported Neal's convict idea. The bolt holes along two walls could have been for benches, bunks or shelves.

Under instruction, the younger of the two officers collected the bones and stacked them in a pile near the skull so they wouldn't lose them. He had the green–blond hair of a swimmer and no neck. 'How about some gloves, Nick?' he said.

'Hardly think he's a candidate for STD,' his partner replied without moving to help.

'Should we be walking around the scene like this, Nick?' Kevin was on first-name basis already.

'He's not going anywhere.' The police and Kevin shared a loud, uncomfortable laugh.

'Maybe he's neanderthal.' Neal was mock-thoughtful as he tilted his head to look at the skull. 'He looks neanderthal, don't you think, Nick?' He addressed the senior police officer solemnly.

Nick nodded slowly. 'Know what you mean. Maybe he is.'

'Brisbane Man, that's what we'll call him, and we'll be famous, Harriet, because of the find,' Neal said. 'They'll have us in *Archaeology Australia*. You with your flaming red hair at the door of the tomb under that hardhat, could pass as a pith helmet, me in lumber shirt and jeans. First Java Man, then Ice Man, now Brisbane. We'll need an agent to negotiate the deal.'

A loud voice called down from the sacristy for them to clear the chamber immediately. 'Sounds like the big boys,' the green–blond told Nick. He tossed a last bone on the pile. 'We're outa here.'

Back in the sacristy, they were greeted by a small wiry plainclothes officer who paced out the length of the room while addressing a large hirsute colleague. 'I'd wager just about anything this time, Bruno.' He stopped talking when he saw them emerge from the stairwell and turned and glared at Nick and his partner. 'No one's touched anything, have they?'

The two officers looked at one another. 'Course not, Jack,' Nick said. Harriet thought of the bones they'd stacked neatly below.

'Who found the body?' They pointed over to Harriet. 'You mind waiting here till I go have a look at the body, ma'am?' She nodded. He disappeared down the steps and returned a few minutes later.

Detective Inspector Jack Champion was seriously bald and had gone to considerable effort to drag long wisps from one side of his head to the other. They looked liked stripes. 'Why did you go down there in the first place?' he asked Harriet after they'd introduced themselves.

'I was trying to get a sense of the dimensions of the room.'

The sacristy was filling with an assortment of uniforms, overalls and suits. Jack led Harriet outside. The smell of Brut aftershave followed them.

His eyes darted round the chapel. 'What do you do, Miss Darling?'

'I'm a conservation architect. My firm has a contract to do a study on the church and house for Archangels University.'

'Guess you're pretty upset about this then.' Harriet nodded and swallowed. 'What are they planning to do here?'

'Nothing if I have my way.'

'They listen to you?' He asked these questions as if he had little interest in the answers. He looked around the chapel and at other people as he spoke, and interrupted Harriet to issue instructions.

'The university put us on to provide advice,' she said. 'We're the experts. You can't destroy the past these days.'

'Looks like someone's had a pretty good go though, doesn't it?'

'They say it was an electrical fault.'

'And what do you say?'

Harriet lowered her voice. 'There was a demolition team in here this morning. They were told the chapel's unstable. It's not, of course. I think they simply want to make life easy for themselves for rebuilding. I think they want to finish it off. I'm worried they'll be back.'

'I just might be able to help you there.' Jack moved his hands and spoke in a loud voice in a way that reminded Harriet of her father. Stan was taller and more graceful, but the resemblance was enough to leave her feeling more at home than she might otherwise have felt faced with a senior detective in a tacky suit smelling of cheap aftershave. 'Our preliminary investigation will take at least a couple of days, even if the body's as old as you think. And then, if we're doing a full investigation, could be tied up for weeks.'

'How do you decide whether it's a full investigation or not?'

'Depends how old the bones are. More than fifty years we won't bother. Less than that, we gotta go all the way. Now, if I was a betting man, I'd say we're looking at something newer than fifty years, maybe even newer than ten.' A hint of a smile made Harriet think he might know more than he was saying. 'Either way, no one's going to do anything to this church till I say they can. I can call you if you like. You local, case I got any more questions?'

Harriet had what she wanted, a temporary stay for the chapel. 'I'm here for at least the next month. But I don't know any more than I've already told you.'

He flipped closed his black plastic notebook and replaced it in his coat pocket. 'You'd be surprised what people know.' He looked at her for a long moment as if he'd finally shifted his attention in order to commit her to memory. 'We'll be in touch.'

The police cordoned off the sacristy and the clean up resumed elsewhere. Harriet gathered her team outside. 'This could work for us if the skull's old, Tim,' she said to the engineer, 'but we only have a couple of days. We need to find out how the crypt and this new chamber work together, and what else is down there. Did we find anything in the original tests?' Tim shook his head and said they'd only been looking for the crypt according to the building plans. 'Neal thinks the skeleton might be a convict. If he's right—' Neal started to interject but Harriet ignored him, '—we're set as far as preserving the rest of the chapel goes. Let's face it, guys, no one will care if it's a priest, but everyone loves convicts.'

'Didn't the police say the skull was more recent?' Neal said as he was leaving to head back to the New Farm office.

'You had good reasons for your theory, Neal.' He started to protest again but Harriet stopped him. 'Trust your judgement. What would that policeman know? You're the historian.'

Brisbane where the big things are, Richard Corsair had said when Harriet told him she'd accepted the consultancy. Bris-Vegas, John Maple, the other third of Corsair Maple, called her temporary home. 'They have a big pineapple there,' Richard added, 'three storeys of fibreglass *avec vue*. They carve into their history without a second thought. And this private university consortium, they bought that land from the Catholic Church and promised to keep the school name and leave the old buildings intact. Five years on, they've crowded out the site with a bunch of unsympathetic buildings. Now they're saying they want to develop the church and house. A job is one thing, Harriet, but if they do you over, you'll be branded a fake by the people we need on side up there, like the Trust and the Heritage Council.'

Harriet hadn't told Richard that the big pineapple had spawned a big cow, a big mower and a big kangaroo that sold used cars. He wouldn't have understood. What she did say was that she had to get out of Melbourne. He understood that. Her work was flat. He hadn't said as much, but he thought it and so did Harriet. She hadn't done a job she was happy with since the break with Martin. Her life in Melbourne now was dull projects punctuated by fundraising cocktail parties where old men put friendly (and sometimes more than friendly) arms around her waist. Fossicking about in the past, her father called it. 'When you gunna do some drawing again, HD?'

Initially, the plan had been that Harriet and Neal would set up the Brisbane practice and return to Melbourne. Already they'd moved into their own offices at New Farm and had taken on a couple of drafters and an architect. Harriet should be thinking about going home. Richard had asked her in vague terms, and when she pretended not to understand, he'd tried to excite her with new work. But she'd told him not yet. She was flying on automatic pilot here, doing just what her body told her to do, and it felt good.

Until now, Richard had been wrong and had admitted as much. The job had been going well and she'd done a preliminary report that had convinced Max Palethorpe and the Archangels University Board they couldn't touch the chapel and house when they made over the rest of the campus. The chapel could continue to be used for services by the university ecumenical chaplaincy, and the house was appropriate for its current use as a vice-chancellor's residence. The Board had agreed. People said Ted Dawes, the vice-chancellor, might see things differently, but he'd been away and she had Max's imprimatur. Harriet was starting to like Brisbane and its size large preference. Sure there was big advertising and big backyards, but the smiles were big, too, and the sky. She was glad it was Neal who was going to call Richard. She didn't need the inevitable 'I told you so'.

CHAPTER FOUR

Harriet had set up her site office in one of the three pink sandstone buildings that formed a U around the grassed quadrangle at the top of the hill. The quad was the transition between Old Archangels and new, where the university encroached on the old world. On its open side, it looked past the Virgin down the grassed terraces to Old Archangels and the river. But inside the U, recycling bins slouched over the grass, the tatty remains of bill posters littered walkway walls and Apple Macs on ergonomic desks stared out blankly through double sash windows. Behind the quad, nineties university buildings crowded round in dully precise landscaping. Today sprinklers threw sheets of water onto the perfect grass while students stood in groups and stared down the hill towards the ruined chapel.

At her desk she dialled the city council and was put through to a help desk where a woman's broad soothing voice made Harriet feel she might cry. 'Well, of course you're concerned,' the woman said. 'It's no wonder you're upset dear. Ye-es. My Katie's at Archangels and she had trouble settling in, you know what it's like, uni's so different from school. Your people were so kind. Ye-es.' O God, Harriet thought, she thinks I'm from Archangels.

'No, you don't understand,' Harriet said. 'It might be the university that's done this. We must act to prevent further damage.'

'I don't know dear,' the woman said kindly, 'but I'm going to try to find out which department might be able to help. We have so many.' She didn't sound confident.

Heritage was the responsibility of every level of government and none, like the environment and children, too large to comprehend but too important to ignore. The project officer from the state government department was less helpful than the woman from the council. 'You can try for a temporary stay or something, I think. Funny it isn't already on our register.'

Funny indeed, thought Harriet.

'Maybe we can get you a stay at the next meeting,' he said as an afterthought. She pictured him in tight pants and a short tie throwing paper rockets at young women in the office.

'For godsake,' Harriet stood up and walked around her desk, 'I suspect they're trying to blow the bloody thing up. Can't you at least come down here and have a look?'

He was busy that day, he said, but he could come the next. Harriet took what she could get. She phoned a colleague at the national Commission as well.

'We'll write to them, Harriet,' he said. 'It's all we can do from here. Why wasn't this place listed in the beginning?'

It was a good question, although, as her colleague added, listing was no guarantee of anything in the land of the Big Pineapple.

The phone rang as soon as she put it down. It was her father. 'Just wanted to check you got back all right, love.' She'd left a note on his door on her way to the airport before dawn. He'd worried because he hadn't had time to phone the airline and check the plane, he said. Stan had been a maintenance engineer on big planes, and since he'd retired he never flew anywhere. Harriet grew up travelling with him and loving flight, in every kind of plane. It was the notion of being in the sky that drew her. She'd not been nervous, not until lately when her father's horror stories crept into her mind, especially at takeoff and landing. She'd even started imagining she might fall from the sky.

'We nearly crashed,' she told her father now. The plane had bounced onto the tarmac and skidded so heavily the passengers applauded when the pilot managed to set the big jet right.

'Not surprised. It's because they don't have faith in the pilots anymore.' Stan had left just as computers were taking over flight.

She chuckled. 'Faith? That's great coming from an engineer.'

'We're talking thousands of tonnes of metal thirty thousand feet straight up. Last thing it's inclined to do is stay there. If we engineers don't have faith, what hope is there?' Before he hung up, he said, 'You all right, love?'

'Sure, Stan.' She realised she hadn't told him about the fire. 'Busy day.' She continued to watch the phone for a moment after she'd replaced the receiver. And what a day. She needed to clear her head.

The university swimming pool was shoved between two buildings constructed in the 1940s, monumental architecture recalling the grand sandstone days, now so crowded in they'd lost scale. In Melbourne Harriet swam in the 1870 city baths. In Paris, it had been the vintage Piscine de Pontoise. Here in Brisbane, she swam in this steamy modern glasshouse. It felt like an artificial womb around her.

She swam hard and fast, and barely noticed the effort of a mile on her arms. When she sat down in the change room to dry her feet after a shower, she realised one of her boots was missing from the bench where she'd left them. A poster on the wall said, 'Protect Your Stuff: Thieves Are About'. The thieves had stolen one of her boots. They were expensive worksafe boots. Why would they steal only one? And they were size five. Hardly anyone was size five. She looked around. Three or four women, most likely students, were dressing or undressing. Harriet went back into the shower cubicle and locked the door. So far, she'd managed to hold back tears, which was good, strong. But now her boot was gone. She noticed her arms and torso were red. Suddenly, the ache of the swim took up in her shoulders and calves and the sting of the too-hot shower stretched over her skin. In her mind's eye, she saw, for the first time since this morning, the Archangels Chapel in ruins. She turned on the faucet and let the tears come.

Back in her office, the woman from the city council phoned. 'I've found Morrie Stewart from Parks,' she said. 'He's dropping over to see what's going on. He'll ring you personally when he's done that. Says he knows the church well.' Apparently Morrie was a plant biologist. Harriet thanked the woman and wondered what good a biologist from Parks would be with a church. At least he could check the fig for stress. Perhaps he could check Harriet for stress while he was at it. She threw the lone boot into the corner of the room.

Harriet did a once-around the quad on her way down to the chapel. What would Martin do in this situation? she wondered. Never believe anyone from the heritage lobby, he told her once. But that was before she became a heritage specialist and moved from his firm to Corsair Maple. They're all fools or off with the birds or both, he said. Martin wasn't part of the heritage lobby, although he did a lot of work on listed buildings. He was a signature architect, left his fabulous mark on every fabulous thing he did. And whatever private disdain he held his clients in, they were always happy with the outcome. What would Martin do? When you're down, you have to look as if you're up, he told her. 'So, we're having a poor month. You know what I do? Put on a lunch. Expensive. Buy a new suit.' Maybe Harriet should buy some clothes or lunch for the man from the state government or the plant biologist.

She thought out loud as she walked. 'We're powerless to stop the university. I need a decision tree.' She drew in the air. 'If old skull, police stop investigating, I only have two days protection, then demolition might start.' She drew the other branch. 'If new skull, police investigate, I have unknown time but demolition might start eventually. If old skull and convict, no one will blast. The best outcome is old skull and convict.' She stopped and looked back towards the rest of the university. 'Of course, I'm still thinking inside the square. I'm the consultant. They know what I tell them, and I can tell them what I like. No one knows who belongs to that skull yet. No one knows we're vulnerable.' Harriet was impressed with her guile. That's why Martin bought suits. She could tell the university anything and they'd believe her. She was in control, not them. All she needed were some little lies about listing and convicts, hardly significant in the big picture of Old Archangels. She hurried down the hill.

CHAPTER FIVE

The morning's emergency workers had moved on to the next real-life drama, and from outside the chapel, the smell of burned wood over spring flowers was the only hint of what had happened. The police had boarded shut the front doors so Harriet climbed in through a window. She noticed a butcher bird behind her as she lifted herself up onto the ledge. 'You following me?' she said. She'd have sworn the bird nodded. When she looked back again it had flown away.

Afternoon sunlight filtered through the dust and smoke to create a new softness inside the chapel, and Harriet took a moment to let her eyes adjust. She crawled under the tape marked 'CRIME SCENE' on the entry to the sacristy and went into the sacristy itself where the trapdoor had been sealed with a large padlock. 'Spoil sports,' she muttered. 'Neal and I found it, not them.' She could smell a hint of Jack Champion's aftershave, less intense and more pleasant as a memory.

Harriet felt less hopeless about the chapel now, whether because she'd let herself cry or because she'd come up with a strategy to save what was left she couldn't say. Perhaps at some level she already knew that one day, this would become just another incarnation of the building. This was fire damaged. It followed built, overbuilt, extended, altered, flooded, painted and restored. The slow story of a building is told in the layers, the surface over surface. Eventually, Harriet might even accept the fire and its damage as just another layer of the story. If there's still a story to tell, she thought.

She went out onto the altar, taking the route the priest might have taken as he strode out each morning with the confidence of the Lord to say mass. And what a glorious mass it must have been, the nuns in full voice, their sweet faces upturned to God's representative here on earth. Priests could do almost anything: forgive sins, join couples, baptise the living and anoint the dead. As she stood behind the altar, Harriet wondered if they became vain. They probably did. All that adoration of God may as well have been for them, and all that power might have vested in them.

'In the name of the Father, the Son and the Holy Spirit,' Harriet said in a loud voice. 'May the love of God and the fellowship of the Holy Spirit be with you all. Go in peace, to love and serve the Lord.' She held out her left hand, two fingers extended in a blessing, with her right hand over her heart.

The last mass Harriet had attended had been at the end of her final year at St Pat's, over a decade ago, in what were probably the Catholic Church's finest contemporary years. Catholics were renewed and enriched by Vatican II, and they hadn't started talking about what happened to them as boys and girls in the care of nuns and priests and brothers. It was before the press decided that no one was sacred, and before the flow of vocations slowed, stalled and then stopped. That's what Old Archangels reminded her of, the small enfolding church of St Pat's with its safe stone, so different from the adult world in which she found herself now.

Harriet had loved school. She'd been a good kid, a rounded sporty loud kid with frizzy red hair and in just enough trouble to be interesting. She'd believed in God, too, at least sometimes. On school camps and at masses she felt filled with the Holy Spirit, especially when they sang hymns and played guitars. She'd been a liturgical dancer in the final St Pat's mass, solid and lithe for the Lord, dancing to a St Louis Jesuits hymn about the earthen vessels that carry the bread and wine turned into the Eucharistic body and blood. She was sure she could remember the steps of that dance if she thought about it.

She was crouched with her hands crossed on her chest, having done the wheat gathering routine, and was about to start grapes for wine, when a noise—a shift of a pew or a clearing of a throat—told her she was not alone in the chapel. At first, she thought it must be Neal. But she saw jeaned legs in boots in the back of the boarders' chapel, perhaps twenty metres from where she stood in front of the altar. The rest of the person was in darkness, and the legs were too long for Neal.

'Aerobics?' It was a man's voice. As he stood up a shaft of sunlight through the window turned him into a silhouette so she couldn't see his face.

Harriet could feel herself blush. She was reconstructing the last few minutes when she'd thought she was alone. She hadn't talked to herself. No, that wasn't correct, she'd recited part of the liturgy of the mass when she was pretending to be the priest. Then she'd done the dance, the liturgical dance, the mid-eighties bread and wine liturgical dance, with pirouettes and an arabesque. Her face felt hot and the late afternoon sun was like a spotlight. 'You should have said you were there.'

He walked down the aisle. 'I didn't want to intrude. Are you a priest?'

She could tell from the angle of his head he was looking at her. He was much taller than Harriet, at least six foot. 'Not exactly,' Harriet said. 'I'm an architect.'

'The architect?' His surprise was nothing new. People were often thrown by the tiny young woman as architect, they expected a bigger person, a male person, although in this case Harriet suspected the surprise had more to do with the fact she'd been practising the mass as an architect.

He moved away from the ray of light and she saw his face for the first time. He was perhaps forty, with messy dark brown hair and one of those sunbleached, week-old beards and face tans that movie stars work hard to maintain. 'Was that some sort of building ritual?' His voice was warm and deep, which didn't quite mesh with the rough exterior, and he was trying not to smile. 'I know you wet the roof of new buildings. Was that a variation for old churches?'

'You should have said you were there.'

'I should have.' He smiled down at her now and it was this smile she remembered later. He raised his eyebrows, cocked his head, parted his lips to reveal a crooked front tooth, and then his whole face broke up into lines and light. It was a smile she couldn't help responding to. There was irony rather than sarcasm as she recalled it later. He looked around the chapel. 'On the other hand, if you wanted privacy, you might have thought before you did that routine in a public place.' He paused. 'I'm dying to know, what were you doing?'

'It was a liturgical dance I did at school. When I was saying the mass prayers, it came back to me and I got carried away. It's been a long day.' He smiled down at her again and this time she joined him. She told him about the weekend fire. 'I have to keep saying it to myself or I forget. This was my project. I was supposed to protect the chapel.'

'Sometimes I come here on hot days and watch the river through that fig,' he said. 'It gives me time to think.' He was wearing a dark green workshirt that matched his hazel eyes. He looked like a forest ranger. 'Mostly I sit up there with my back to the altar and let the world go still.' Harriet was about to say 'Me too', when it occurred to her that the stranger might be lying. What if he'd watched her in the church before and knew her habits? Serial killers sometimes spend months stalking their victims. Maybe he was a serial killer. But although there was something that didn't ring true about him, he wasn't thin and sweaty and he didn't smell clean like a dentist in the way Harriet imagined a serial killer would. In fact, he smelled of lemony flowers, the aftershave she'd mistaken for Jack Champion's. I'm overwrought, Harriet thought. We both like to watch the river from the altar, that's all. We have something in common. The thought pleased her. 'It's an original Moreton Bay fig, that one,' he said. 'One of the grandest old trees you'll ever see, probably been here since before settlement. Are you the one who's doing a conservation study on this area?'

She remembered, the city council, he must be the plant biologist. What was his name? 'I am,' she said. 'I'm worried about the fig.' They'd walked together down the aisle and across to the sacristy side of the nave. She pointed towards the river window. He nodded but said nothing. He was leaning against the wall with his arms folded loosely and one leg bent behind him. Light came in through the open window and shone on his hair and strong forearms. Harriet noticed his shadow along the floor. His shoulders were elongated like wings. He looked like an angel. She was about to say something about shadows and angels when he stepped forward and closer to her and the angel dissolved into a man. What was the name? Malcolm? 'I was thinking you might check the fig for us,' she said when he didn't respond.

'The fig? Sure, I'll have a look.' He stood up and ran his hand over his chin. 'Do they know how the fire started?'

'Security system blew a fuse supposedly.' He raised an eyebrow. 'Makes you wonder, doesn't it? Especially since I gave the university my stage one report last week which ruled out making any changes to the building. Then the fire.'

'You're kidding. You don't think?'

'Well, what do you think?'

'This is a church, for goodness sake. The university wouldn't burn down a church.'

'Hah! From what I've heard, real estate's the only religion here. I could tell you some things. After the fire, which didn't finish the job, they tried to sneak in a demolition team on the grounds that it's unstable.'

He looked at the ceiling. 'Is it?'

'My engineer says it's fine.'

'This is so odd. The vice-chancellor of Archangels spoke at the National Trust's annual conference. Why don't you talk to him? He was excellent, at least on conserving natural heritage.'

'He's not here at the moment. And anyway, I wouldn't be so sure he's on side from what I've heard.'

'Sleeping with the enemy, you reckon?' He folded his arms and shook his head.

It was so nice to meet a friend. 'Yeah, that's a good way to put it. I've heard from people who know he's more white-shoe developer than white-shoe developers.'

'I'd never have picked that listening to him talk. My grandmother used to say you never know people. And you never do.' He was shaking his head. 'I'd have thought this place would be safe forever.'

'In my business, you learn nothing's forever.'

'What about the state government?'

She told him about her experiences on the phone. 'They'll do what they can, but they can't move quickly. It's fallen between the cracks, the state thinks it's listed nationally and the feds think the state's covered it. And neither has yet. People forget that as well as being an 1890s church, it's also an 1850s building which was the first cathedral.

'I was thinking maybe the city council could put some pressure on in terms of town planning.' She paused but he looked to the floor. Perhaps he didn't have that sort of pull. She let it drop. 'The good news is I don't have to let the university know how powerless we are.' Harriet smiled conspiratorially.

He walked past her towards the altar. 'Is that ethical?'

'What do you mean?'

He had his back to her. 'Well, not that I blame you, but you're hardly being loyal to your client, are you? The university, I mean, if you're going behind their back.'

'I can't let any client destroy our built heritage. If it comes to that, I'll quit the consultancy. But it won't come to that. They need me as much as I need them. I give them credibility.' He nodded thoughtfully. 'At least we've got some breathing space. We found a skull this morning, so the police won't let them touch the chapel.'

He wheeled around quickly to face her. 'Whose skull?'

'The police are investigating, but I think it's a convict. That's why the sacristy is boarded shut.' She saw Neal waving to her from one of the windows at the other end of the nave. He was early. 'That's my appointment.' She'd have liked more time with the plant biologist.

'So it is,' he said, 'and I should go, Harriet.' Had she told him her name?

Neither of them moved. He continued to look at her face and shrugged. She tried to think of a way she could suggest they meet again without suggesting they meet again. 'I've heard of stress taking some time to develop in trees,' she said. 'Maybe you could come back to check the fig again. I'll be here the next few afternoons working.'

'Tomorrow then.' He disappeared out the window. Harriet watched until Neal called again from the other side.

'Who's your friend?' Neal climbed in after handing through the camera equipment.

'A guy from the council. A tree doctor.'

'Very nice. Noticed you smiling sweetly.'

'Can you smell flowers?'

Neal looked over his glasses. 'You really are under the spell. What happened to this morning, "I can't cope"?'

'Fickle, probably PMT, bloody women, but what can a man do?' Harriet was still looking after the plant biologist. She turned back to Neal. 'You're right. Let's get on with it. How'd you go?'

'Not much joy, I'm afraid. Richard says to tell you to be good.' Harriet frowned. 'Don't shoot the messenger. He says there's not much we can do. And we should go easy with the press. It could go either way and they might get behind the university.'

'Surely not. They'd be on our side.'

'Our side is the university, Harriet. Remember how this works? They're our client, we're their consultant, we work for them, they pay us money.'

'I've been thinking. We should release the report publicly. It rules out development and we can point to the fire as proof that the university isn't on side. These guys play hard-ball, Neal, we know what they've done.'

'No we don't, and if we come in heavy now we might lose them altogether.'

'Neal, they tried to burn down the church. If that's not coming in heavy—'

'That's pretty grassy knollist, Harriet, even for you. They're not going to sneak around in the middle of the night lighting fires. They don't need to. They could have done whatever they wanted in the first place without taking us on. But they didn't, they decided to put you and me on, the best heritage team in the known universe.'

'And our report told them they couldn't do anything round this area, and the chapel burned down.'

'They must have known we'd rule out major development. Face it, HD, there was an accident with the security system just like the investigator said, and that's awful. Maybe someone at the university thought they'd use the opportunity to finish it off. We stopped them. That's good. But you've got to start looking on the bright side. You're so bloody . . .' He looked past Harriet out a window.

'Bloody what?'

'Negative. I mean, I used to be the depressive in this relationship and you'd cheer me out of it. Now you see conspiracies everywhere, like everyone's ripping you off.'

'Maybe they are.'

'Yeah and maybe the world's going to end today. But I doubt it. Anyway, we have to be careful. We can't exceed the brief. We do work for the university, that's what Richard said. You'll have to talk to him yourself. He's read the report, says it's a bit reactionary.'

'Reactionary? Did you tell him about the Board?'

The Archangels Board were twenty suits in high-backed leather surrounded by portraits of old nuns and priests left over from the school days. They'd bought tradition and history along with the real estate. Harriet had done her best to present the preliminary report, but she'd felt as if she couldn't make enough noise to fill the room. There had been one question, from the octogenarian Sister Mary Cecilia, former principal of Archangels School, former Provincial of the Sisters of the Blessed Redemption, and now a member of the University Board as part of the handover deal. My mother went to Archangels, she'd said while her blind eyes found a middle distance nowhere near Harriet. I don't want them changing anything. Harriet had smiled and said things never stay exactly as they are. The old nun misheard. She nodded and agreed things should stay as they are. There was no other discussion.

Leaving the meeting, Harriet had been struck by a portrait at the head of the table, different from the others, of a bright-eyed nun, Irishly pretty, transparently happy and pink-skinned in a way that suggested red hair. The grey eyes glowed and she looked squarely at Harriet. She might have winked and said, 'It's all right, sweetie.' Harriet had nudged Neal at the time but he hadn't noticed.

'No, I didn't tell him,' Neal said now. 'He wants you to call.'

'Doesn't he know you and I are out here on the perimeter? I mean, if we're talking reactionary.' She let it slide. 'Do you remember that portrait we saw in the boardroom? The one at the end, the nun. Was that Mother Damian?' It had given Harriet hope that this wonderful young woman was watching over the Board's proceedings, so much hope that she wasn't at all surprised when Max Palethorpe had phoned to say they'd accepted her report without a quibble.

'Yeah, Mother Damian Ryan.' Neal smiled. 'Reverend mother here for about fifty years. I always figured her for a mate of yours, HD, an early feminist, and difficult. Maybe she should ring Richard for you.'

CHAPTER SIX

From the evening ferry, Harriet stared at the lights on the river. She hadn't stopped since three-thirty am in Melbourne. She needed to tell Max Palethorpe about emergency listing, make threats about what the government might do. Tomorrow. And maybe she could leak the report without telling Neal and they'd get some press. The plant biologist had asked about ethics and Neal had been unhappy this afternoon. In a way, they were right. But how ethical had the university been, especially if they'd had anything at all to do with the fire? The investigators were saying it was an accident. But Kevin McAnelly knew Harriet and Neal were in the chamber. He probably had a hidden camera. Was his security system back in operation now? Would it blow another fuse and finish the job? He smiled when she said they mustn't knock it down. Maybe they were coming back. Harriet dismissed this thought. Detective Inspector Jack Champion had given her at least a couple of days. She was too tired to think.

At home, she changed into a tracksuit and opened a Margaret River chardonnay that was corked on first sip. The only other cold bottle was a riesling, more suited to scampi than the lasagne she'd picked up for dinner. Even so, it was better than corked chardonnay. She drank the first glass while she zapped dinner. She moved to the lounge and absently flicked television channels, unable to settle. She drank quickly and before long she was thinking about Martin. She wanted to call him, that was the problem. She wanted to hear his voice, be reassured. It wasn't fair, it had been so long. She fell into that comfortable, familiar feeling that made her sigh. But almost before the sigh was out of her mouth, reality kicked it out of the way. Martin Jamison would never provide reassurance to Harriet.

The first thing she'd noticed about Martin was that he had no shoulders, which made him vulnerable and strangely attractive. I like what you do, he told her at the uni exhibition, the way you think about design on the page. Want to come work with us? She was the only one in her class to be employed in his chic firm, Jamison and Jamison (I'm worth two of any other architect, he told her). He had waves of silver hair and white teeth. She was nineteen, and it was the best news of her life. There was so much work and so many people to meet. She needed more confidence, Martin told her. She was awkward with clients and not used to being with people. She was just a teeny-weeny bit off when it came to dress. But she'd learn, he assured her, he'd teach her. He announced their first date like one of the building projects they worked on. Harriet didn't have a choice and wouldn't have exercised one if she did. She adored his self-assuredness. His passion for her knew no limits. They married just after her twenty-first birthday in a garden he'd designed. The bridesmaids wore mauve gingham. His mother cried. Her father wouldn't come to the wedding. It's not his age, Stan said, you're wrong about that, it's the way you act around him, like you've got no brains. It was a cruel thing to say, and it simply wasn't true as far as Harriet was concerned.

Within a year, Martin's limitless passion had drained away like one of the prune-shakes he drank for breakfast. When she moved to Corsair Maple, he talked enthusiastically about the new architect he'd brought into the office. At the other end of the day, he drank cognac from a brandy balloon or sticky port from a tiny glass.

After they separated, Harriet went to a counsellor, something she thought she'd never do, and made pronouncements: her life was finished, she was worthless, no one. The pronouncements brought tears and a little relief. She'd cry for a billable hour, watching the children's drawings that covered the grey walls instead of the grey counsellor, and go home. She'd ring Martin and cry some more. She'd write him long angry letters she never intended to send and send them. She'd dial his number to listen to his service over and over again or his real-time voice. He knew it was her, he even said so once. 'Harriet, you've got to stop this.' She sat frozen in terror at discovery until he sighed and hung up.

And here it was again, that old familiar feeling of wanting to call, an almost welcome yearning. We love our pain if it's all we've got; she'd read that somewhere. It had been nearly two years. It wasn't fair. She'd suffered enough. The counsellor taught her to hold two fingers of her left hand with her right and to breathe through her fear and sadness. He said when she had the urge to call Martin she had to think about what was in it for her, not him. She had to put herself first instead of Martin. For a while, she tricked the counsellor, she tricked herself. When she wanted to ring, she constructed a careful reason, with something in it for her, something he'd said once that she needed to confirm or investigate. But over time, almost in spite of herself, she realised the counsellor was right. There was nothing there. Martin was a prick. The prick faded. Martin used to tell her the first rule of negotiation is never tell the truth. It didn't occur to her that she was a negotiation, too. He took the house and practice while she wandered

Melbourne in a dream. For the first time, here in Brisbane, she'd started to feel she could have a life ex-Martin. She mustn't pick up that phone.

She was well into the second glass when the black leather purse she'd pocketed popped into her mind. She'd forgotten about it in the excitement that followed the fire and skull discovery. She nearly knocked the wine bottle over in the hurry to get to her bedroom. She found her dungarees on the floor where she'd left them and the purse in the pocket. She went back to the lounge and cleared the mess from the coffee table. She fingered the leather of the purse, savouring its soft reassurances. She ran her hands over its surface, noting the small scratches and faults, feeling lumps likes jewels. She pulled at the silver foldover clip, which came away easily, and emptied the contents onto the tabletop. A set of bright blue beads clattered onto the glass, followed by a neatly folded one pound note. They were rosary beads, indigo blue in the lamp light, surely lapis lazuli, threaded on a silver chain, with a silver Jesus dangling on a lapis cross at the base. They were expensive, Harriet reckoned, possibly Egyptian azure, perhaps even blessed by the Pope. So much for the convict. Less and less likely. A priest or nun? The pound note wasn't quite the image she had of either a religious vocation or a convict.

Harriet hadn't told the police about the leather purse. It hadn't been her intention to deceive, but when Jack Champion asked whether she'd seen anything else that might help them identify the body, she'd forgotten. When she remembered briefly at the end of the interview, it was too late. It would have looked suspicious. She'd put it out of her mind and had lost it until just now. She could always call the police tomorrow and explain.

Neal could date the pound note. She could just hear him. 'A convict with rosary beads in a chapel, HD?' But they could be anyone's rosary. Which was more believable: that a convict had a rosary or that a nun had money? Harriet thought this was very funny as she poured her third glass and imagined the look on Neal's face. Lying back on the couch listening to Willie Nelson's 'Stardust', she fingered the rosary and absently started a Hail Mary, but she couldn't remember the last lines.

Rosary beads had been before Harriet's time, although she had owned a scapular in primary school with an image of St Christopher carrying the baby Jesus across the water. It was made of shiny card and hung on a leather thong around her neck. If she kept it against her breast all day for a month, she would go to Heaven, guaranteed. The first time she'd showered with it on, the little plastic wallet had filled with water and afterwards the ink from St Christopher ran onto her nightie. Three days later St Christopher developed mildew and Harriet gave up.

Rosary beads were different. There were ten beads in each group, and five groups, plus five beads on the tail; you recited the rosary as decades of prayers so you had to be able to count to ten. Each decade had ten Hail Marys. Or was it because there were ten of each kind of mystery? What were the mysteries? The sorrowful, the angry, no not angry, righteous, perhaps happy, no that was joyful. There should be a travelling mystery, Harriet thought. The first decade of the travelling mystery where Jesus goes to a wedding at 'Cana and turns corked chardonnay into riesling.

They'd seen many things, these beads, priests and nuns and girls coming and going from Archangels in its school days. Convicts even, and settlers. Whose fingers had worn this holy abacus smooth? Who'd sat in that chapel over the years, hoping the next life might be better, or absently fingering them, as Harriet did now, like worry beads? She told herself she needed dinner and had work to do. But she fell asleep, all thoughts of Martin quite forgotten, feeling close to happy, with the blue rosary beads wound loosely around her hand and the cross falling over her chest.

CHAPTER SEVEN

Mother Damian Ryan sat under the rose trellis to watch dawn bleach the sky and the Brisbane landscape take shape. It was five am, the year was nineteen forty-nine and Damian should have been saying office. She sat on the green garden chair in front of the Virgin. She watched the Story Bridge and felt the ambivalence of a soft breeze.

It was a view she hadn't tired of in half a century. Her hair, which no living soul in Australia had seen, had turned from deep auburn to white at Archangels, so that now, if it weren't crewcut and hidden under her veil, it would match her pale blue eyes and highlight the thin red lines of her cheeks. She fingered her rosary and opened her office so as not to be disturbed. She had much to think about and the bishop would arrive soon for mass.

She'd woken at three that morning. 'Is that you Vincent?' She'd found Sister Mary Vincent perched on a high stool, legs wide, in the convent kitchen, wolfing down toast thickly spread with butter and strawberry jam. Vincent was frankly overweight and doing nothing to develop a more circumspect approach to diet. And the flatulence was terrible. She never owned up but Mother Damian had long ago realised Vincent was the only common denominator in the terrible odours that emanated from the folds of someone's habit. And she was completely undiscriminating, passing wind through the drawing room, study, even the chapel. Damian thought of speaking to her but wasn't sure how to be delicate and clear at the same time. Thankfully, Vincent spent most of her time in the well-ventilated kitchen. She was stricter with the novices she supervised than with her personal regimen, and Damian suspected she didn't much like novices. In fact, she didn't much like anything other than eating and the ballroom dancing lessons she gave the juniors at the school. On dancing days, she wore a white habit with a short skirt she'd made herself and dainty white shoes which looked like fancy pins at the bottom of her fat legs. She always partnered with one of the taller girls and waltzed around the Pride of Erin as if she were free as a bird and light as a feather.

From the rose trellis, Damian turned and looked back to the quadrangle where pink stone was turning to gold and white with the sun. She saw their newest novice emerging from the square where the new buildings were underway. By the time Sister Mary Angelina reached her, the full glory of Archangels was revealed.

'This is early for you child?' Mother Damian said. Angelina had missed mass more than once of late. She was just turned seventeen, and the love of sleep didn't change quickly when a girl became a woman.

'Yes Mother, I've been in the grotto.' Angelina had been a scamp of a child who'd grown into an adult grace at Archangels. Her hair was a mess of loose plaits. It was so hard to comb without mirrors at first. But even with messy hair and dressed as she was in the plain wool skirt and sweater of a junior novice, the girl had a beauty that suited her chosen name. She also had a gift with little children, and Damian wanted her for head of the primary school when the building was finished, if only she could convince the older sisters. 'Mother, can I talk to you?' she said now.

'Sit here with me awhile.' Damian looked over her spectacles. Angelina was frowning hard. She'd been pale and distracted of late, too, and Damian had meant to ask the other novices if they knew what was wrong. Why were there never enough hours in the day?

A breeze greeting the new day reminded Damian of the first hot blows of summer when cut green grass would smell fresh and her aging bones would warm. 'I've been happy here.' Angelina sat down and looked straight ahead to the river.

'That's good, child.' Damian took the girl's hand in hers; it was feverish.

'It's so hard to be sure sometimes.'

Mother Damian was about to agree when they saw Vincent, who'd probably eaten half a loaf of bread by now, marching up the hill with the certainty of a general. 'Where are your office and rosary Sister?' Vincent called out before she'd reached them. 'And what are you doing disturbing Mother at prayer.'

Angelina stood up. 'Yesta, I mean I was going to reflect quietly this morning so I didn't bring them.'

'Were you now? Did it ever occur to you that your office and rosary are your means of quiet reflection Sister? Well, did it?' Vincent narrowed her brown mouse-eyes at the girl.

'Yesta.'

'Off you go please and get them.'

Vincent replaced Angelina on the seat with Damian, her considerable weight making a discernible difference to the balance at Damian's end. 'She wasn't bothering me Vincent,' Mother said.

'They must learn,' Vincent replied emphatically. Damian wanted to tell Vincent she was being too harsh on little

Angelina and they'd lose her, but she knew better than to push. Instead she suggested more tea and toast despite the fact they'd be taking the Blessed Eucharist in less than an hour. With the bishop, Damian thought to herself. I must get off on my own for a few moments.

Damian poured a cup from the teapot that warmed on the stove all day. On the pretext of prayer, she left Vincent to the sweet comfort of strawberry jam after assuring her that the novices were virtuous girls who'd make fine sisters because of Vincent's intercessions with the Virgin on their behalf. Damian was worried about Angelina, who was unhappy, and about Vincent. But there were more weighty matters to be dealt with. She went up to her room and penned and dated a letter of resignation, a prop she might need if His Grace was difficult. She was running out of tricks. Somehow, the building work had reached halfway without stoppage. She'd told Mr Stanley to finish, the cheque would be in the mail, God would provide.

CHAPTER EIGHT

Harriet woke to the bright light just after dawn. She'd rented the apartment sight unseen from Melbourne based on just this picture of a sun-filled bedroom, which she'd seen in a real estate brochure. It also boasted cathedral ceilings, loft life and fine finishes. In facsimile, it was perfect. The real thing was on the top floor of a renovated woolstore in a semi-industrial area, a ten-minute ferry ride or forty-five minute walk from Archangels. The ceilings were more country church than cathedral, and it was no loft, but the finishes were fine enough. Burgundy jarrah and blue laminate contrasted with white walls, and double sash windows looked out to the river. Originally, the building had been designed to maximise light for wool classing, and louvred vertical windows along the zigzag roof meant light streamed in at different angles during the day.

In Brisbane, Harriet was learning, wild things grew uncontrollably because of the sun which was without modesty. At night from the sky, it was beautiful like any city, but by morning it was a jungle. From the back verandah off the kitchen, she could see the red roofs of Teneriffe hill. On Sunday walks, she'd taken careful notes about the single-skinned wooden houses beneath these roofs, raised on stilts against heat and flood. They were like old men on rickettsial legs, farting and shifting in the day's heat. Harriet had gone into the yards to get a closer look. On the verandahs warm breezes and sleeping dogs made her think of Victorian beach towns in summer. She talked to herself and sketched. Occasionally, people came to their front doors and were mostly kind even if they talked a little more loudly than needed and watched carefully as she removed herself. But it was the forest that surrounded these houses, ready to engulf them, that was starting to grip Harriet now, the trees and vines and flowers and birds and insects that once owned Brisbane. New estates might carve into the hills and old buildings disappeared from the city streetscape just as Richard said. But Harriet had started to see that the whole place was underpinned by a forest that was unstoppable, a forest that would overwhelm everything if the people left for a decade or so and let the summers do their work. 'Our most livable city', the signs from the airport said. But livable for what? Harriet had asked a taxi driver the week before. He'd fallen silent. She'd assumed he was reflecting on the idea.

As she was heading out the door the phone rang; the pool manager. 'We found your boot under the bench in the change room. I don't know how you missed it.'

'Silly me,' she said. 'I thought . . .' She let it go.

The first ferry from Teneriffe had three passengers, a thin woman with too much magenta lipstick for any time of the day, a grey-whiskered parks worker in a different coloured green shirt from the plant biologist, and Harriet who edged close enough to read the worker's name badge. It was Jack. 'Do you know a plant biologist whose name starts with M?' she asked him.

He thought for a bit then nodded. 'I reckon you mean Morrie Stewart,' Jack said. 'Great bloke. Knows his ferns.'

'Do you know where I could reach him?'

'Jeez, he used to work out at Brisbane Forest, I think. Best bet's ring our switch and get them to find him.' Harriet thanked Jack, who instructed her to have a good one as he alighted at New Farm Park.

The river was flat gold and quiet, which accentuated what noise there was. Ropes clinked against masts around the New Farm reach where yachts moored and trucks sounded as loud as trains as the ferry trundled under the Story Bridge. They passed Archangels, too, the chapel, the gentle house with its pretty lights shining, the school buildings of the quad and the ugly university that had invaded the campus beyond. Harriet alighted at the top end of the still-snoozing city, wondering if Morrie Stewart would come back to the chapel today. If he didn't, it wasn't meant to be, she decided. And if he did? She looked along gritty Princess Street and passed a man sleeping in a doorway. She felt she loved the sleeping man, she loved Princess Street, Brisbane, the whole world. Perhaps if Morrie didn't show she could flip a coin, tails she'd ring him, heads she wouldn't. Perhaps there would be a sign. She'd go back to the chapel this afternoon and check. She knew she was being ridiculous, but she walked more quickly, feeling she'd accomplished something even though she hadn't.

The first view of Archangels from Princess Street is of the high stone wall that flanks the site on two sides and does not welcome even the brashest visitor. From a distance, the white turrets peep over the wall to entice interest. But at street level, it is powerful enough to shove a visitor backwards onto the footpath, and is broken only by green metal gates at one end. Archangels could have been an invincible fortress in a war, and it would have made Harriet's work easier. War monuments were protected by every level of government as well as by the hush of those who stared in wonder at the lists of dead young men. Archangels' real history was dull in comparison, and there was only so much Harriet could do to embellish that history while Neal had breath in his body.

Harriet's report told what she liked to think of as the truth. Once, the Archangels hill was a gentle rise out of a valley covered in dark forest. It was an important place to the Aboriginal owners, who lived along the bank of the river for thousands of years. When soldiers and their governors arrived, they cleared the forest, murdered the owners and created a prison for recalcitrant offenders. They made Moreton Bay in their own image, and they built Archangels House as the home of the first Catholic bishop, and Archangels Chapel as his first cathedral.

The settlers who sailed with Bishop John Ambleton from Dublin on the *Fortitude* in 1848 were promised land and work in the new free settlement of Brisbane town. But there was neither land nor work, only the enduring fact of convict transportation, so the faithful put up humpies and slab huts in the wounded landscape. They mixed with the worst of men and lost all sense of propriety. Perhaps as those perfect hedges took shape on the hill, they looked up and thought of a former life in Ireland. Keep the faith, the bishop would have told them as he surveyed the mess of their lives. Too many men and too few women made for too few decent unions and children. Convicts committed new crimes, free men became criminals, and emancipists lived as if their sins were atoned. It was a frontier town in all the worst ways.

His Grace must have sighed with relief to greet the first Redemption sisters to arrive twenty years later. The fair rosy servants of Our Lord's redemption came in the middle of the night on the ship *Perseverance*. Hailing from cold grey Dublin they were amazed by the sticky heat, the large trees and the implacable black faces of the natives. Their serge habits dragged through the mud and their winter boots became mildewed. They developed prickly heat and boils in their armpits. Initially, they taught school in makeshift classrooms throughout the city which made them vulnerable to thieves and vagabonds. In 1880, their bishop announced his decision to make his house a school for girls. He moved into town where the roads were paved, gentle folk wore suits and he was no longer forced to look over the mess of human life and tree stumps he'd created in the valley.

The sisters named their school Archangels. They planted hydrangea and geranium, put verandahs and a tower on the convent house and built themselves the new twin-spired chapel. They ordered the construction of a wall, whether to keep the faithful out or to keep their girls in, no one knew, but it grew higher each time the government flattened Princess Street, and eventually turned the gentle hill into a sheer cliff. The wall became a symbol. Faithful and faithless alike could see it from all over town.

With a bit more spine from Ambleton, the Catholic Fortitude Valley might have had a mind to secede from Protestant Brisbane. And Harriet would have had her story, a messy war map on which to pin names and dates, and now a rescue mission for the entire nation to support. They'd send an Army PR officer in a shortsleeved poly shirt and a red lanyard. There would be no university, no new buildings, just memories and a modest entry fee. Archangels would be a monument, to a bloody civil war that raged for decades before the Catholics won. Of course, the Catholics won. They may not have had the numbers or the common sense, but they held the key strategic position which was Archangels. The only access was the narrow front gateway, the lane behind Old Archangels or the water, and the hill afforded views. They could have fought for months and lived off their own produce. Surely the Protestant city would have given up and moved to the Gold Coast. And now Archangels would be safe from harm, a truly sacred site, the site of civil war. Even in

Brisbane, the authorities wouldn't let them demolish the memory of war.

When Harriet had tried her war idea on Neal, only half in jest, he'd given her a look that suggested she was slow-witted. Archangels had a messy, motley history as a presbytery, convent school and university, he'd said. It was enough. If Harriet's job was to go too far, Neal's was to hold her back. She had to unbuild buildings, peel back layers until she had a core of meaning, and then build a believable story which captured the imagination of many. Within broad guidelines, the story had to be true. Neal's job was the detail, too much detail sometimes, which he misconstrued as truth. He collected pieces of paper like a bower bird collects blue, stored them in masses of neatly labelled files and regurgitated them as soon as Harriet pressed the button. He was always right, he made sure of it. Harriet went for the overall narrative, the beginning, middle and end of the story that would get the cheque, stop the wrecking ball, or win public support. She had less respect for small details than Neal and perhaps less respect for the truth. After all, what was truth? she'd asked him more than once.

In terms of the national criteria for listed properties, Neal was right, Archangels had enough heritage to keep it safe forever. But to most people it was a big dull brick wall that told even the friendliest to piss off. Harriet's challenge was to create a story that would excite the casual observer and commit them to conservation. Neal had said no to the civil war, but a convict in the chapel might just do the trick. Everyone loved convicts. And it was possible that rosary beads might belong to a transported felon, however unlikely it had seemed at first.

The buildings that surrounded the quadrangle were constructed in the last decade of the nineteenth century in the style of the house and chapel. They'd been designed by an architect, but Harriet and Neal had decided they were actually the master plan of the second bishop, Gerard O'Hare. When the first bishop had given the nuns his home and church, he'd stripped out whatever wasn't nailed down and had subdivided the hill to sell it off as portions to free settlers. With the proceeds, he'd constructed on a nearby hill a boys' school in the best style of boys' schools. As Archangels chaplain, O'Hare could see the girls struggling to educate themselves and live in the twelve-room house. There was more housework than schoolwork done, and they were dirt poor. When he became bishop, the situation was reversed and the beautiful buildings of the quad had taken shape.

In her office, Harriet was hunting for interview records in the filing cabinets that Neal had carefully systematised. She could never fathom his method which relied on a logic outside the range of the expected. In among building certificates, plans and historical photographs, she located one or two interviews. She was looking for something specific, something to do with blue rosary beads. But by nine o'clock, when Sam D'Allessandro appeared at the door, she had found nothing of any use and the neat folders were in various stages of interrogation on the desk.

'Hah! Is that a small detective–architect?' Harriet looked up. 'YOU FOUND A SKULL!' Sam D'Allessandro was at least a foot taller than Harriet, heavy set with purple lips and eyeshadow, and black eyeliner as if she were trying to put frames around her keen eyes for news. 'OOOooo, I just LURV a mystery.' She wore layers of pink and purple crepe like something from the *Mikado*. 'Look at this place!' The drawing board was covered in partially unfurled sheets, and on almost every other surface were piles of photographs, slides, books and papers. To Harriet, they were promises to be fulfilled, problems investigated for a while and abandoned where she'd lost interest, on the drawing board, floor, coffee table and desk, which was now overlaid with this morning's effort.

Harriet was excellent at focusing on the problem. It was just that the problem kept changing.

'A skull! Where's the chancellor? I want a picture of Frank and the skull. Spot the dead person.' Sam laughed loudly, especially at her own jokes. 'I went down to the chapel yesterday, sweet as pie, and said—' She sat on the corner of Harriet's desk. '"Excuse me, officer, I'm from university public relations. Don't suppose there's any chance of me getting a photographer down there for a teeny picture? We think it might be a rare find".'

She deepened her voice. '"You'll have to wait, ma'am, until forensics has had a look".' She laughed again and slapped her thigh. 'All I can say, Harriet, is some people will do anything to get into the press.' She opened the morning paper to page four where there was a brief story on the skull which mentioned Kevin's name. It ended by saying the police were investigating. 'Any idea who it is?'

'Could be a convict, or one of the priests or nuns.'

'Listen, lovey, you get anything firm, let me know. We could run a story, you know, Archangels history and a skull, could work well. At the moment, there's all sorts of talk.' She paused as if weighing up what to say. 'And it would be good to be public about who it is.'

'What do you mean "talk"?' Harriet was all for the idea of getting the press involved but suspicious when the suggestion came from the university.

Sam looked at her carefully. 'You know what a university's like. It's not such a good idea to have skeletons in your closet who don't have ID bracelets.' She smiled lipstick teeth. 'It's cleaner if we know, that's all.'

Sam D'Allessandro was the university's media adviser. She'd been the first Archangels person to meet Harriet other than the Board-appointed interview panel, and it was a contrast. Sam had found the young architect in her office on her first day, kneeling on the floor in a corner behind the desk,

scratching into the plaster with a key. 'Morning prayer?' she'd
asked. 'Just checking it goes all the way through,' Harriet had
said. 'Of course,' Sam had replied, 'we wouldn't sell you a
fake.' She'd taken Harriet on a confused tour of the campus,
charging ahead, stopping to introduce people, then charging
off again. They went around in circles. Harriet had been
unable to make sense of the site, and it took her a week to
find her bearings. 'He wants to see you.'

'Who?'

'Teddy red, he's back this morning. And he's not too
happy with my little girlfriend architect.' Sam had befriended
Harriet after that first day, taken her on a driving tour of
Brisbane and included her in a dinner with her large circle
of PR-style friends. 'We're meeting, he said, you, me,
Marguerita and Max. A council of war, he's stormin' the top
floor right now. Ten o'clock.'

'Not Max.' Harriet screwed up her nose.

'In Ted's words,' she said in a broad accent, 'Max is the
one who's responsible for this mess. He can explain how the
expletive deleted we got to here.' In normal voice, 'I think
he's looking for you.'

'Professor Dawes?'

'No, Egoboy. He's retracing his steps just a little now Ted's
back.'

'But he agreed with the report.'

'Sometimes he agrees with the last person who told him
he's handsome. That must have been you. But mostly he
agrees with Ted who pays the bills. You'll see. The dynamic
changes just a wee bit when Teddy's home. Max gets back in
his box.'

During the interview when Harriet had tendered for the
Archangels job, Max Palethorpe had been neat in his questions, verging on nasty. Later, Harriet learned he'd run school
education for Queensland before they'd recruited him to
Archangels. He still had something of the teacher about him.

When Harriet had met with him on her first day on the job, he was dressed in a singlet and shorts, about to go running, despite the fact she'd booked an appointment. 'What sport do you do?' was his first question. When she said she liked to swim, he wanted to know times, what time she did a fifty, what time a click, a mile. Harriet didn't know her times; it had never occurred to her to look. She noticed six miniature blow-up penguins on his desk in bowling pin formation. 'You got a job to do,' he said, adjusting a penguin, 'and the panel want you to do it. Me, I'd have preferred we handle the project in-house.' He looked at Harriet's breasts as he talked and played with his penguins, but he might just as easily have been sizing her up as thinking of what to say next. 'By the way, one thing I want clear, you report to me, not Ted. They got that wrong in the job spec. I'm in charge of the campus redevelopment. Think of me as the client.' He smiled although it looked like he didn't want to. Then he did a series of stretches, starting with hamstrings. He reminded Harriet of a priest who'd visited St Pat's to talk about Africa, intensely neat and openly ambitious. Harriet was a person who liked to think of texture and depth, layers of meaning, not only in terms of finishes on buildings where wood was under plaster or bricks but also finishes on people. But she was a lot more canny about building finishes than finishes on people, and they remained opaque to her most of the time. And Max was a difficult person to get to know.

It had been a different kind of first meeting with a client, but Harriet gave him the benefit of the doubt and said, 'The joy of running,' as she left him prostrate on the floor in a position that made him grunt.

She'd only seen Max twice since then, once to make an inquiry into her payments on which the university had lagged, and the second time to deliver her preliminary report. She'd made it clear to him that development of the site was out of the question. He'd smiled and said that was just fine, not to worry, and he admired her integrity. She'd felt chuffed. He talked about the chapel and house as if they were old friends. She was starting to believe he'd shifted to her side.

'I'll be there,' Harriet said to Sam in her office now.

'I just love a drama,' Sam said. 'Ted's gonna EX-PLODE!' Just then Harriet's phone rang so Sam took her leave mouthing, See you at ten.

It was Marguerita Standfast, the Archangels lawyer. 'Max is doing a number on you.'

'So I've heard. Tell me more.'

'Don't know much, and I'm already late for a meeting. Just stand by your report, that's all. I'm with you.'

Harriet thanked Marguerita and put down the phone, which rang again immediately. 'Ted's not exactly satisfied with where we're at.' It was Max. 'I just thought you should know.'

'But you were, Max, you thought everything was fine.'

He hesitated which told the truth, then lied. 'Of course. But I always said we'd have to take into account many factors in devising a strategy. Ted left me to run the thing and that's what I've done. My way. We need to be strategic.' Harriet didn't like his use of the word 'strategic'. Like 'quality assurance' or 'performance management', it was used by people in suits whose eyes met hers squarely while their mouths told lies. It was back to scratch.

Harriet racked her brains for proof that Max had supported her. At their last meeting, he'd said everything was fine. He'd taken the report, he'd read it that night, called the next day, given her the green light on stage two, told her about the Board meeting. He hadn't put it in writing. 'But you told me to go ahead with the conservation plan.'

'Not exactly,' he said. 'We need to hear what Ted has to say.'

Max left Harriet with the impression she was being isolated by the power brokers, and would have to fend for herself against Ted Dawes, the vice-chancellor who'd managed to keep one of Australia's first private universities afloat through tough financial management.

It seemed Marguerita was Harriet's only support, and the corporate view of Marguerita was anyone's guess, but loose cannon came to mind. She was a tall, straight-talking feminist who could carve up the strongest anger with the things that came out in her silky voice. Harriet had first met her two years before at a cocktail party at the University of Melbourne. They'd hit it off immediately, swapped cards and shared a meal sometimes when Marguerita was in Melbourne. Harriet had been pleasantly surprised when she'd phoned a few months before. 'We need someone to advise us on some old buildings and a sympathetic development,' she'd said. Marguerita wasn't the type to be interested in heritage. 'Depends on what you mean by sympathetic,' Harriet had replied. Heritage, according to Marguerita, was simply another manifestation of the patriarchy. Middle-aged white men, she'd told Harriet, that's who those buildings belong to. And they've had their centuries in the sun. Now, it seemed, Marguerita would be Harriet's only ally against some middle-aged white men who had all the sunshine they needed.

Before Harriet left for the meeting, she phoned Neal. 'Do you remember something about blue rosary beads?'

'Where from?'

'I don't know, one of the interviews, something you read.'

'Doesn't ring a bell.'

'Where are the transcripts?'

'In the filing cabinet drawer marked "Interview Transcripts". It's a smokescreen, I put things where I say I'll put them because no one thinks to look there.'

'There is no filing cabinet drawer market "Interview Transcripts".'

'Yes there is, I'm looking at it.'

'Did you move the records to New Farm already?'

'You don't think I'd trust you with them? I shifted all the important files down here when I moved in.'

Harriet glanced over the mess on the desk. 'I remember something, Neal, something about rosary beads. Who's in the crypt?'

'Gerard O'Hare and a couple of others, I think.'

'See if you can find out. I might come into the office later today and have a look.'

'Anything I can do?'

'No, we'll talk later.' She told him about the meeting with Ted Dawes.

'Want me there?'

'No, I'll come to you when I've finished.'

'Lunch at Cosmo?'

'Sounds great.'

Harriet walked up three flights of stairs to the vice-chancellor's suite. She heard voices within, Sam's and another that sounded familiar although she couldn't place it. The receptionist told her to go straight in. She knocked lightly and opened the door. Sitting around a glass-topped coffee table were Max Palethorpe, Marguerita Standfast and Morrie Stewart, the plant biologist from the city council, in a suit. What was Morrie doing here? Harriet stared at Morrie and then noticed Sam standing behind the large oak desk at the other end of the office. Sam was looking at Morrie, too, beaming. 'Ted, this is Harriet, the reason for all the excitement.'

CHAPTER NINE

He was a liar. The stranger from the chapel who was supposed to be Morrie Stewart, the handsome plant biologist and the first man to arouse anything more than base level irritation since Martin, was Ted Dawes, vice-chancellor of Archangels University, Harriet's client, Harriet's nemesis. She didn't say anything. She couldn't speak. He stood up, he had no trouble speaking. 'Harriet, what a pleasure to meet finally.' He was extending a hand which Harriet knew she was supposed to take in hers. He was smiling that bloody smile she'd thought about so often in the last twelve hours. She was finding it difficult to get her arm to move and only managed when all eyes in the room were on her, probably wondering why she'd become a lump in the doorway of the office. I'm not a lump, she told herself, my legs can move. Finally she strode forward, more like someone trying out artificial legs than a one-time liturgical dancer. She gripped his hand. The next step was to let go. He was still smiling, that lovely open smile with the crooked tooth, but now it seemed so false she expected the tooth to straighten. Sam was talking. Harriet could feel his warm dry hand surrounding hers.

'She must be over-whelmed by the whiff of high office, Teddy,' Sam said, 'because it's the first time I've seen Harriet Darling speechless.' High office looked different today, neatly waxed hair combed straight back, babyskin shaven and a lightweight suit. High office smelled like flowers or lemons, Morrie Stewart's cologne.

Ted smiled. 'Do I know you from somewhere?' He made no attempt to release her hand. They stood at the coffee table where Marguerita and Max sat and watched their interaction. Sam had got the intonation and cadence just right when she'd done her Ted impersonation earlier. It was Morrie's voice that belonged to Ted and Harriet hadn't made the connection.

She knew she had to regain her composure. 'Ditto,' she said. 'I feel I know just about all there is to know about you, at least about the way you work.' She was smiling as if this wasn't important, all the while trying to remember what she'd told him and whether it mattered. Somehow she managed to get her hand out of his and back down by her side.

'The way I work. I just say yes and nod at the right times, Ms Darling. Gets me a long way.'

'Call me Harriet, Professor Dawes,' she said. 'Is that ethical for someone in your position?'

'Ted, please. Depends on how you see ethics really. I'm elastic on those kinds of things.'

Sam looked from Ted to Harriet. 'What are you two going on about?' Suddenly she drew a loud breath. 'Ted, where on earth did THOSE SHOES come from?' She'd walked around from behind the desk. Harriet followed her eyes to Ted's feet and saw he was wearing white moccasins.

'Picked them up somewhere,' he said. 'Suit my image, don't you think, Harriet?' She didn't reply. 'Sam, you know what I reckon?' He didn't take his eyes off Harriet. 'I think your architect might see us as the bad guys, destroying our precious heritage down there on the river.' For the first time, he wasn't smiling and a flush of what might have been anger crossed his face. His slicked hair gave him a severity. He took a deep breath and looked out towards Old Archangels. 'A kind of white-shoe developer. But do sit down, Harriet,' he said. 'We don't trade in flesh.'

The office was dim and overbearing in a way that didn't suit Morrie Stewart but probably suited the more sinister Ted Dawes. Two sets of heavily draped french doors opened to small curved verandahs, while dark wood panelling covered the walls behind original art and neat bookshelves. It was an office dressed for success, male success, and a spittoon, moosehead and tiger skin would have fitted right in.

Dawes still looked like someone who'd been in the sun, but in the context of this office he was an executive just back from a holiday in the south of France rather than a plant biologist with parks. The dark suit was only silly when the white shoes came into view. He was right, he'd simply said yes, and she'd made all the assumptions. She'd been the fool, confiding in a stranger. Exactly what had she confided? That she'd been in touch with all the regulating bodies, that she'd go to the press if needs be, that she was powerless although the university didn't know it. But now they did, because she'd told their chief executive. It could be worse but at that moment Harriet couldn't imagine how. She'd figured out her plan for this meeting. But she hadn't figured in a variable, as they say, hadn't planned for the contingency that Ted would already know her true position, and he'd know because she'd told him. And so now she had to revise the plan. She wondered if he was going to sack the firm. He certainly had grounds. Richard would kill her.

Ted was talking. 'So, we have this report that tells us the chapel and my house are significant.' He sat forward, opened her report and smoothed down the spine. His fist was large and brown. Of course, thought Harriet, Archangels House is the vice-chancellor's residence, that's why he was down on the river, that's why she'd seen the lights on this morning from the ferry. 'Quite frankly, we knew they were significant. My reading is that we have to take things slowly.'

'What?' Harriet had to pull herself together.

'No, Ted,' Marguerita said, looking at Harriet as if she expected more. 'Harriet is saying no to what we want to do.' Marguerita's red mouth had a way of putting a point that brooked no argument. 'We mustn't develop the site. We have to find an alternative source of income. I think it's straight-forward.'

Max turned to Ted. 'We have commitments for next year, and a chance to do something about our finances. We need the money for the new business building. Ted, you can't be taking this report seriously.' He wasn't even paying lip service to his earlier support for Harriet, and perhaps because he was backpedalling so fast, she started to regain composure. When Max looked her way, his eyes were cold.

'We're not talking about just any building here, Max. You've read the report. You know how significant Old Arch-angels is. You agreed. You said my report was fine.'

He didn't flinch. 'I told you there were many factors to take into account,' he said flatly. 'You're the consultant. You should have thought of them.'

Harriet was about to respond when Ted put his hand forward. 'I have some questions.' He was gentle, which only made Harriet feel her disadvantage more acutely. He knew her game plan, but she didn't know his. He knew where her loyalties lay, but she didn't have any idea about him except that he liked to sit in the chapel and watch her and pretend to be someone else. 'I reckon some of your facts are wrong, and I want them sorted out so we get a true picture. Max is right. We have pressing commitments for next year. Your report allows no room for negotiation. You've set the chapel up as some kind of monument. And it's not that, however you look at it.' Harriet agreed it wasn't a monument and said she didn't remember using that term in the report. In fact, she remembered very well that good old Neal deleted 'monument' whenever she did use it on the grounds that it was melodramatic. 'You do realise, Harriet, that you work for my university, not the National Trust, and it's our interest you should put first.' Harriet nodded meekly. He had a point.

She felt a little better as they wound their way through the report, and made a mental note to thank Neal for removing all her unsubstantiated claims and exaggerations. He'd cleaned up her grammar, too, which was bad on a good day, and he'd made it work mechanically. But as they turned the pages and read the story, Harriet also commended herself for the wonderful narrative she'd made out of Archangels. The beginning theft, the convict shame, Catholicism and all its trappings, and the school. In what she now saw as a lack of political savvy on her part, she'd given the university just two lines at the end of the history, albeit to say how committed they were to their heritage. She felt she could have given them a bigger wrap, appealed to the Ted Dawes' vanity. Was he vain? Harriet had trouble knowing what he was. He seemed a mass of contradictions, but she guessed that was because his face and body had until this morning been someone quite different. A daggy cardigan on the back of his desk chair reminded her he'd been Morrie. The rest of him was pure chief exec.

Harriet did not resile from the report's conclusion that development of the site was out of the question. 'Far as I'm concerned,' Max said when they'd finished, 'we've got a design that won't interfere with what's here.'

'What design?' Harriet said quickly.

Ted levelled his gaze at Max. 'No we don't. We have two architects telling us two different things. It's a bloody mess, Max. They should have been working together. What am I supposed to do? And as for you, Harriet, Max is right. You've got to start working with us, not against us.'

'It was Harriet's job to advise on the site,' Marguerita said. 'She's the one with support from the National Trust. That's why the panel appointed her. We have her imprimatur, we look good. We can't ignore what she says, whatever we might wish to do. There are government regulations we must follow here. And a casino, Ted. I mean, really.'

'What casino?' Harriet said.

'Max has engaged a second architect off his own bat,' Marguerita looked at Ted sharply, 'who disagrees with your findings. A private developer wants to build a little casino and five-star hotel around the chapel.'

'Just a minute, Marguerita,' Ted said. 'That's no help. My problem is this,' he was addressing Harriet. 'We're a private university that must keep an eye on the bottom line. We're still in our establishment phase. We get no government sub-sidy and we're squeezed every year. We need a new building next year so we can grow enough to tide us over for the following years.' He smiled weakly.

'A casino?' Harriet was stunned. 'For gambling? You can't be serious.' The tender specification for the job had said the university was considering options to refurbish the chapel and house and make them more useful. Never in her wildest imagination could Harriet have believed they meant a casino.

'A boutique casino,' Max said as if it made a difference. 'A little Las Vegas.' He turned to Ted. 'What choice did I have? You were away. My hands were tied by the bloody panel.' Harriet figured the bloody panel must have been the panel that interviewed her. Max must have been the dissent-ing vote. 'Everybody's sweet with what we want to do. I've got the architect, the investor, and the Heritage Commission thinks it's all fine.' Harriet couldn't believe what she was hearing. She asked who in the Commission Max had spoken to. He ignored her. 'What do you reckon Ted?' He looked as if he'd shaved with an energy verging on self-abuse that morning so that instead of a five o'clock shadow he'd taken on a ten o'clock pink.

'How much money?' Harriet said to Ted. 'How much money are they paying you?'

'Five million,' Marguerita said. 'That's what the lease is worth.'

'Marguerita,' Max said sharply.

'She may as well know. She is the architect we've engaged to do the study.'

'Look, Ted,' Max said. 'We have no choice. You know that. I did what I thought was right.'

'I know.' Ted was sitting forward with his head in his hands. 'It's just the way you've done it, Max,' he said to the floor between his feet. 'Marguerita's right. We wanted a heritage consultant, and I wanted us to look after the church and house. We promised the sisters we'd do that.'

'We are looking after the church and house,' Max said. 'We're building around them.' He sat back with his arms folded. He'd won. Harriet had been a bigger fool than simply blabbing in a church. She hadn't slept with the enemy. She'd served herself and her reputation up and fed them to him on a platter. Max had accepted the panel's decision to recruit Corsair Maple, and had let her write this report to lend credibility to what they wanted to do. Meanwhile, Max had been working with another architect to design some tarty little casino. He'd probably gone to the Commission with the blessing of Corsair Maple. Her name would be mud in Brisbane. And Ted might not have liked what Max had done, or might not have cared for all Harriet really knew, but now he was going to let it all happen.

'We found that skull,' Harriet said, 'and we believe it may be that of a well-known convict, which will make the chapel even more significant. I don't think you can do what you're planning in those circumstances.' It was weak but it was all she could think of.

'How do you know it's a convict?' Ted said quickly.

'We're still researching,' Harriet was careful. 'We'll know more after we get in and have a look. Even if we're wrong, important people are buried under the church, and a casino.' Ted looked at her but didn't respond. 'You'll be hated for this,' she was appealing to the Morrie in him. 'Don't you see that? No one wants to hurt that church, not even you if you're honest.'

He got up, arched his back and walked out onto one of the verandahs where he noticed a butcher bird on the balustrade. 'A week,' he turned around and told the meeting. 'I'll give you a week, Harriet.' The butcher bird started a long call. 'Spring's nearly over,' he said. 'Bet he's calling a mate.'

Max stood up and started for the verandah. 'Ted, what do you mean?'

'I mean a week,' he said as he walked back inside. He turned to Harriet. 'Come up with an alternative proposal for the lease, another place they can put the casino, a different design. On the river. A week. We need certainty or the investor will go elsewhere. And there's plenty of sites in this city at the moment. They want the river view, the old buildings. You figure out another place that doesn't cause us any pain and we'll leave the church and house alone. And forget about the skull, which is hardly a winning argument.' He smiled. 'Be good for you, Harriet. Spend some time designing something new instead of digging up graves.' Was he trying for reconciliation? Harriet wondered. Not a chance.

'The past matters,' she said.

'For sure it does, but you topped your year at Melbourne, in design, which is a tough school. You should be creating instead of crawling round ruins.' He'd read her curriculum vitae.

'Ted,' Max said.

'I've made up my mind, Max.' He didn't take his eyes off Harriet as he continued to address Max. 'Another week won't matter to you. And if there is another site and a better proposal, that's good. We recruited Harriet Darling to do a job. Let's give her a chance to do it.'

Harriet wasn't sure there was anything she could do, even if she had a year, but she had a week. Martin had told her that design skills were what was important. University's one thing, he'd said when she won the medal, but the real world is where it counts. You've got to do better. The counsellor nodded when she told him this and said he found that curious, that someone as obviously bright and talented as Harriet would take at face value everything Martin said. Well, now she had a chance to prove Martin wrong. All she had to do was come up with a creative solution to a problem. That couldn't be too hard.

The meeting broke up with Marguerita smiling down at Harriet and whispering to her that this was a good outcome. Sam paced the room, perhaps disappointed there hadn't been more sparks flying and keen for the next drama to unfold. Max left quickly without saying goodbye. Ted wandered back to the french doors where two butcher birds were side by side on the railing. 'I think I was wrong about you,' he said to the first. 'You're the girl.'

CHAPTER TEN

Harriet was singing to herself on the way down the stairs. When she opened the door to her office, she knew something was out of place. She found Max Palethorpe sitting in her chair. He turned it round slowly. 'Just who do you think you are?' he said quietly, his mouth and jaw hardly moving as he spoke. He looked controlled like a robot. Harriet hoped someone sensible was holding the controls as she walked over and stood on the other side of her desk. 'Don't ever embarrass me like that in front of Ted again. You understand? I tried to tell him. Fuck.' He punched the arm of the chair in a small way as he said it, his control slipping. Harriet's breath was catching somewhere down in her bowels and her pulse was getting faster in her head. Calm, she told herself, I'm feeling calm, but her body wasn't listening. She'd heard about Max's temper, how he destroyed people with his cold voice.

'I wasn't trying to embarrass you. You gave my report a green light.'

'You got that right. We do a professional job here and you just don't have it. You messed up at Melbourne too.' He stood up and walked around the desk. He was six inches from Harriet's face. 'In future, you stay out of my business. You hear me.' Harriet was still. His breath was sweet. 'I said, you hear me!' She nodded just before he walked past her and slammed the door so hard the Margaret Olley painting Sam had organised, an Aboriginal woman with a vase of flowers, fell to the floor. Harriet stood in the middle of the room unable to do anything for several minutes. She walked around to her side of the desk, checked her chair for she didn't know what, a bomb perhaps, and looked over her papers. There was nothing missing as far as she could tell, but in that mess who would know.

'Okay, you win,' Neal said when she told him about the meeting. 'Archangels is an evil place, the world's going mad. A casino?' He shook his head. 'That Max is a bully.'

'He was annoyed we've got another week,' Harriet said, and smiled. 'But it was like he and I were in competition to win something from Dawes, I have no idea what.' She hadn't told Neal about Morrie being Ted. 'I told you they were up to something.'

They were seated under a striped umbrella at one of a dozen small cafes in a grubby mall in Fortitude Valley, five minutes walk from Archangels. To the first group of nuns who'd arrived to build the school, this had been a dangerous place where blacks killed whites and Chinamen sold potions. The sisters had needed their wall. To Harriet, who shopped for Chinese vegetables here on Saturday mornings, fresh food markets and light industry were putting up a brave but unwinnable fight. Overnight, young trees and olde paving stones replaced bare chewing-gummed asphalt, and a warehouse became a hundred apartments. Harriet looked over to the groups of young professionals who fought each other for seats at the best cafes. The valley was still dangerous to that extent.

Neal was doing his best with a large piece of sundried tomato and eggplant pizza. 'Okay, HD, you were right, I was wrong. But how do you figure Ted Dawes in all this?'

She bit into bruschetta. 'Maybe he's for real, doesn't like tricks. Maybe he likes old chapels more than casinos. I don't know. He's only given us a week. I'd hardly call him generous.' Neal nodded and pulled at the ropes of cheese trailing his bite of pizza. 'I mean, what can we do in a week? There's nowhere else on that site they could put a casino without interfering with the university.' Harriet had been drawing matchbox-sized buildings on her serviette with a felt pen which had left smudgy balls wherever she paused. 'Unless.' She was looking at her drawings.

'What?'

'You know the wall side of the site, up high. There's a couple of temporary blocks and a low rise. What about there?'

'That's where the graveyard is.'

'Don't suppose we can move it?'

'Harriet, you're supposed to be a heritage architect.'

'I know, it was only an idea.' But she turned the serviette a few times and examined the idea privately.

They walked back to the office at New Farm, which was on the upper floor of a two-storey redbrick tudor house in a suburban street. Neal had done a wonderful job finding retro furniture including a meeting table and chairs that looked as if they'd come straight out of 'The Jetsons'. No chair matched any other but they worked as a group. 'By the way,' he said when she was rolling plans to take back to Archangels, 'I found your blue rosary.'

'Where?'

'Vincent. Remember, the one who took over from Mother Damian?'

'She the one we interviewed in the rest home?'

'That's her. For some reason, she came into my head after we got off the phone, so this morning I looked at her interview.

And bingo. I must say, you have a good idiosyncratic memory.'
Neal went to his desk and took from his neatly stacked pile of
papers the copy of the interview transcript.

Vincent was a big woman in convent photographs, but
she'd shrunk to the centre of the bed. Her interview had been
slow, Harriet remembered, made more difficult by Vincent's
dementia.

Neal had highlighted a section near the end of the interview. 'Mother was too close, too close, and vicious. The noise
the two of them made with their silly laughing. Dear God in
Heaven. Laughing now they'll be, their filthy laughs. Mother
was very distressed when she lost her rosary. Blue they were,
the Virgin colour, and the colour of sin. Poor Mother, poor
Mother. Got them from her daddy at postulancy like the rest
of us. In that beautiful box. Who does she think she is
parading around with that dog like for all the world she's just
a girl. Hah hah lost your beads.'

Vincent had mentioned Mother Damian Ryan as the
owner of a blue rosary. Granted, it was one comment in the
middle of the rantings of a demented nun, but to have
mentioned the rare blue rosary at all gave the account ver-
acity. Neal had said that Bishop Gerard O'Hare was buried in
the crypt, along with a few nuns. Surely the crypt included
Mother Damian, who'd been the reverend mother for half a
century. 'Did you find out if Damian's in the crypt?'

'It's a bit confusing. She has a plot in the graveyard
according to the convent's records but I don't think she's in
it. The nuns often shared plots and headstones to save money.
Hers is with Mary Angelina, one of three nuns who died of
pneumonia after the war. But that dig they did found no
remains in Damian's grave.'

The dig Neal referred to was an archaeological exploration
for Aboriginal artefacts in the 1970s. 'Is there a headstone?'

'Yeah, but only the other nun's name's on it, on the left,
as if they never filled out the other side. At first, they

suggested Damian would have decomposed completely by now, but there were remains for all the others and the soil's good for bones here, so they concluded she mustn't have been buried there. I'm wondering if maybe they prepared a gravesite for her but by the time they buried her she was so famous they put her in the crypt instead. The crypt records postdate the graveyard records.' He paused. 'So, what's this about?'

'Nothing,' Harriet said. 'I just thought I remembered something about the rosary beads.'

'Oh yeah, and then you thought you remembered something about who's in the crypt. Come on, cough up, what is it?'

'Nothing, Neal. Give it a rest. How are you going with your skull research?'

'Not great.' He looked miffed. 'If it's a convict down in the chamber, I don't know how the hell he got there. Bishop Ambleton doesn't strike me as the type to harbour criminals. Maybe some of the nuns were involved. They certainly settled into life in the Valley. Maybe they got close to some of the ex-cons. Maybe they ran a brothel for all we know. It's all speculation, HD, and I wish you'd come clean with whatever you've got.'

'Keep working. Maybe the police will tell you something.'

'Not likely. They've gone very quiet. That detective we talked to was obliging at first but now he won't tell me a thing. Come on, you have to tell me. You're dying to.' He leaned over and nudged her arm.

He was right, she decided, she was dying to tell him, and the convict story looked thinner by the minute. She'd have to save Archangels with her alternative to the casino. She closed the conference room door before she took out the black pouch. 'I took it when you and Kevin were chatting.'

He stared at her. 'You shouldn't have done this.' He was fingering the beads. Harriet noticed how beautiful they were. 'You have to tell the police.'

She snatched the beads from him. 'Why should I? If we find out who it is before they do, we can get Archangels to run a press release. Anyway, these belong to us. We found the skull.'

'HD, this is serious.' She screwed up her nose. 'Well at least you've got some interest in something for a change.' She let that pass.

'So, the skull is Mother Damian's,' she said.

'Probably, if the crypt and chamber are linked. But we can't know for sure until the police let us in.'

'I wish we'd unsealed the crypt in those first two weeks and checked it out.'

'Well, I did suggest—'

'Yeah, I know, but Kevin was difficult about it and I figured it could wait. I wanted to get the preliminary report done.'

'Even without getting into the crypt, we can find out more about Damian and age this pound note.' He looked through the crisp bill. 'It's British, not Australian, and good condition, be worth a packet I imagine.'

'Have we still got the original tape of Vincent's interview?'

It was on the table. 'I knew you wouldn't trust my transcript.'

'It's not that, Neal, it's the voice, it helps. You do a great job. You know I think that.'

'It's still nice to hear it sometimes.'

Harriet sat down at the table. 'You're right, I haven't been very fair, have I?' She sighed heavily. 'I'm afraid I'm not good at all this burning down churches and doing secret deals with other architects. I know I couldn't get through this without you. Today in that meeting with Ted Dawes, I was so thankful for all your work on the report. He said I'd made rash statements. And I had, until you pulled them. They couldn't find a thing, Neal, and that's because of you.' He was trying not to show his pleasure at the praise. Neal spent most of his time in libraries and cellars uncovering small facts about the past. It was hard work, often unrewarding and provided little feedback. He needed to know when he'd done a good job, just like anyone.

Harriet had worked with Neal on a casual basis for five years and had recruited him to Corsair Maple when she'd taken on the partnership. He was quiet by nature and didn't talk much about his personal life but he did tell her once he'd made some life changes, including a new career in research when he finished an honours degree in history. Before that he'd been a drafter. From something he'd said, Harriet was pretty sure he'd been married and that his wife had died, maybe just before they started working together. He'd have been in his late thirties. Harriet had tried to ask him about it once but he'd looked at her so viciously she'd dropped it quickly. It wasn't worth risking their relationship. He was perfect for architectural research because of his experience in drawing and his knowledge of history. She couldn't do a project like this without him now.

Neal had found the owner of the blue rosary beads. It was Mother Damian Ryan. Surely she was also the one reaching for them in the chamber. The crypt and chamber must be joined. The engineer's report certainly didn't rule out a link but they couldn't confirm it until the police granted access. Of course the chamber and crypt were joined under the church, thought Harriet. Who needed an engineer to confirm that? The rosary beads belonged to Damian as Vincent had suggested. She'd been buried in the crypt. The crypt and chamber were joined. It was Damian's skull that the police had taken away to their bright fluorescent offices for testing.

CHAPTER ELEVEN

Located in the old gatehouse at the bottom of the drive, the convent archives hadn't been touched in twenty years. The nuns were supposed to move them to Stanthorpe where the mother house had been re-established after they'd sold Archangels. So far, they'd taken some papers, but they'd left this place and a shed behind Archangels House. The university hadn't needed the gatehouse space yet, although references were made in the draft site plan to a caretaker's cottage there. Max had told Harriet to tell the nuns they should collect their junk if they didn't want it thrown out. In her meeting with the provincial, she'd tactfully suggested they engage an archivist to find out what they had, and that they do this sooner rather than later in case anything was inadvertently lost.

Harriet hadn't told Neal about the archives. Faced with all this information in one place he would have swooned, and she hadn't wanted him distracted by facts while they were working up the preliminary report. In overalls and cotton gloves, she stopped on the stoop and knocked on the large green wooden door, bearing a flashlight and several bunches of keys. 'Open up, narrative police,' she said. All I need's a pith helmet and a little fireman's axe, she thought.

A musty breeze hit Harriet's face as new air flowed through the age old vents when she opened the door. Inside it was cool and smelled of paper and dust. She walked down narrow stairs to the ground floor at street level. In dim light, she saw that the room was chock-full of desks, chairs and school paraphernalia. Near the stairs, she noticed an unfurled banner for the 1949 Archangels spring fair leaning against a wall. She decided to start back upstairs where smaller items were kept.

Originally the kitchen and living area of the porter's cottage, this room was packed. Harriet picked up the 1962 tennis cup, a dress sword and baton, a pink tulle skirt, some silver shoes, one of two plaster fox terriers (the one with an ear snapped off) and an unattached brass doorknob. She put on a grass skirt and took up a pair of castanets. On top of an ivory-inlaid walnut box on a stand, she found a yellow mixmaster with a silver label. The box was locked and there was no key but next to it on the floor were cartons. Some were labelled—SCHOOL YEARBOOKS, REPORTS, PLANS TECHNICAL SCHOOL, LETTERS—but most were not. Harriet opened the first box, pulled up a fruit crate to sit on and started work.

It was a slow process. A carton labelled with much dark black authority—LETTERS, CONVENT—could have anything but letters in it, from photographs to cotton reels to chalk. After an hour of dead ends, she came to an unmarked carton next to the ivory box. It was full of letters, initialled rather than signed, SDR or MDR, Sister or Mother Damian Ryan, and undated. They must be Damian's letters, in draft. Harriet sat back on the fruit crate and started reading.

It's a grand place we found for me, Mother. I know you experienced some trepidation about my call, but I have never been so happy nor felt so useful. I am home.

MARY-ROSE MacCOLL

Our little school continues to grow, with fifty boarders now and twice that number of day girls. They are good children, Mother, with bright eyes and more freckles than you would think possible. We are making a life here in the service of Our Lord with them, despite the heat which is at times overwhelming and the insects which are enormous, as SM Patrick will have told you. We find the sicknesses here are different from home, too, as are the remedies, although the basic rules still apply . . .

Mother Joseph has asked me to be bursar. I told her you would be pleased. You always said I had a head for figures. Part of my responsibility will be the new school to be built on top of the hill. It is indeed a daunting task, and I pray daily for the skills that will be needed. Looking at the blue of the sky here, Mother, I cannot describe it to you, but I have a clear picture of rose stone buildings in a square and an ivory statue of Our Blessed Mother to the Glory of God. I can hardly wait to start, although there is much to be done beforehand to raise sufficient funds.

The rose stone buildings Mother Damian mentioned must be those of the quad, built at the turn of the century. Damian arrived in Brisbane in 1890 and would have been at Archangels through both its major building periods.

We have two black children at the school now which caused some consternation in the valley below us and among some of the parents. I do not believe we could in all good conscience refuse them, Mother. They are people, just like you or me, no different, and yet very different. I do hope you will visit soon, as promised, and bring some more sisters to help.

Harriet read through several letters like this. She chuckled when she found a reference to Archangels' architects. 'We have had to let go of Father Canali.' Carlo Canali, who'd designed the Archangels Chapel, had also done the charming timber verandah and belvedere on Archangels House. 'I feared we were creating some awful thing here, Mother, unworthy of the Lord God, as different from home as could ever be . . . A lovely man filled with the grace of God, but not quite what we need with a set of pencils.' Harriet had seen some dreadful plans for the quad buildings Canali had drawn. She'd wondered what had happened that they were never built.

Harriet and Neal had assumed Bishop Gerard O'Hare had supervised the building works at Archangels. He'd taken over from Ambleton and created the quad precinct. But the letters made it clear that it had been Mother Damian, not O'Hare. Neal had found records of another architect who'd complained to the state government about Archangels in the late nineteenth century. He and Harriet had concluded, in a sexist way Harriet realised now, that the master planner had been Gerard O'Hare. They imagined Archangels was like the Vatican, a separate state where O'Hare could do as he liked, and he'd sacked the architects on a whim. But it wasn't the bishop who did as he liked, it was Mother Damian. She'd have been barely thirty when the quad buildings were finally completed, Harriet's age, and she was master planning a site like Archangels. She'd sacked Carlo Canali who, up until the quad, had virtually owned Archangels. Mother Damian had established herself as a judge of design, an armchair architect as Martin would say, but Harriet agreed with her assessment. None of the first plans for the quad buildings worked with the chapel and house to create the stunning symmetry she finally achieved. Harriet smiled and wondered what Mother Damian would say about the work she and Neal were doing. With the old nun watching over, the casino didn't bear too much thinking about. She read on.

The first school buildings have now been redrawn. I see a beautiful future with Our Lord Jesus at the head, His

Mother at His side and our girls in prayer. Mr Campbell, whom you may know through our sisters in India where he built St Mary's, has agreed to take on the commission and for this we are fortunate. He has not only the most exquisite eye but also the most agreeable nature and a solid faith in what we are trying to achieve at Archangels.

His Grace the Most Reverend Gerard O'Hare formally took up office as our new Bishop this month. As you know Bishop Ambleton had been ill for some time. Father O'Hare has been a constant source of support and inspiration as our mentor and confessor. Already he has indicated a need to press ahead as a matter of urgency with my buildings. I know I have come to my mission, Mother. You were right. I could not be happier in service.

Harriet looked at her watch and realised she was due in a meeting with Sam D'Allessandro. She left the letters and the open box on a table, locked the gatehouse and made her way back up the hill. She hadn't found an answer to the question of how Mother Damian got into the chamber, but already the words for the final report were forming in her head: 'Mother Damian Ryan, Archangels Architect, a woman of great achievement'.

On the way to Sam's office, Harriet called at the swimming pool. The smirk on the faces of the attendants told her their opinion of her, and they were right. She'd screamed thief when all the while her boot was obvious under the bench. She'd considered saying, in her defence, that the thief must have put the boot back, but decided it would only make things worse. It was easier to find a new pool.

'I know Mother Damian was terrific, Harriet, but we don't want to draw attention to the skull right now.' Sam D'Allessandro stood behind her black desk with her arms folded. Harriet stood at the door nursing the boot. 'Simple.' Her office was in one of the new university buildings, with a plateglass view over Brisbane. It was finished in black leather, glossy plastic and fat red cushions.

'Who's we?'

'We the university,' Sam said.

'But it's Mother Damian. You said this morning we should do a story.'

'I did, but I changed my mind.' Sam pursed her lips.

'It's the chapel, isn't it?'

'What?'

'Because of the meeting this morning, the casino. You don't want the church in the press.'

'Don't be silly.'

'Then what?'

'I just want to go easy, pet.'

Harriet pointed her boot at Sam. 'You guys are incredible. I tell you, Sam, you can't develop the church site.' Sam looked puzzled. 'I get this, okay? I get it. And it stinks.'

'You think we don't want to do a press release because we want to blow up the chapel?'

'Yes,' Harriet said curtly.

'For goodness sake, Harriet, you are so unsophisticated. Come in and sit down. I'll tell you why I can't do a release,' she lowered her voice to a whisper, 'on the skeleton.'

Sam swept over and closed her office door, motioned Harriet to sit on the lounge and from her desk told the telephone to hold calls. 'I assume the entire world knows because that's what it felt like at the time.' She sighed loudly as she sunk into the lounge opposite Harriet, and then moved forward, elbows on knees, legs apart. 'Here we go.' Black eyeliner and green to purple shadow rainbowed from the outside edges of her eyes up to her hairline. 'But you have to promise to keep it to yourself.'

'Of course,' Harriet said, still miffed but warming to the intrigue.

'Ted's wife left him.'

'So?'

'So she not only left Ted, she left everyone, family, friends, her two jobs, a house in Sydney, us. Without a word!'

'And you think the skull?'

'Don't be silly, but there was talk.' Sam narrowed her eyes. 'Frankly, it was more the way it happened than anything else.' She lowered her voice and leaned further forward. 'It was two years ago now, and Ted was at a meeting down the coast, came home, no Mattie! If you'd known her, Harriet, she was so bright, such a good balance for him. She had something, charisma, pizzazz, I just wish . . . Anyway, late that night, still no Mattie, so Ted calls the police. They don't take him seriously of course. He's had a few drinks, and I suppose wives are fickle like that, they disappear all the time! She lives half-time in Sydney so the police suggest that's where she's gone. Next morning, still no Mattie, Sydney house still not answering, Ted's a mess! Hung over and I have to come in and hold his hand. No idea!

'Slowly, little details emerge. She's taken a suitcase, frocks. There's money gone from the account. He finds a letter. I never saw it but he pulled us all into his office and told us Mattie had decided to leave and we'd just have to get on with life. He was nearly in tears! He's never mentioned her since, not once. I used to try to talk about her, or at least about her staff who he treats terribly now, as if they're not even part of the university. He'd give me his YOU'RE GOING TOO FAR SAM look. And that would be that.'

'She worked here?'

'Oh yeah, she's Professor Mattie Hamilton, the gynaecologist, she ran our largest research centre—infertility. We're big on fertility here, we make babies, and Mattie was world class. She and Ted were a package when the university started. They were great, Harriet, young, well connected, at least on her side, a real darling, one of the reasons I took this job actually. A dream to work with, such a gift with the press.

Bit like Max.' Harriet screwed up her nose. 'Don't frown. Some people just have a media instinct, they know what to say. Max managed all those terrible changes in school education and got quite a name for himself. Ted's a nerd scientist, too cautious. He was completely stuffed without Mattie.

'But it gets worse. She didn't turn up for work, not even in Sydney where she ran a clinic. Friends and family didn't hear from her either. A week goes by, another, then it's a month and suddenly the police are really interested. They interview us all, and we go through it again. That was the worst time. It would start to die down, and something would happen. Someone painted PIG on Ted's car in red. Probably students, probably not even related, who knows, we were all paranoid by then. I had to manage him. He wouldn't have coped without me. I never want to go through that again.

'Frankly, if I'd known she was going to drop out like that, I might have managed it differently right from the start. I could have made Ted into a nice grieving husband whose wife has vanished, instead of the separated vice-chancellor. Disappearance is a mystery, but separation is scandal material.'

'These days? Even royals divorce.'

'We're not some tatty little monarchy. Case you hadn't noticed, lots of our money is old. Or if it's new, it'd like to be old. We may not be religious, but many of our backers are either large C Catholic or large C Conservative, or both. Divorce and the CEO; not a good idea. The board was UN-UN-HAPPY, believe me.'

'Did the police think he had something to do with it?'

Sam shrugged. To her, it seemed, the whole thing was just another PR problem. 'Knowing Mattie, she's probably having a great time in some exotic island resort laughing her head off at us.' Sam chuckled. 'I'll admit it's been a while, but Mattie was so very much alive, I just can't imagine her dead. When we found that skull yesterday, it didn't even cross my mind that people might put the two things together. And, as you say, it's good old Mother Damian. To be completely honest, I'm with you. A story would be a good strategy, even given everything. But Mister boring Ted took me aside after our meeting this morning and said he wants to keep it quiet. I suppose he thinks the more it's in the press, the more people will talk.'

Back in her office, Harriet phoned Marguerita. 'Sam's big mouth will get her into trouble one of these days,' Marguerita said. 'We all agreed we don't talk about this.'

'Is it true?'

'Sort of, but she puts a spin on it. Wait there.' A few minutes later, Marguerita was standing at the door of Harriet's office. 'The only thing I'm sure about is that Mattie left Ted and that's all I care about. I saw the letter she wrote which we showed to the cops at the time.'

'Sam said there was an investigation.'

'Of course there was. She comes from one of those we're-so-important families. They're successful and they're bloody rich. They weren't going to put up with their daughter leaving with no explanation. They kicked up a hell of a stink, especially her father.'

'What do you think happened?' Harriet couldn't believe no one had mentioned it before.

'Who knows? I always figured she got sick of being the great Professor Mattie Hamilton and cleared out. Made sense to me. She certainly took enough money to set up somewhere else, emptied their accounts from what I understand. Left Ted embarrassed for a month or so until he got into their savings. I had to lend him lunch money. And if you'd heard her father Alexander Hamilton, on television about his perfect daughter. What a creep.'

'What about the police?'

'They questioned us, stood around drinking coffee for a bit then gave up. They were always polite with Ted. I'm sure they figured Mattie had left but couldn't say so because of old

Alexander. He was terrible, Harriet, said Mattie was a dutiful
wife with a great future, implied those close to her were
jealous of her success, all but accused Ted of lying.

'Who knows, maybe she came to some trouble after she
left. Mattie was a pretty adventurous girl and sometimes
adventure can lead to misadventure.' She looked at Harriet.
'At the time, Ted's media adviser was his worst enemy.'

'Sam?'

Marguerita nodded. 'She started off with the idea that no
publicity is bad publicity. In her mind, it was better that
Mattie disappeared than that she left Ted because this would
make him look better with the Board and less of a failure in
the community.'

'She mentioned that.'

'Did she also mention that she actually encouraged the
press? Ted was furious when he found out. Then she got this
idea she'd fix it for him. She found an academic lawyer and
did all this stuff to get her and Ted in the social pages, to
show he wasn't flawed with women or something. The two
of them had nothing in common. You know Ted, he's so down
to earth and she was up there.' Marguerita reached above
herself. 'Beautiful and a thorough snob. Anyway, when his
picture's in the press with this other woman, it all starts up
again. What a mess. Ted doesn't do media stuff now and he's
better off.'

'Sam said Mattie was really something.'

'Yeah, something. I don't think she liked me much, but
she was Sam's type. She certainly had a way of getting support
for whatever her centre was doing.'

'Sounds like you didn't like her much either.'

'She was hard. So am I. We'd have clashed if we'd got to
know one another well.'

'It's silly not to do the story now. We think the skull in
the chapel is Mother Damian, but Sam said no because Ted

doesn't want to draw attention. Surely it's better to have the facts out in the open.'

'I'm totally behind Ted on that. I don't think we should do anything. My advice was wait and see what the police come up with.' Marguerita looked flatly at Harriet. 'You never know.' She ran her finger along the sill as if checking for dust.

Harriet stopped at the Archangels library to find a short biog on Mother Damian. The old nun had made it into *Who's Who*. 'Born Dublin Ireland 1870; Nora Mary Ryan, daughter of Patrick and May, three siblings Patrick, Michael and Sean, arrived Australia 1890, Reverend Mother of the Sisters of the Blessed Redemption (RC) 1897–1949, died 1949.' A life reduced to a few lines in a fat book. After she'd copied the entry, Harriet went to the computer terminals, logged on to the Internet and typed in 'Mattie Hamilton' in the search menu. There were a hundred or so references, mostly dealing with the work of the Archangels Infertility Centre, the AIC whose GIFT breakthroughs had doubled the number of couples who could benefit from IVF. She found a short newspaper article on Mattie's disappearance with a photograph. It said she'd disappeared from the couple's Brisbane home and an extensive police investigation and family-offered reward had so far failed to provide any clues as to her whereabouts. Harriet peered at the grainy photograph and pressed 'print'. On the way out, she picked up the photograph of Mattie Hamilton from the reference desk and put in her satchel without looking at it.

CHAPTER TWELVE

She heard his step on the choir stairs. 'I'm not in a dancing mood.'

'And the fig looks fine.' He was wearing the expensive suit of their meeting, but his long legs finished in black shoes now rather than white. 'I'm sorry about this morning.' He walked towards her, hands thrust in pockets. 'I was going to drop down and see you before the meeting, but I doubt it would have helped.'

Harriet's natural inclination was to feel sorry for Ted Dawes after what Sam and Marguerita had told her, but she knew enough about him to be cautious. 'You seem to spend a lot of your time doing the wrong thing and the rest apologising for it.' He was standing in a circle of the light that spilled into the nave through cracks in the boards on the high windows.

'That's a pretty good summary, although I'm usually more in control.' For someone who wasn't in control, he was doing a good imitation, Harriet decided. He knew everything about her plans. She knew nothing about his. He'd given her a week, but why wouldn't he? The police could take that long anyway, and she might come up with something he could use. Her firm's name was associated with his project. She had the heritage credibility he needed. He had to keep her on side. Max might have gone behind her back to engage a second architect and be happy to ignore her report, but Dawes had deceived her, too. He was kicking at the floor in what she saw as contrived coyness. 'You're not exactly squeaky clean,' he said. 'I was right in what I said. You work for us, not the Trust. You shouldn't be digging up dirt on what your client wants to do.'

'So you said, but this morning certainly vindicated me. You've been going behind my back.'

'Fair enough, I won't try to convince you I didn't know what Max was doing, although I didn't.' He flashed a smile. 'You still have your week. That was good of me.' He walked closer. 'They tell me you're interested in the skull.' His voice was even.

'I'm a researcher,' she said carefully. 'Maybe there's some history in it.'

'Sam called me after you spoke to her. I thought you said it was a convict.'

'Yesterday you were a plant biologist.' He smiled. 'We did think it was a convict, but we now think it's Mother Damian Ryan.' Harriet wondered whether Sam had also mentioned to Ted that they'd talked about his wife. It didn't appear so.

'The old matriarch herself. How'd she get here?'

'There's a crypt underneath us. We think it's joined to the chamber where we found the skull. I went to see Sam about a story. But she said you're hesitant.' She looked at his eyes.

They blinked. 'Not at all. But the police have asked us to keep things quiet until they've made an announcement.' Harriet nodded. If he was worried the skull in the crypt was his wife, he didn't show it. 'They came to see me last night.'

'I'm pretty sure I'm right,' she said more gently.

'I was wondering if you'd like to join a group for lunch at my house on Saturday. Just casual.' He was kicking at the floor again and not looking at her. She had an impression he hadn't given a personal invitation to lunch for a long time. 'It's a chance to get to know us, see if we're as bad as you think.'

'I'd love to.' It wasn't what she'd expected. Once again, he'd caught her off guard.

Someone called to them from the back of the chapel. 'Hello?'

'Up here,' Harriet answered.

'Look at this mess. What a terrible shame.' A man, late fifties, in jeans, work boots and a green shirt, walked towards Harriet and Ted. His lined face was ruddy and freckled and his sandy hair fell in thin sweaty wisps over his bare head. He held a straw hat in his hands and gloves hung from his key clip.

'You're Morrie Stewart,' Harriet said.

'Everybody's Morrie Stewart.' Ted was standing close behind her.

'Pleased to meet ya,' Morrie said. His hand was dry and rough. 'Bloody awful mess.'

'Yes,' said Harriet, 'and here's the man you should write a letter of protest to.'

'Ay?'

'Never mind.'

'This isn't really my department,' Morrie reflected. 'I'm forests. They oughta send someone from environment and heritage.'

'Yes,' said Harriet, 'although you might check the fig.'

'I thought I was supposed to check the fig,' Ted said.

'I think Morrie's more qualified.'

'Actually, my research is ferns, but what the hell.' Morrie left through the side door of the chapel which had been opened to allow the clean-up to continue.

'I might go with him,' Ted said. 'I happen to like fig trees.' He confirmed the time for lunch. 'Look forward to it,' he said, and smiled that smile.

Harriet wasn't going to be charmed. 'Likewise,' she responded.

After Ted had gone, she paced out the distance from the crypt to the chamber under the sacristy. She tried to imagine how a link might work, tapping the floor in a few areas to see whether there were sound differences. There weren't, not that it meant anything. Finally, she went into the taped-off area and checked that the police padlock was secure on the trapdoor. It was.

Walking back up the hill, Harriet felt light and happy, and a niggling thought drifted just far enough away to tease her consciousness. A soft breeze off the river caressed the back of her neck, and she touched the blue rosary in her pocket while the thought wandered closer. Was it to do with the skeleton? No doubt the police would announce its age in the next few days, and she should return to the archives to build a better story. She turned around and looked at the chapel. She ran her fingers over the smooth cool beads and tossed them from hand to hand. She watched them catch the sunlight and piled them into her palm. She felt time slowing, one of those significant moments that doesn't always reveal the secret of its significance. What was it? Sam said Ted Dawes' wife had disappeared. She'd left him and flipped out of sight. It was the way relationships finished from the point of view of the one left behind; the beloved is gone with no satisfactory explanation and you're left wondering what's wrong with you. That's what it had been like with Martin. But it was more than that for Ted. Mattie had left him and then she'd left the world. She'd vanished. It was indeed mysterious. The niggling thought persisted and Harriet stared at the beads in her open palm for a moment more. Then she knew. It was not, surprisingly, this latest version of Ted Dawes, a man with a disappeared wife. Nor was it a concern about what had happened or whether Ted himself might have been involved. No, what was nudging Harriet Darling's consciousness on that pleasant spring evening was that he'd asked her to lunch and she was looking forward to it.

CHAPTER THIRTEEN

Harriet spent the next day at the New Farm office and it wasn't until late afternoon that she had the chance to return to the archives. She'd decided to read every letter systematically and order them chronologically to build a timeline of Mother Damian's life. Most of them grouped around one or other of the two major building periods, the first at the turn of the century and the second after World War II, with fewer in the period between. Harriet wrote, '1890s then post-WWII?', and felt good to have made a note. But she quickly became bored with the systematic approach and took to picking up letters at random again in the hope she'd find something interesting. Damian's style changed over the period, from an immature, conservative hand to something more flamboyant and rich, and from hesitant reportage to comfortable authority. The later letters were of most interest to Harriet, approaching the time of Damian's death. These became recognisable by the different handwriting as well as by the paper which was less yellowed. Harriet read on as the sun made long shadows then disappeared beneath the gate-house window.

The Good Lord is smiling on your sisters although the Government has now confirmed its intention to require training for teachers. Loud voices in the Legislative Assembly say religious education is unsuitable for our youth, and they are being heard, Mother. It's the work of the devil, to be sure, but I am lost to know how we would manage without the supplementary funding we receive from the State. Vincent has finished her teaching certificate and will be back to school next week. Her health has failed to improve, however, and I may be seeking your assistance at a later stage to provide her with passage home.

Angelina and Oliver will take first vows with myself as spiritual adviser on the twenty-seventh of next month. SM Oliver is trained to teach and we are thrilled to have another two sisters and establish a truly local presence here. I only wish our dear Bishop O'Hare might have lived to see them. Angelina is a beautiful bird in song for the Lord, and she has had her crosses to bear as you well know, Mother. She is still so young for the life, and I worry she doesn't have enough lightness in her spirit. I do hope she will be able to visit the mother house before long.

I understand that SM Bernadette has been in contact with you by recent mail with private concerns about the school and convent. I realise she has a role to play as Head of School. But she has raised the matter with His Grace, which is not appropriate despite any prior relationship they may have enjoyed during her postulancy in Ireland. Bernadette would like us to run our school and house in a more disciplinary fashion. Let me be frank, Mother. She wants more of the cane. I have no intention of resiling from my position which has always been in Him, His Mother the Blessed Virgin and our Foundress, to recognise the goodness of every single person.

I stopped the practice of monthly examinations of the girls by His Grace because it was an upsetting and humiliating experience for the girls themselves who were expected to know what they had not been taught. They are clever and capable young women, Mother. Two from this year's graduating class will go on to university studies. Without seeming critical, His Grace is a daunting examiner, and the girls feel he sets out to trick them into making a mistake, which is not my idea of education at all. Without wanting to compare, I must say our dear Bishop O'Hare, God rest him, always made a point of visiting the girls, too, but it lacked the terrible hammer of judgement I feel the new Bishop wields.

Perhaps I am unwise to write of these things so plainly, but times are difficult enough with the Government attitude, and I need to know I have your unfailing support. I await your further advice upon the matter. In particular, I would appreciate some instructions as to my response to SM Bernadette. I cannot stress to you the seriousness of these matters. For the meantime, I will continue as Reverend Mother to carry out the responsibilities vested in me.

If Neal had been there, he'd have told Harriet not to muddle the order of papers because it would help with dating. She looked to the stack of opened letters on the floor. Oh well. At any rate, the bishop Damian mentioned in this last letter was James Douglas, who replaced Gerard O'Hare in 1943. The building period therefore was the second spurt, in the late forties. Damian died in 1949. There was no mention of a rosary, but conflict was a good start.

Harriet found it hard to read under the weak overhead bulb. She'd been using her torch for an hour when it started to flicker. She stood and stretched. Her back was sore from sitting bent over. Her hands were dry and dusty with paper. The time had gone so quickly, and yet she'd only made that initial note about the two periods into which the letters grouped. It was as if Damian herself were talking to Harriet, about life in the convent and school, her difficulties and small joys. Harriet had been surprised by the young energetic portrait in the boardroom. Damian was an extraordinary woman, and Harriet looked forward to recognising her achievements in the final report.

She was about to lock up and take her gear back to the office when she noticed, at the bottom of the box she was repacking, a small black prayer book. When she ran her hand over the soft leather, her heart jumped. It looked and felt identical to the leather of the rosary pouch. The pages were finely edged in gold which rubbed off in sparkles onto her fingers. The book opened naturally at a page where a small sheet of Damian's writing paper had been glued in. There was a single prayer, in a script that must have been Damian attempting neatness.

> Lead kindly Light, amid the encircling gloom,
> Lead Thou me on;
> The night is dark and I am far from home,
> Lead Thou me on.

Harriet read and reread the prayer. It was the sort of thing you might find comfort in, near the end of your life, or if you knew there was no more life to be had. Maybe Damian had this book in the chamber. But that couldn't be right because it couldn't have then found its way to the archives. Harriet had to think logically and stop her imagination running away with her. She couldn't wait to tell Neal about this. She held the prayer book close to her chest. She felt happy with her discovery and also immensely sad. She joined her hands under the book and in a rare moment of faith said a prayer for Damian. 'Dear God, I hope you cared for her at the end. I hope your kindly light was there in the chamber to take her home.'

CHAPTER FOURTEEN

Harriet was locking the gatehouse door behind her when she realised she'd left her torch and was still clutching the prayer book to her chest. She rolled her shoulders, which felt as if they'd been winched tight. As she reopened the door, she heard something rustle. Rats? She crouched to replace Mother Damian's book, and a gust of wind ran around the room with a loud whisper. The prayer book slipped from her hand and into the box, open at the page where the prayer was glued in. She picked up the book and as she did the prayer fell out. Underneath, she noticed a folded sheet of notepaper. Harriet's torch had given out completely. She unfolded the paper, held it up to the light, then stood on the wooden crate to read it against the bulb. Even then, she could just make out the words.

I must see you. Please don't deny me. I must, just once more. We are made to be with one another. My darling, my love, life, light.

It was unsigned, undated, perhaps unsent. When was it written? It was a note to a lover, with that formal intimacy borne of desperation, that neediness which knows only one remedy. Mother Damian had a lover.

At home, Harriet drank the rest of the riesling and ate crackers absently as she stared at the prayer book which sat in the middle of the coffee table. When she looked at her watch it was after two am; she had no idea where the time had gone. She imagined telling Neal, 'Mother Damian was the power behind Archangels, not the bishop. And she took a lover. I really have found something this time.' And Neal, gentle, intellectual and largely cynical Neal, would look over his bifocals with his head down in the note. He'd nod slowly and say, 'Yes, HD, you most certainly have.'

A bright morning woke her from a light sleep on the couch. She checked that her treasures were on the table where she'd left them, and while she made coffee, looked round the corner from the kitchen several times to make sure. Lack of sleep and yellow sunlight sped up the world. She took the note in her hand and ran it against her face. It was scented. The paper was a finer grade than Damian's normal writing paper. It was the sort of paper Harriet would reserve for her most important correspondence, intimate moments she wanted to preserve, moments she might have shared with Martin. Damian was much the same. She looked at it again. The note still said what it had said the night before, 'I must see you'. In the light of day, she noticed a few faded pink stains on the paper, like rose water. The hand, surely Damian's hand, was desperate.

Harriet needed a few more hours sleep, but a thousand thoughts rushed through her head. When was it written? Was the affair consummated? Was it over a long period? Who was it? Who knew? She'd been led to the letter by that inex- plicable gust of wind in the archive, the way the book had fallen open and the paper had slipped out and onto the floor. She'd been praying for a peaceful end to Mother Damian's life. Harriet hadn't believed in God or prayed for years but the way the gust led her to the note was disturbing.

Her head was full. She was wearing day-old clothes and the kitchen was wicked with two-day old lasagne, thankfully vegetable rather than beef, sitting in the sink where it had turned it into a science experiment with the heat. She threw the lasagne and a couple of cultured pears into the rubbish and took it downstairs. There was no mail, but squeezed between her box and the wall was a police calling card. 'We see you're not home,' it said in its printed script. 'And we'd like to talk with you. Please call Detective Inspector Jack Champion,' the name filled out in a large loopy hand.

Sitting on Harriet's minimalist lounge an hour later, Jack Champion looked to Harriet like her father Stan and not like him at all. His quick neat movements were something like Stan's, and his voice was slightly too loud for the room in the same way. Like Stan, he was definitely the one in charge. But Jack was tightly organised in his body, verging on niggardly, in short sleeves and a tie that had seen better days, and his eyes were hard. He said they were investigating. 'You've done the work on the chapel so far, that right?'

'Yes, and that's how we knew about Mother Damian. She's in the crypt and we think it's linked to the chamber where we found the bones.' He'd taken careful notes as she'd told her Mother Damian story. She hadn't mentioned the rosary beads. It was too late now to explain why she took them, and she'd hardly need them once she could prove Mother Damian was in the crypt. She didn't mention the note either. Harriet wasn't sure she wanted to tell anyone about Mother Damian's love letter. She felt it would be a betrayal.

'What makes you think there's a link?'

'The chamber isn't on the original building plans but the architect must have put it there for a reason. If he put in two underground rooms, he'd almost certainly link them.'

'What was the chamber used for originally?'

'We don't know. I wondered at first if it was a place to hide convicts, but that's unlikely. Maybe it's an extension of the crypt.'

'But you're not sure there's a link?'

'We're waiting for you to give us access so we can run some tests. But we know Mother Damian is in the crypt.'

'Pretty long bow to draw.' He was looking through his notebook when Harriet noticed the prayer book and the open note on the table facing him. She picked them up quickly along with her dinner plate and wine glass.

'When you live alone, there's no one to keep neat for. Let me clear these things.' In the kitchen behind him, she put the prayer book and note up on her recipe-book shelf, then offered coffee. He'd followed her and was standing on the lounge side of the kitchen bench. He said yes to coffee. Harriet thought he was looking up towards the recipe books, and didn't dare follow his eyes there. She got out two cups and noticed her hand was shaking.

'You told me they were trying to demolish the church, that right?' Jack Champion watched her as she slid his coffee across the bench.

'I sent them packing just before we found Mother Damian.' He asked who had arranged the demolition team. 'Kevin McAnelly, who I think you met.' He nodded. 'But he was acting under instruction from Ted Dawes.' Harriet was relieved when he followed her away from the kitchen and back to the lounge.

'Good coffee. That would be Professor Ted Dawes, the vice-chancellor?' He made a note. 'But he wasn't in Brisbane on the weekend.'

'No, he was overseas, but Kevin spoke to him on the phone.'

'Have you spoken to Dawes or McAnelly since?' Harriet told him she'd met with Ted to discuss her report. 'Did he seem concerned?' She asked why he should. 'Well, you stopped him knocking down the church. Was he upset about that?'

Harriet shrugged. 'To be honest, I think I may have been a little hasty in my judgement of him, Inspector. He's given me a week to come up with suggested alternatives.'

'You know what they're planning for that area around the church?'

Harriet thought of Max. 'My firm advised them to leave the chapel site alone. It's a significant building because it incorporates one of the oldest buildings in the city within its structure. It's not something you can mess about with.'

'But?' Jack didn't have much interest in Archangels' history.

'The university has also engaged another architect. They are quite advanced in planning a building for the chapel site.' Harriet made a mental note to find out the name of the other firm.

'Professor Dawes put on this other architect?'

'No, Max Palethorpe did.'

'The deputy vice-chancellor.' He made another note. 'Was Dawes supportive of the plans?'

'I don't think so, although we didn't discuss them in any detail. He was certainly annoyed that two architects were telling them two different things. And as I say, he gave me a week to come up with an alternative.'

'Maybe he knew you wouldn't be able to do that.' Harriet must have shown that she felt slighted because he added, 'I mean, maybe he knows there are no alternatives. It's a riverside casino, isn't it?'

'I believe so.'

'Well, there's only one bit of riverside, isn't there?' Harriet nodded. 'You seen the plans they got?' Harriet said no. 'We believe Professor Dawes was going to cover that little church of yours with a great big building.' Jack had made himself comfortable on the lounge. He'd put his notebook on the table and was leaning back with his hands behind his head. He was watching Harriet carefully. 'Like a shroud. Why do you think he might do that?'

'Who said that?'

'I've seen it on paper.'

Harriet was suspicious of police, naturally wary of authority in all its forms. But Jack Champion seemed different. 'To be honest, it wouldn't surprise me, Inspector. Archangels has been a difficult client, and they appointed another architect behind my back. That's quite unethical.'

'How long you known Professor Dawes?'

'I've just met him.'

'How's he strike you?'

Harriet was surprised to find herself blushing, which only made her blush more. 'Why, I don't really know. He might be a good fellow. Why are you so interested in Ted Dawes?'

'He runs the university where you found a skull. I like to know who I'm dealing with.'

'Did you ask him all the same questions about me?'

'Matter of fact, I did.' He paused.

'What did he say?'

Harriet got up and walked back to the kitchen to pour more coffee. 'He said you're a person of high integrity. Is that true?' Harriet said that it was, and thought immediately of the rosary beads and prayer book. She should have told him, she knew that, but it was too late now. He asked for a copy of her report and she took him into the study where his eyes took in the mess on the desk, the walls where she'd pinned pictures and colours for inspiration, and the corkboard above the desk where he stopped. He turned and looked at her. 'What's that doing here?'

It was the picture of Mattie Hamilton she'd printed in the library. 'Oh that.' Harriet felt like a child caught stealing sweets. 'It's a friend.' He looked closely at the photograph and then at Harriet as if he might say something. She buried her head in a filing cabinet to find a copy of her report. She hoped he wouldn't know who it was. 'Here it is,' she said. 'It's brilliant.'

As he was leaving, she asked whether there was any news on when the chapel would be released. 'Still with forensics,' he responded.

'Any clues about the skull you can share?'

He looked at her for a moment. 'Nice place you got here. Bright.' He smiled. 'Still with forensics.'

Harriet felt bothered after Jack Champion left. At first she attributed this to her failure to disclose relevant information to a crime, or whatever they called it. But as she went over their conversation, she realised that he, too, hadn't been entirely honest. He knew more about the skeleton than he let on, and he'd listened to what she'd told him about Mother Damian as if he'd already figured it out. Perhaps he already knew how Mother Damian had reached the chamber, or perhaps something Harriet said had told him. He certainly knew more about Archangels than she did. She realised, too, he'd know full well who Mattie Hamilton was. He probably investigated her disappearance in the first place. Cheap aftershave lingered and left Harriet nervous. She couldn't help thinking she'd ended up implying something she didn't mean, although she had no idea what it might be. She called the New Farm office and said she wanted to work from home for the rest of the day. There were half a dozen messages to return, and a couple of letters for signature that could wait until the next morning. Neal had a client for them to see but agreed to go on his own.

Max's office had refused to give her a copy of the other architect's drawings. She'd managed to weasel the original specification out of Sam D'Allessandro, but even that had been difficult. 'The things I do for you, Harriet Darling! You owe me lunch. And not some crappy uni cafe.' Sam had stood behind her desk. 'Maybe I should check with Max and Ted first. What if you use it against us?'

'Don't be ridiculous, Sam. What could I possibly do with it?' What she could do was tell the media that Archangels was selling out to a developer who wanted to take over the riverside for rich foreign gamblers. 'Please, you won't regret it.' Harriet thought of Sam's fat bejewelled fingers handing over the brief. She'd asked about the lunch at Ted's. 'He mentioned it. I need to look around the house,' Harriet had said.

'Good, I'll see you there. Might liven up the old place a bit, you and me. Sure could use it.'

'Does Ted have someone now?' Harriet said casually.

'No, and he needs a nice girl.' Sam raised an eyebrow and smiled. 'Like you.'

'I didn't mean that, I just meant who would be there and so forth.' She backed into the doorjamb on her way out.

Sam said, 'You know what's funny? He asked the same thing about you. I told him you wear that ring.'

Harriet smiled to herself now as she remembered this conversation. Sam would think she was interested in Ted, and she'd behaved like a silly schoolgirl leaving the office. She must explain some time, but just what would she say by way of explanation? She'd blushed when Jack Champion mentioned Ted's name. She decided none of this warranted too much thinking about.

It had taken Harriet several years of practice to find a comfortable work style that sat easily with her creative talent but ensured she got things done to a deadline. When she was involved in a difficult problem like this, she'd learned, it was better to give herself time and space alone to mull before moving to design. In Melbourne, she often did her mulling at home where she could listen to music, sleep, think and wander unfettered. Once she'd finished mulling, she could work quickly and efficiently to complete the design phase. Archangels was difficult and she had less than a week to come up with a solution that would work. It was a new building, too, not a renovation, and she was excited at the prospect of creating something from nothing. She also knew she'd have to keep the mulling to a minimum and get on to the design by the weekend.

Options for a casino and hotel according to the spec were limited. They'd need separate street access, a small footprint and river views. Easy, Harriet told herself as she paced around her study, although with less confidence than she'd have with a restoration where the rules were clearer. The site was already crowded and whatever they did would mean they'd lose something. She spread the site drawings over the floor and studied them from different angles. She cut out building footprints and placed them in various locations.

By early afternoon the floor was a mess of drawing paper, but she hadn't come up with any ideas she could use. While she cooked herself some macaroni with parsley and garlic for lunch, she decided to have a glass. She found a passable red blend of grenache, mouvedre and shiraz that was spicy and suited the nutty wholemeal of the pasta. She took the food, wine, prayer book and love letter back with her to the study. She spread out her latest plan on the drawing board and set the prayer book and love letter on the shelf above her desk with the leather purse and rosary so that she could look at them as she worked. It was then she noticed the picture of Mattie Hamilton.

She pulled it off the corkboard and looked at it closely. Mattie was turning to face the photographer, and her black hair fell messily to her shoulders. Her dark eyebrows were raised which accentuated her full, slightly parted lips. She looked surprised, but ready for whatever might be coming. In the foreground a blurry face leaned towards her. Harriet leaned towards Mattie, too, she couldn't help it. Her eyes kept shifting back from anywhere else in the frame. Mattie was stunning, one of those people you just want to look at, with coifed hair, big dark eyes, heart-shaped faced and this winning smile. She was perfect. Harriet wondered if Ted was the blurry face and he'd held the camera at arm's length to take the photograph.

CHAPTER FIFTEEN

An alarm pulled her out of a deep sleep. The drawing board lamp was on but the rest of the apartment was dark. The telephone. She stumbled out to the lounge-room, fell over the couch, which seemed to have moved of its own accord, and picked up the receiver as the answerphone kicked in. 'We were right about Mother Damian.' It was Neal. How did he know about the lover? She hadn't told him yet. She managed to stop the answerphone.

'What?'

'I checked on site. Damian is definitely in the crypt. There's a gravesite for her, but they never buried her there.'

'Hang on.' He didn't know about the lover. Harriet went over to switch on the light. She was blinded, and she rubbed her eyes and stumbled back to the phone. 'What time is it?'

'Eight-thirty.'

'Still Wednesday?'

'Yeah, HD, night-time. Are you okay?'

'I was sleeping. Go through it for me again slowly.'

'I went and looked at the cemetery. There's a headstone on the double plot but it's only got one name on it, the other nun's. And the pound note is late nineteenth century British. Damian arrived in Australia in 1890. So it fits.'

'Are you saying she's in the crypt?'

'Yes, with the bishop, Gerard O'Hare, which is consistent with the crypt records.' O'Hare. Damian's lover. It certainly wasn't his replacement, James Douglas, if her correspondence home was anything to go by. Harriet blinked and opened her eyes wide. O'Hare was about the right age, maybe ten years Damian's senior. He lived on site until he was elevated to bishop, said mass for them every day, heard their confessions, ministered to their sick, died in forty-three. Mother Damian had taken the bishop as a lover. 'That archaeological dig in the seventies,' Neal was saying. 'I found this medico who was involved. I'm seeing him next week. Want to come?'

Harriet said she'd see. 'Neal, this is great.' She told him about the prayer book and the love letter. 'It says, I must see you. Desperado city, Neal. Do you think Damian and Gerard?'

'Who knows? Why didn't you tell me about the archives?'

'You know as well as I do I'd never have got you out of there. We can go back tomorrow and look for more clues.'

'Gerard and Damian, wow, that would be a find, the creators of Archangels, the big bishop and the nun, a couple. It makes the civil war idea look dull. Let me go back through the interviews, see if we can find something. We should talk to Cecilia. She might remember something. I'm dying to get into those archives. You haven't disturbed anything have you?'

'Of course not.' Harriet would need to go in early and clean up. She told him about the police visit. 'Something about that fellow makes me uncomfortable.'

'I'm not surprised. You're withholding evidence in an investigation. That's serious. You have to tell them. So, Mother Damian had a lover.' Neal chuckled to himself. 'We should be able to build a good story with the archives.'

'I don't want to do anything to slander Mother Damian.'

'What if it's the difference between saving the chapel and not?'

'If it comes to that. But for now, it stays between us two.' Reluctantly he agreed. 'How was your new client this morning?' He told her they'd taken on a small job to restore a listed property at New Farm, a late nineteenth-century worker's cottage. 'Well done,' she said. 'How about you run with it?' Harriet had been giving Neal more responsibility in the firm. He was a good manager who had no trouble completing tasks on time. 'How was everything else today?' She'd wandered back into the study with the phone to look at what she'd been doing before she'd fallen sleep.

He was telling her she had a quick hello in the morning with another new client. 'He's rich, Harriet, and he owns a big house at Hamilton. He wants to do everything properly.' Harriet said absently she'd heard that before. She tilted her head looking at the site plan. Neal was talking on about the client.

'Neal, I've got it!'

'What, are you all right?'

She dropped the phone and turned the site plan around so that Princess Street was at the bottom and the river was at the top. She picked up the phone. Neal was calling her name. 'I'm here,' she said. 'The Archangels' job, I know where they can put their casino.'

'Harriet, you sure you're all right? I thought you must have been shot or something.'

She was grinning. 'You got a copy of the site plan?'

'No, Harriet, I don't. I'm home. It's eight-thirty at night. I'm about to snuggle up with my Mussolini biography and a muscat.'

'Let me explain. You know you said I couldn't put the building over the graveyard?' Neal wasn't interested, she could tell. He thought they shouldn't be dabbling in casinos and hotels, they should be writing history and saving chapels. He was probably right. 'I'll show you tomorrow. You talk to Richard today?'

'Yeah, he said to tell you to stop avoiding him.'

Harriet went to work in earnest on her idea. She didn't have all the data at home. Never mind, she could get the rest tomorrow. She'd found a spot they could put the casino and hotel without invading the site. It was a small area Max had pointed out to her when she'd first started. It was obvious. She'd circled it in red before she fell asleep and then dreamed the solution. What a wonderful mind she had. What a star she'd be. They'd have views and access and they could be isolated from the university. It was a better solution than the chapel site. It looked better, would work better and was just brilliant. She hadn't done this kind of work for such a long time. It felt good. She put Mattie Hamilton in a bottom drawer and talked to Mother Damian's things on the shelf above her desk as she worked on rough sketches. 'They might even name the building after us, Mother D.'

She tried Ted Dawes' office from seven am until his secretary answered at a quarter to eight. The secretary said he had a window at ten.

'Good. I'll see you then.'

She took her time showering with the jet on massage. Breakfast food didn't fit with her body's view of time so she made chips and tomato sauce. What to wear was the next question. A meeting like this was important. She finished the chips while she looked through the large walk-in wardrobe. There was so much hanging space, a ballroom dancing team could have practised in there, and Harriet's meagre collection sagged sadly into the middle.

Growing up with her father and brother in Fern Tree Gully, Harriet's role models in the fashion stakes had been the other girls at St Pat's who mostly laughed at her red hair, white skin and lack of grooming skills, and her mother's mother who took her to expensive cafes in the city and twirled her hair behind her ears and told her tomboys never got ahead. 'If only your mother . . .' It was a sentence she never managed to finish.

Harriet had arrived for work the Monday after she and Martin broke up sporting a blonde crewcut and nose stud. Richard and John hadn't said a word. But they were relieved after her next holiday when her hair was back to frizzy red and the nose stud was just a small hole you'd never notice unless you were looking. Richard told her so later. She hadn't told them about the tattoo. Since then she'd been a bland architect, unable to find expression of a self, unable to find a self to express and frankly uninterested anyway. She bought big suits and hid in them. She felt like a child playing dress-up in a mother's clothes.

Not today, she decided. Today she was going to look great. After a longish fashion parade along the catwalk (the real estate agent called the walk-in a 'robe), she selected a green lycra T-shirt and black leather jacket with checked tencel pants and Docs. The outfit worked. She wore lace undies, too, which the big-busted woman in the store had called 'femmy'. 'Here I am,' she said to the mirror. 'I'm a hip young architect and business person of my generation.' Harriet's eyes smiled back. She teased her hair, which didn't need it a bit, and donned thick black-rimmed glasses to give herself a hint of seriousness. Her body felt lush, boticelli-esque, a body hankered after by a renaissance man. She kissed the mirror and left wet pink lips there.

CHAPTER SIXTEEN

It was an idea, a good idea, and she clutched the rolled-up drawings and took the steps three at a time up to Ted Dawes' office at five to ten. She walked straight into the inner sanctum, oblivious to the protests of the secretary. Ted, Max and Marguerita were sitting round the coffee table. Harriet was annoyed. What were they doing here? She had an idea overflowing from her brain. Her head was a light bulb. She heard the secretary's voice, 'You can't go in there.' She started to withdraw with a breathless apology, realising she'd walked in on a meeting, but Ted was smiling, standing up, saying it was all right. 'We're nearly finished, come in. You might be able to help us.'

On the few occasions Harriet had seen Max since his outburst in her office, he'd treated her as if she'd been the offender, addressing her only if he had to, and then making sure he used a minimum number of monosyllabic words, primarily the word 'No'. She looked over towards him gingerly. He had his arms folded like a sulking child, even his bright bow tie sagged. Harriet could ignore him, she decided. She was going to be the star.

She sat down with the drawings under her arm and smiled acknowledgement at Marguerita, who ran her eye over Harriet's outfit. Marguerita was tailored as usual, in a black suit with two rows of gold buttons, fawn stockings and heeled black sandals. Ted was all smiles as he, too, looked at Harriet's outfit. He poured her a coffee from which she took a big swallow without tasting anything. She put the roll of drawings on the floor, but they sprang free, and she turned them over so as not to spoil the surprise. When Ted crossed his legs, she saw a small section of his ankle between the cuff of his trousers and sock. For some reason, it made her feel tender towards him. He was wearing a cotton shirt which wasn't tucked in all the way round and a sunny tie. Harriet wanted the meeting to end so she could be alone with him and tell him about her solution. She was finding it difficult to remain seated. There's a good girl, she could hear her mother's mother say. Sit still or I'll prick you.

'The Board's not going to blink twice about this, Ted,' Max shot a wary look Harriet's way. 'It's their job to keep an eye to the bottom line. We had a majority vote.'

'A slim majority, Max,' Marguerita said. 'You know the Board doesn't like this much dissent.'

'Max chairs the tenders committee,' Ted said to Harriet, 'and they're recommending an architect for the new business building. It's ten million so everyone's a bit nervous.' Harriet asked who'd won the tender. 'Steel Armstrong.'

She nodded. 'Who else bid?'

'Leichardt, Flynn Morecross.' Marguerita added some other names. Flynn Morecross was a firm Harriet knew. They were good. Steel Armstrong, the recommended tenderer, had an industry reputation for cutting costs at the expense of good design. Harriet didn't say anything. 'Marguerita's pointing out that the committee was divided about the proposal,' Ted said. Max started jiggling his knee. 'What do you think?'

All eyes were on Harriet. This was unfair, and on a morning when she wasn't feeling as chipper, she'd probably have shown better judgement and stayed out of it. But today, convinced she was invincible, she said: 'Why not have a design comp?' Ted looked a question. 'Go back to the committee, take the top three tenders, give them a few thousand dollars each and run a competition to design the building. You'll know what you're going to get.' And Steel Armstrong will fare poorly, she thought.

'That's a great idea,' Ted said. 'And Max, that would include the ones Marguerita thinks are better. What have we got to lose?'

'Time and money,' said Max but even he could see it was a good compromise.

'Come on, guys, let's go with it,' Ted said. 'It's got to be easier than trying to convince the Board to do something your committee was divided on.'

Ted told Max to stay on after Marguerita left. Harriet wasn't comfortable about this but she could hardly say so with Max less than two feet away. She picked up the drawings and shifted the coffee cups with a grading arm to one end of the table. She told them she'd considered a number of possibilities around the top of the site, on the street side, but the only one that would work was the western corner. There they had two cheap temporary buildings and an ugly low rise. She blew her fringe out of her eyes and became breathy as she went on. She worked off the preliminary sketches, but she needed three dimensions. 'Mind if I use those?' On the table next to her chair were gifts from Ted's trip—bronze trophies, plastic cases filled with cellophane and ribbons, a sterling silver calendar, ties, a coaster set, a pearl box. She didn't wait for an answer and started recreating the campus on top of the plans, with coasters and cups as buildings. Beyond the table was the river.

'It would mean we could leave the chapel precinct intact,' she said. 'And you'd still get your views. In that area, you could go further in height if you wanted. I'm thinking you could put in twelve storeys without any disruption to the integrity of the site.' The building was gaining an additional floor every few moments. Harriet had to pause to catch her breath. 'I bet we could do it cheaply too. It's perfect.'

'I see where you're headed,' Ted said. 'But what about an alternative on the river?'

'I looked, there's nowhere on the river, and from up here, they'd get better views.'

Without thinking, Ted shifted one of Harriet's buildings into the quad. 'Street access?'

This was the crowning glory of Harriet's plan. 'We'll ramp from Princess Street. There's a long history of that for hotels.' She removed his quad building.

'Town planning approval?'

'I don't think you'll have any problems, especially if they know the alternative. And from your point of view, it's more remote here than down on the river where the gamblers would walk through the campus.'

'Helipad?'

'Roof.'

Max had said little while Harriet was talking. He'd been staring out the window as if nothing she could say could interest him. Suddenly, he sat forward and looked at the site plan. 'You're suggesting we put a twelve-storey building here?' Harriet nodded yes. 'Not a chance. The fill they used when they dropped the wall was from the Newstead gasworks. That parcel of land is on the State Environment Management Register. The soil's contaminated, with cyanide among other things. There's rules about how we have to manage it. The developer wouldn't touch it.'

'I didn't know.' Harriet's face fell. 'I thought you told me you were looking at something here.' She pointed to an area adjacent to the proposed site which she was sure she remembered Max talking about.

'Doubt it.' Max shrugged. 'You should have done your homework.' He stood to go. 'I haven't time for this, Ted, I'm due in a meeting. We must get on with the deal. The police are finishing up.'

Ted said, 'When did you hear this? What did they say?'

'I phoned this morning. We'll have the site back by the weekend.'

'Let's hope it clears this mess up for good.' Ted smiled but Max didn't respond.

Harriet thought that if she spoke, she might cry.

Ted said, 'Seems like it's back to the drawing board.' He looked at her sketch. 'You know, if it hadn't been for the contamination, we could have considered an option like that. It's good.' He gave her the sketch. 'But you should have checked. And we need closure. We're in trouble, Harriet. If I don't get five million to carry us through next year, we could be finished.' He was looking at her but not unkindly. 'Someone else will buy Archangels and they won't care less about your church. They'll knock it down in a minute.' He breathed deeply several times before he continued. 'I asked you to think of ways we could use the river site sympathetically. That's the brief.' He stressed the last three words like an order and got up and walked over to his desk to study his diary. The meeting was finished. Harriet wished she felt strong on the inside.

CHAPTER SEVENTEEN

Embarrassment burned Harriet's face as she walked down the hill in the opposite direction to the stream of students rushing to lectures. She bumped against them consciously without apologising, smarting with the rebuff and her own foolishness in the meeting. She waited for a cab to take her to the New Farm office and then decided to walk. Okay, she thought, I should have checked the site. It was an easy mistake to make at the mulling stage, but she shouldn't have been showing off plans at the mulling stage. She was overexcited and overtired. She should have talked to Neal first, he'd have checked the details, that's what he was there for. Her pants looked wild and silly as they appeared step by step in front of her. She wanted the hot street to swallow her whole. The city sweated.

When Martin's brother decided to marry (a fabulous girl was his mother's description), Harriet sent French champagne. 'This is the stuff on which our dreams are made,' she wrote on the card. When she told Martin, he corrected her. 'Can't you even try, Harriet? It's Shakespeare. "We are such stuff as dreams are made on",' he said carefully. 'Can't you even try, Harriet?' she mimicked his perfect vowels. He smashed the glass door of a display cabinet and cut his hand. 'Don't speak to me like that, not ever.' He sucked blood from his fist. In your own dreams, she said under her breath. Later she refused to make the calls to repair the door and he had to do it himself, but at the time she hid in a cupboard and talked to herself as a way of staying calm. He called his brother and apologised for her. She heard him laughing on the phone. Martin never once dropped a G from a word in all the time she knew him, even when he swore. By then, she'd started to enjoy in an unhealthy way saying the wrong words, any words, to fill a gap, just to make him angry. 'I don't give a filament,' she'd say. It would drive him crazy. After the French champagne incident and without warning, he became opposed to all things Gallic, as a protest, he said, to French colonialism. 'I don't know how you could have given Veuve, not after the Pacific.'

Martin sucked the life out of Harriet like she was one of the prune-shakes he drank for breakfast. Their marriage was like living in bad digs, and she didn't realise how much it affected her until it wasn't there anymore. The night she told him they needed to talk about their future, he lay on top of her and pumped away desperately as if he'd find something inside her that would change things. The bouncing made her sick in the stomach. Asleep afterwards she dreamed she was flying, soaring wingless into blue. But even right at the end when Martin was at his worst, when he was shouting and throwing things around the apartment, even then, and especially afterwards, Harriet thought of what her father had said when they married, that she had made the choice to be brainless when she was with Martin. She nurtured a little thought deep in her bowels that it was all her fault. Sometimes, like now, it grew bigger. She felt the worm was inside her, not Martin, she caused him to be who he was to her, not the other way round. Martin, on the other hand, was happy and married to a radiantly pregnant jewel.

By the time she'd reached New Farm, she'd decided Neal was right; they should be digging up facts for their final report, not trying to find a spot for a casino or a name for a skeleton. She met with the Hamilton house owner who wanted to do things properly and spent the rest of the morning going through her in-tray and returning phone calls.

Her lunch appointment was Joshua Kerry, an engineer who'd worked with Richard Corsair and was project managing the restoration of an old pub. He'd called Richard to get the name of a local heritage specialist. If she'd been looking for someone to bolster her confidence, she needed look no further than Josh. 'I was so excited when Richard said you were here,' he told her. 'I think your work's great.' She smiled and grabbed his arm and thanked him graciously. By the end of the lunch, they already had some ideas for his project and agreed to meet again.

Harriet walked back to Archangels around the New Farm reach of the river, feeling better to have finished her in-tray and to have caught up with staff. Summer was coming like a big friendly smile, and everything had slowed by mid after-noon. Even now, late on a spring day, wobbles of heat came up off the bitumen. In the park the jacarandas were losing their leaves and the roses were wilting. Old Italian women smiled as if they'd known Harriet all her life while black-eyed Vietnamese children played peek-a-boo.

Although there were fewer people on the streets in Brisbane than in Melbourne, they were more open. It made Harriet comfortable and uncomfortable at the same time. She felt like a fussed-over visitor, as if they knew she wasn't one of them but wanted to make her welcome anyway. Today, they buoyed her up. One of the Italian women told Harriet to hurry. She pointed to a line of silver on the horizon and made the sign of the cross. Even now, the sun stung Harriet's scalp and she felt as if she was covered in honey. Rain was the last thing she could imagine.

At first she thought the change in the atmosphere was a change in her own body. She became aware of the intense depth in the greenness of things and moisture in the air shifting. The pace quickened, treetops whispered, ferries knocked against pylons and ropes rattled masts on the river. Light began to shift around from moment to moment, the trees and boats became more restless, as if they wanted to join the crowds of people who walked quickly to wherever they were going. Rather than shifting pace, Harriet wondered how she'd stumbled into the experience.

A front as thick as treacle and green like oysters rolled over the blue of the sky. Lightning and thunder preceded the rain, which fell in isolated drops that touched different parts of her body in tiny shocks, then in sheets of water that drenched her and brought strange relief. Her shoes filled with water and her clothes clung to her. Ted was emerging from inside the quad building carrying a large black umbrella. 'First time?' he said.

Harriet was excited and edgy. Momentarily she forgot their morning meeting. 'How often does this happen?'

'I love the smell.' Her hair was pasted to her face, and her T-shirt stuck to her breasts and upper arms. She could feel runnels of water down her thighs. Ted stared at her for several moments, and said, 'I used to run in storms like this when I was a kid. You look great.' He continued down the steps.

CHAPTER EIGHTEEN

Harriet did her best to towel dry, gathered up her abandoned plans for the casino and ran to make the ferry. The evening was cool and still, and the sun peered below horizon clouds to give a last burst before dying. It was as if the storm had never happened. At home, there was a message from Max Palethorpe. His voice was tinny on the tape and strangely hesitant. 'I just wanted to let you know that this isn't your fault,' he said. She hadn't suggested to him that it was. 'You're caught in the middle. Ted doesn't really understand our position.' There was a pause. 'But he and I talked after you left. He told me to go ahead with my team. I told him I'd keep you in the loop.'

Harriet called him back. 'You haven't shown me the plans,' she said. 'I don't even know who you're working with. I can't see that as keeping me in the loop.'

'We have to get ahead,' he said. 'You don't know all the facts. I'm responsible now. It's up to me, and I'll let you know when I need your help.' He hung up.

Ted Dawes had told her she had a week, but he'd reneged. And he'd seen her on the steps and said nothing. Okay, her design didn't work but she might find an alternative. Perhaps that's what he was afraid of, he didn't want a viable alternative. He'd given Max the go-ahead on the new building. Why hadn't he told her himself? He wanted to play rough. Fine, she could play rough. All thoughts of abandoning Archangels disappeared now. Harriet would save the chapel, all right, with help from Ted Dawes and co or not. She spent the evening on a new plan of action, and went to bed early to make sure she was ready.

The river was slick black just before dawn on Saturday as she made her way up the dark drive. She was dressed in black from head to toe, and the cab driver had asked if she was on her way to a gothic party. She told him she was a cat burglar who'd drawn the line at boot polish for her face as it might have looked suspicious. He laughed. She had a key to the quad building and she slipped up the three flights of stairs to Max Palethorpe's office. Here in the executive corridor it was always quiet but without the weekday hum of air conditioning and equipment it was deathly silent.

She'd planned to call security and tell them she'd left some papers in Max's office but there was no need because his door was wide open. She didn't dare switch on the light. She started on the desk where the six blow up penguins had been knocked over. As her eyes adjusted to the twilight, she could make out the pen stand with two fat black and gold pens in it, and a frame with no pictures in it.

Jack Champion had talked about a shroud over the chapel and it sounded ugly. If Harriet could get a copy of the plans, she could leak them to the National Trust and the press. Surely the Catholic Church would have something to say about one of its ex-chapels becoming a casino. The Redemption sisters probably wouldn't like it either. Harriet looked over the desk and in the credenza behind it but didn't find anything of plan size. Max had piles of shirts in dry-cleaning packs, a cardigan, stacks of singlets, undies and socks. In the bottom drawer of the desk, she found a photograph of a laughing woman with short brown hair.

In one of the work trays on the desk, Harriet came upon an A4 document with an inkpen sketch of Old Archangels on the front. She knew the gold cover and logo in the top right corner, JJ, Jamison and Jamison. It was Martin. Max Palethorpe had engaged Martin to battle Harriet for old Archangels. It couldn't get worse.

Except that it did. She heard footsteps on the stairs outside. She swung around to check she'd closed the office door, which she had, then remembered it had been open when she'd arrived. She stepped lightly across the office to reopen it, then back to get inside one of the tall cupboards along the wall opposite the desk. She could smell Max before she heard him. He was breathing heavily and his sweat and warm body filled the office aggressively. What was he doing at work on a Saturday? He was whistling. 'I'm beat,' another voice said. He wasn't alone.

'Me too. Want a glass of water?'

'Lovely, then I'd better get home. Margot wants the car before Ted's lunch today.' The other man was puffing. 'I'm glad we managed to get together this morning, Max. It's been a tough week for all of us.'

'Frank, about Ted, I've been meaning to call you.' There was a pause while Max waited for a response. 'I'm his deputy. It's very hard for me to talk to him.'

'You want me to?' Frank said.

'It might be a good idea. We're in a precarious position, especially now, and he must know people are talking. This building is worth everything. It could be the difference between survival or not.'

'Of course, Max, but I don't think the two things are necessarily connected.'

'They are in terms of money. We're losing support already.'

'Let's wait a day or two and see what emerges. I'll need to take a few soundings from members anyway, and who knows? Perhaps Ted's right and things will settle down like before.'

'I'd like to be able to agree,' Max said, 'but the talk won't stop.'

'Death by a thousand cuts, know it well. Our job here, Max, is to stick by Ted for as long as humanly possible.'

'Of course, absolutely, and my only concern is for him.'

'I know that, and it's the same for all of us. So let's wait and see.'

Feeling around the dark cupboard, Harriet found hangers with suit coats and trousers. This was Max's wardrobe. He and Frank were saying their goodbyes. Max might need his wardrobe soon for clothes, and, in addition, he'd find an architect. 'You're getting me fit, old boy,' Frank said. The office door closed. Max was whistling again, something sad this time, 'Yesterday'? Harriet's heart was beating in her temples, surely loud enough for him to hear. Momentarily, she considered walking out of the cupboard and making up a story, but none came to mind. 'Yesterday' came closer. Harriet's heart skipped a beat and she held her breath. He stopped at the window beside her cupboard and opened it. From there, he must have turned and walked back across the office. He was in his ensuite. She heard the shower and then singing, Max Palethorpe singing 'Yesterday' by The Beatles. Like Harriet, he needed a place to hide away. She'd have liked to stay and see him naked so she could report to Marguerita, but it was too much of a risk. As quietly as she could, she removed herself from the cupboard. She left the office, closing the door behind her gently, and bolted down the stairs and out of the building, clutching Martin's plans for Old Archangels.

'Shroud' was a good word for Martin's building. Following the rationale that the existing structure was already an ugly mish-mash of styles constructed and altered over decades, he'd ruin the integrity of the site without so much as a yawn. The oldest part of the building, the 1850 chapel on the western side of the transept, would form the base for Martin's new building, a kind of Sydney Opera House he'd graft onto Old Archangels, with the characteristic fish-mouth entry and three canvas sails. It wasn't original, not even with postmodernism as an excuse. In the middle of the sails was a tall white tower, clean and pure, obviously referring to the towers on the chapel and house, but one tower too many.

Harriet hadn't realised just how far Martin had travelled since she'd left the firm, that he could do this with buildings as significant as Archangels, or that his eye could tolerate it. The new structure would completely destroy the original chapel and make a mockery of the rest of the church and Archangels House. Richard had told her Jamisons had gone downhill since she'd left. This was after the split, and she'd thought he was being kind. She'd imagined Martin's creativity untempered would be interesting and original. But this. It was preposterous, vain. It was phallic. It would be easy to prevent this. They'd never get planning approval. She had no idea who Frank was or what he and Max were plotting, but it confirmed that the university's protection of the chapel was nothing but lip service. Perhaps Ted was on her side after all, perhaps not, but either way, Max was determined to make money.

She was angry that Martin was here, at Archangels. She'd come to Brisbane to make a new start, and he'd followed. He'd not only followed, but he was doing it to her all over again, taking what she had and using it for his own ends. At least her foe was a known entity and his proposal was foolish. Her strategy was clear. Solve the Mother Damian skull mystery, and find an alternative to Martin's dick. She spent the rest of the morning reading his leaden prose, getting ready for lunch and laughing to herself about her near discovery in Max's cupboard.

CHAPTER NINETEEN

'Maybe I'll have time,' Ted said to himself as he watched Harriet walk towards him down the gravel drive of Archangels House. He'd selected music carefully, and had been feeling good until the caterer had asked whether he wanted a tablecloth or placemats.

Ted grew up in Maitland, north of Sydney, in a small brick house with three fireplaces to stem the slatey cold. His mother filled the space with tired talking, like a radio in the background, never quite loud enough to hear. Her children smelled of Sunlight soap and their bedrooms smelled of piss. The farm was a large, unfinished building that leaned towards the pale sun. Ted was a gentle boy who spent most of his time alone, hated the smell of the farm and won scholarships to boarding school and university where he learned how not to be himself. He grew tall like his grandfather on his mother's side and quiet like all the Dawes men. He moved more quickly and purposefully than the others in his family and became competitive so he could wish for more. Ted had bright hazel eyes and as a young man with a few whiskies in him, became wry and funny in a self-deprecating way. Alone at night as a hot adolescent with a mess of brown hair, he yearned for something to warm him from the inside.

He worked hard and managed a first class honours degree in biology. His mother came to his graduation with his three young brothers and sister. 'Yer Da says hey-ho,' she said. 'E's caavin.' The boys wore long shorts that started just under their rib cages and revealed bony knees atop high socks. Their hair was greased into three bouffants. Ted shouted everyone fish and chips on Sydney Harbour afterwards. Genevieve sat on his lap in her white party dress while they watched green and cream ferries chug to and from the Quay in golden late afternoon Sydney.

Ted's honours supervisor told him to do a doctorate. 'It's commercial science or academe, and you'll never make it in commerce,' he told Ted. 'Let's face it, quiet guys like you and me don't belong in management.' Ted's research had taken him into biochemistry and genetics.

When Ted met Mattie Hamilton at St Vincent's Hospital where she was a young resident, he thought she'd be that something that could warm him inside. Ted fell into Mattie like a deep cold pool, he was stopped, breathless, underwater. 'I'll marry you if you ask me, Ted,' she said. Theirs was a large apricot wedding with a bridal party you could measure in metres and small children with baskets of flowers to scatter about the church. Next to the self-perpetuating wealth of Mattie's family, Ted couldn't bear to look to his own side of the church where his mother sat in red lipstick and a hat not quite the colour of her handbag not quite the colour of her shoes, next to his clean-shaven, tight-jawed father in charcoal serge that smelled of mothballs. Ted liked most that Mattie knew rules he could only guess at. She knew when to use tablecloths or placemats, when to smile or speak. Mattie could talk to anyone about any subject. She made people feel special, wanted, not alone. She made Ted feel that way, too, at first.

The other guests were on the verandah, Ted told Harriet. 'If you stay after, I can show you through the house,' he said as casually as he could. 'Do you know whether it's tablecloth or placemats for lunch?'

Harriet wore a new white dress with turquoise flowers and black leather sandals. 'Neither?' She was examining the plaster in the entry hall in a spot where the wallpaper had chipped away. 'It's magnificent.' She'd walked to the house from the chapel on the morning of her interview. That day, she'd been greeted at the gates by half a dozen crows that rarked flatly at one another when they weren't picking the cold watching eye out of the video security camera. The paranoia of high office, she'd figured at the time. Now she couldn't so easily reconcile the tight security with casual Ted in his jeans, runners and white T-shirt.

The house was on a grander scale than anything Harriet had seen in Brisbane, but the verandah and belvedere meant it lacked the austerity that often accompanied large homes in the southern capitals. Inside, it was just as she'd pictured it, and today she had that good feeling of arriving at a place she already knew in her imagination. The grand entrance hall was big enough for a rock concert, with high moulded plaster ceilings, double sash windows out onto the verandah where guests gathered, dark silk wallpaper and crystal chandeliers. Carved wooden fixtures had soaked up wax and wood polish over decades, and these smells mixed now with the aroma of roasting capsicum and cumin, which Harriet hoped was lunch cooking; she was hungry. 'I only use a few rooms,' Ted said. 'It's ridiculous having the big house.'

Harriet noticed the set table in the formal dining room and the eat-in kitchen where starched white aprons bustled. 'Who's the John Denver fan?' They were walking through the sitting room overlooking the river. A hefty CD collection with an eclectic group of styles and musics lined a bookcase.

'Mine.'

'You're not serious.'

'Well who else?'

There was an uncomfortable pause. 'I'm not quite sure,' said Harriet. 'But it's not something I'd admit to if it were me.'

'I have nothing to hide.'

'So it seems. You know, the more I get to know about you, the more I think I like Morrie.'

'I bet he'd sing along to John Denver all day.'

'Where did that come from?' Harriet pointed over to a small carved Virgin Mary. She was in the typical white robe and blue cape of the Mother of God, but nothing else about her was typical. This Mary was luscious, with curvy hips and accentuated breasts. She smiled broadly from big red lips, and she was black.

'It was in the convent,' Ted said. 'I took to it.' Harriet had only seen one Black Madonna before, owned by a St Pat's girl from one of the islands. They were probably popular in over half the Christian world by now, but when Harriet was growing up the very idea of a black Mother of God was wicked. A convent icon? How on earth had the convent accepted a Black Madonna as a gift? This one was thirty centimetres high and mounted on a plinth in a corner. Above her was a painting of her fair-skinned son, a pale wimpish Jesus with blue eyes that followed people around the room and a red heart glowing through his robes, squeezed by a crown of thorns and emanating gold rays to the edges of the print. His black mother was the more beautiful.

'When they showed me through the house, they had it hidden up in the attic. Story has it that your Mother Damian confiscated it from one of the girls,' Ted said. 'The girl stayed on after she finished school and became a nun. You know

Angel Square?' It was a pretty group of postwar buildings off the quad that had been the primary school. 'That was named after her. She was very good with kids, and she left the nuns a small fortune.' Ted looked at the Black Madonna. 'I hope old Mother Damian felt bad she took this from one of her benefactors.'

'Damian was a saint, incidentally,' Harriet said. 'But how did you get this?'

'I made the nuns an offer they couldn't refuse.' You're not bringing that in here, Mattie had said when Ted put the statue in the sitting room. It's ghastly. He looked at the Black Maddona proudly now. 'I bought the Sacred Heart painting as well. The contrast appeals to me.' He took Harriet's arm to steer her outside to the verandah and the other guests. She could still feel the warmth of his hand after he let go.

CHAPTER TWENTY

What was wrong with a Black Madonna? Mother Damian wondered. Maria Di Maggio was a dear *bambina* who wouldn't stop crying because she wanted to go home to the country, an eminently sensible idea in Damian's opinion. The reverend mother had never seen anyone so out of place and lonely. The girl's dark skin stood out at Archangels, and the loose messy plaits in her thick black hair constantly threatened to come undone. Girls can't help it, Mother Mary Joseph had told Damian, and our job is to enforce silence and order. But those large dark eyes. Maria didn't belong. She was just turned eleven, wetting her bed every night and on the way to what decades later would be called a behavioural problem, but what was then called brazen or sassy. The girl's only comfort was this Black Madonna she'd been given by her papa to protect her at school in the city. Sister Mary Vincent had confiscated Maria's Black Virgin and had led a delegation to petition Damian. It must be destroyed, Mother. What are we coming to? Indeed. It was a test, clearly. They wanted to know what

Damian would do now that the monsignor had taken up office as bishop. Dear God, thought Damian, what a test. Maria was irreconcilable. She loved her Black Mary. 'She's our Mother of God, Sister.' Her plaits shook as sobs racked her skinny body.

Cecilia, the young postulant who wanted to write the school's history, had asked Damian about her vision when she first came to the school. A vision? Damian muttered. Of course a vision, said Cecilia. As Cecilia told the story, Damian brought the Archangels Hill itself into being. She must have started with a vision. But in Damian's mind, visions happened to the blessed and she didn't count among the blessed. She remembered like yesterday the rare sunny day in her village when Deirdre Nolan saw the Virgin move. She was a ghostly white in the soft late afternoon (the statue, not Deirdre, although Deirdre was pale enough to be sure). The hands of the Blessed Mother of God, joined in humble prayer, had moved from just below her ghost-white chin to halfway down her ghost-white chest. Deirdre had been chosen by God to make the village famous and Damian was jealous. She was smug and vindicated a year later when Deirdre was squashed under the milkman's horse. But the legend of the Virgin was only strengthened by the visionary's unexpected demise, and Deirdre's family raised enough money for a plaque in front of the statue and a holiday in Rome to meet the Holy Father.

But what Sister Mary Cecilia of the school history meant by vision was intention, and Damian did have a vision in those terms. As a girl named Nora, she watched her poor mother wither away like a dying tree for want of company and intelligent conversation. Your father can't help it, Nora's mother said just before she folded up and died to oblige him. When Nora joined the order soon after, her father turned up at her novitiate with slick steel hair, big wet lips, a trinket box with a fancy rosary inside and the smell of the grog on him. When she went to Dublin, she'd already decided things should be different for girls. She didn't go back to her old convent school and her slick father. Instead, she found a frontier, Australia and Archangels, where she brought her vision of sweet release for Christian girls and her blue rosary. She was just twenty.

Damian grew stronger and more crafty in her years as bursar. She was quiet and ready when Mother Mary Joseph died. It was a clean election; Damian had done nothing she was ashamed of. Then twenty-seven, the youngest reverend mother ever, she set about a program of work that had taken her life since. Years in convents had taught her that needle-point, fairy cakes and dancing were less useful than carpentry, mathematics and a love of literature. She established new rules to give the girls a sense that they owned the school. She set up a student council, unheard of in those days, and a system where older girls big-sistered their younger col-leagues. She was fierce about democracy where the girls were concerned. Her rule of the convent was more of a dictator-ship, mostly benevolent. It wasn't that Damian didn't listen to her sisters, it was that she rarely agreed with them, and she knew she was right.

Damian could close her eyes and believe nothing could change Archangels now, whatever the monsignor did once he was in the bishop's house. It was nineteen forty-three. In a few years the school would be finished and Damian herself would probably be six foot under and pushing up daisies, as the young soldiers living in the junior dormitory would say. They'd commandeered the building, the Americans and their Coca-Cola, and there was nowt could be done about it. Damian felt she was the only person on earth who had no desire to help the war effort, but it made little difference; the war effort helped itself.

Maria's parents ran a store in a small town too far away for their daughter to attend as a day girl, otherwise they wouldn't have made her leave home. They worked hard and had a fortune hidden in their house that would buy suitable graves for themselves in the Italian section of the cemetery and a wealthy future for their adored child. 'She is good girl,' her father told Mother Damian. 'You take care of her for me.' He wore a black three-piece suit with a white shirt and felt hat when he visited, whatever the time of year. He brought a basket of food and wine for the sisters and left a smell of coconut oil and cleanliness. He told Damian he prayed only for his daughter's happiness.

It was a passion for reading and writing that Damian first loved in little Maria. God knows, she hadn't made herself easy to love in other ways. Vincent had disliked her on sight which wasn't surprising, she disliked almost everyone, but in Maria's case, dirty was added to the usual list of epithets she gave her charges, and dirtiness got under her skin. 'She doesn't make her bed, doesn't do chores, doesn't come to study.' In her first few months they called her parents back. There's only so much fear one can instil in a small child's heart and Maria was oblivious to threats anyway. She just became more intransigent. Mother Damian secretly admired her spirit. To her parents, Maria was the model of good behaviour. 'Papa,' she'd cry, 'Papa, you've come to take me home.' He called her 'little one'. And her stories! Merciful God. She'd have them all in stitches in English classes or after study at night. Mother Damian smiled just thinking of them.

There it was, prostrate across Mother Damian's lap. A Black Virgin. Why couldn't the Virgin be black? All God's children was what he said, all God's children, although Damian had an idea this might have come from a singer rather than from the Lord Himself. Damian had been chuffed three months earlier to accept the commission from the Provincial for a record fourth term, and happy with the election result which demonstrated majority if not overwhelming support. Surely the war would end soon, and she could get back to the building program. She was sure of everything, the right-ness of what the school was doing, the goodness of God, bricks and mortar. But so many of her sisters didn't share her views now, and some of them would go straight to the new bishop when they didn't like the answers they got. It rattled Damian to take decisions so many thought were wrong. She wasn't made of steel. And now Gerard had gone, to a better place he'd kept saying. It was cold comfort.

Damian knew what she had to do. It was just a question of finding the way. After three days, she came to a solution. To her sisters, she said she'd reflected on the Black Madonna. Here it was in front of them. She'd consulted scripture which continually told her of God's perfect love for imperfection. She'd prayed. God had replied. He'd told her to give the Black Virgin back to Maria. Her sisters were completely satisfied by this, accepted the story with the conviction of blind faith, even Bernadette who was anything but sheep-like in her devotion. In Mother Damian's opinion, it was only a small compromise of the truth anyway, a white lie. She had con-sulted scripture and she did find constant evidence of God's perfect love. She had prayed. But God hadn't actually spoken to her and told her to return the doll. God never spoke to Damian at all, certainly never told her to do anything. God wouldn't have dared. To Maria, Damian said the doll would be their little secret, she could take her to bed and nurse her in the evenings but she wasn't to parade her around the school. Maria was as grateful as could be and immediately recovered from her homesickness.

Over time, Maria became happier at Archangels. She was bright if lazy and sang like a bird. She rounded out as girls do and grew into a beautiful young woman with a way of gazing out at the world that suggested she understood more than she let on. When she was fifteen and told Damian she wanted to join the order, the older woman was thrilled. Many of Damian's contemporaries were dying or otherwise acquiescing to her will by then. They'd lived through a war in which their American guests had smashed the apse window. The nuns had made sacrifices, developed camaraderie. Some of them had grown to respect and even like Damian. But little Maria would always represent to Mother the independent woman she'd worked so hard to develop in her girls. 'My child,' she said to her, 'obedience will be your struggle.'

Maria chose the name Angelina because it rained the day she decided on religious life and her father had told her that rain was the angels turning on the taps in Heaven. Sister Mary Angelina was a brilliant teacher with sometime doubts about the path her life was taking. But she wrote herself indelibly on to Damian's heart that morning when she clutched her Black Madonna to her breast and leaned up and kissed the old nun's face with an open mouth. She thrust a bunch of sweet lemon myrtle into Damian's hand. 'Thank you Mother, from the bottom of my heart. Thank you. And God bless and double bless you.'

CHAPTER
TWENTY-ONE

Today in slacks and frocks, the dozen Archangels Board members and their partners on Ted's verandah looked more like a contemporary bowls club outing than the unresponsive governors to whom Harriet had presented her preliminary report. Max was on the lawn with the woman in the desk drawer photograph, probably his wife. Harriet wondered if he'd come straight from the office. The weather was easy but the conversation was difficult until wines had been poured and refilled. They dined alfresco despite the placemat-set table inside. The couscous was good, lamb, chicken, capsicum and fruits, and Harriet went back for seconds. She sat on the verandah steps to eat and watch the river. She asked Sam about the heavy security on Ted's house.

'Kevin,' Sam said, as if that explained everything. 'When Mattie first left, it was like hacking into NASA just to get an appointment, let alone visit him here. They set up all this stuff and we had to have pin codes and swipe cards and bi-lock keys. Did you know the french doors in Ted's office are bullet-proof glass? It was just silly. No one could get in or out.

And as you can imagine, Ted got more and more isolated. Peaceful, I'll say that. But the day we locked the chancellor out, Ted just unplugged the whole bloody thing.' Sam said people had been quite paranoid. 'I guess that's what you do. Maybe it's a way of controlling the world when it's out of control.

'Used to be so different when she was here,' Sam said behind a hand but loudly enough for people near them to hear. 'Good God! Your tag's sticking out.' She tore at the back of Harriet's collar and produced the price tag Harriet had forgotten to remove that morning. 'Nothing cheap about you.' She laughed loudly. 'She ruled the roost, you mark my words. Mattie Hamilton would never have put up with all this security nonsense.'

Suddenly, Harriet heard the voice of Max's running partner, Frank, behind them on the verandah. 'Would you excuse us for just a moment,' he said. Harriet turned around. Frank was Sir Francis Lynch, the Archangels chancellor, chair of the Board of governors and titular head of the university. He'd sat at the head of the table when Harriet had presented her report, but he hadn't spoken that day, and she hadn't known he was called Frank. Max had some powerful friends. Right now, Sir Francis was taking Ted aside to speak with him. Harriet listened.

'I got a call yesterday from Bob Hannigan,' he said. 'We go back a long way you know, Ted, and he's been good to us.' Harriet knew Bob Hannigan was the state government minister responsible for heritage. She concentrated to hear Frank's low voice above Sam. 'His youngest wants to do law with us, real asset if you ask me. He's a good kid, too, went through with one of mine. Don't know what his chances are. But if I can put in a good word for him, you know, I think it might calm things a little.'

'I'll have a look.'

Harriet glanced around again and noticed Ted's jaw was set as if he'd been asked to comment on something and wouldn't.

'I don't want special treatment or anything, Ted.' Frank winked and smiled, showing gold on a line of dull teeth. 'But it might smooth the way for the redevelopment. Max tells me it's go go go.' He grabbed Ted's elbow.

'Of course.' Ted said. He noticed Harriet watching them and smiled over as he raised his glass offering a drink. She stood up and excused herself and walked over to where they stood.

'Did I hear that right?' Harriet said after Frank wandered off. 'If you let the minister's son into a course, you'll get a smooth ride. I thought you were ethical.'

'That's not what he meant, Harriet,' but they both knew it was.

By five, the caterers and most guests had left and those remaining sat around drinking coffee from mugs. Ted was talking about the USA, where he'd done a postdoctoral fellowship. 'It was the moon that dragged me home. Here, when the moon's waxing, it's a smile.' He smiled. 'We used to call it the fingernail moon when we were growing up. But in the northern hemisphere it's a sad mouth, curving down not up. Of all the changes I've had to make living in other countries—new houses, cities, people—it was the change in the moon that finally made me homesick for Australia. We'd lived all over by then. But I only made a year in the States and came home to Sydney. The southern hemisphere night sky and its happy moon pulled me home.'

'I have a Swiss friend whose first language is French,' someone said. 'She says she can think of the words for moon in seven languages but only feels pulled by the French, *la lune*. She believes our emotions reside in our first language and can never go anywhere else however practised we become.'

'Do you agree?' Ted said to Harriet.

'I don't know, I never worked hard enough at languages.'

'*La lune*,' Ted said softly. 'Makes me think of love not the moon.' He looked away from Harriet when their eyes met.

When the others had gone, she made him walk the house several times to get it clear in her head. They finished the tour on the upstairs verandah where the view stretched up river to the Story Bridge written in fairy lights across the night sky and down to the city centre. Ted was looking at the chapel. 'You were disappointed about your idea for the other site. I thought about your proposal after you'd left.' He smiled and looked towards her. 'They were good drawings. It's the wrong spot, that's all. But they were good. You should do more work like that.' Harriet hadn't mentioned her failed idea again. 'Anyone could have made the mistake you did,' he said. Two pigeons were doing a courtship dance on the grass below them, he strutting like a prince with his chest puffed out wide, she coy as a princess, both of them disoriented by the day-lights flooding Ted's garden.

'I know that,' she said. 'I just didn't want it to be me.'

'At this rate, we'll have to go with Max's plan.'

'I was wondering if you were going to come clean about that. Max called me. So much for your promised week.'

'What did he say?'

'Just that, you told him to go ahead.'

'I told him to work with you.'

'"Keep me in the loop" were the words he used.'

'That's not what I said. I want both you and Max on this. I'm sure we can solve the problem if we work together as a team.'

'I'm not.' Harriet winced at the thought of a team with Martin and Max as the other members.

'He must have misunderstood. I'll talk to him again about including you. Your week's nearly up anyway. Got an alternative?'

'I'm working on it.'

'I'd have let you know if I was going to break our agreement. I keep my word, Harriet.' He looked at her. 'You believe that, don't you?'

She didn't respond straightaway. Then she said, 'You can't knock it down, Ted.'

'I don't want to knock it down, I want to make it better. And I want you to convince the government and the Trust and my Board that I can make it better.'

'I'm never going to support major development around the chapel.'

'You know, I reckon you're right. You never are. We should just knock the bloody thing down after all, and put up a nice fat high rise. Why try to integrate the church? Hell, let's turn it into a carpark.'

'Seems to me you were well on your way until the fire was put out.'

'That's right, I burned down the chapel. I sent in a covert team in the middle of the night. Also, I blew up the *Rainbow Warrior*, I made the Watergate tapes, I was there on the grassy knoll, and I drove the white Fiat. Forget the carpark, let's make it a fast food cafe with a high rise next door.' He stopped and looked at Harriet's scowl then shook his head. 'I'm kidding. We're not going to knock anything down. I just wanted to see your reaction. It was a joke, Harriet. I respect the church, believe it or not, and I respect history.'

'There are some things I have very little sense of humour about.'

'So it seems.' He looked over at the chapel again. 'And I don't particularly enjoy being called a white-shoe developer. My interest here is the university's survival, and I believe we can do something that's sympathetic. You can help me, or not.' Harriet was about to ask for more time but he was turning to go inside. 'Kevin!' Kevin McAnelly was standing in the middle of the room. 'Don't sneak up on me like that, you'll give me a heart attack.' Ted had his hand on his heart as if to check. 'You two met?'

'Sorry, sir, but the office paged and said you wanted me. Yes, we've met.' He didn't approach Harriet or attempt to shake hands. 'Miss Darling.'

'Kevin's the guy you have to know if you want anything to happen here,' Ted said. 'People say I'm the VC but Kevin's the real boss. Harriet's just making suggestions for how we could finish off the chapel. You still got the number of that blasting company?'

Harriet started objecting. 'I don't think that's a good idea,' Kevin said. 'The police have told me we're not to do anything just yet.'

'Until when?' Ted said. 'I thought they were finished.'

'Another week. I got a call this morning. They let the facilities guys in, then changed their minds and closed it off again.'

'Why, what's the problem?'

'I don't know, they wouldn't say more, but they're still investigating.' They exchanged looks.

'Damn,' Ted said. Harriet silently gave three cheers for Jack Champion.

'I can come back later if you like,' Kevin said.

'No, it's fine. I just wanted you to have another look at the alarm. It still goes off every time I open the door. It's driving me bananas.'

'You swiping your ID card like I showed you?'

'Of course.'

Kevin smiled. 'Well the system's pretty robust, sir. I'll try your card if you like. Or maybe you could show me what you do.'

Ted smiled. 'You try it. I'll be down soon and you can give me another lesson.' He flipped the card from his wallet and handed it over.

After Kevin left, Ted said, 'It looks like you have another week. It's a charmed life you live after all, Harriet Darling.' He leaned down and looked as if he might say more, then stood back. 'I'll walk you out.'

They waited together for Harriet's cab in the crisp starry night. She saw Venus and made a wish for goodness without saying so. When she got in the cab, Ted motioned the driver to wait. He leaned in her window. 'I'm going down to the hinterland for a walk tomorrow. Don't guess you'd like to come.'

'I'd love to.'

'I'll pick you up at seven.' He kissed her softly and quickly on the lips. 'That's better.' He waved the driver on and walked back to the house.

CHAPTER
TWENTY-TWO

Brisbane in late spring is a warm fecund place ideal for love. The days are long and sleek and summer's a hot promise. Dark figs turn frog-green, jacarandas lilac, bauhinias blush pink, and poinsettias shock red. Magpies, butcher birds and rainbow lorikeets streak the sky. The air buzzes. The earth creaks and moves. Angels sigh.

From Harriet's verandah, the hills in the far distance were clean and blue after a night shower, and even the dirty river looked fit for swimming. She ate cereal while she thought about the day ahead. She'd phoned Marguerita. 'I think Ted Dawes has asked me on a date,' she'd said. 'But I'm not sure.'

'What did you tell him?'

'Yes?'

'Classic patriarchy. If he can't beat you up, he'll charm you. Fuck the consultant for a glowing report.' Harriet imagined Marguerita making the word 'fuck' with her perfect mouth. Marguerita quite liked Ted, she said, he was all right for a man, and she was surprised he'd sink so low. 'Like all of them, he's weak. Wants his own way. He'll do whatever he has to get it.'

'What should I do?'

'You should go, absolutely. For one thing, it's a great national park. But more than that, you can watch him. I'll guarantee he'll try to persuade you into just a tiny compromise on the chapel. You mustn't. It's what you believe in, Harriet, and we've been giving in to them for too long.' Marguerita had no concern for the future of old Archangels. When Harriet had commented whimsically that the towers on the chapel and house achieved synergy, Marguerita had said that men even wanted to fuck the sky. Having seen Martin's plans, Harriet would have been inclined to agree with her. 'If you don't stick up for what you believe in, what's left?' That was the point as far as Marguerita was concerned.

And she was right, Harriet had decided. She should go along with Ted, get what she wanted and beat him at his own game. This is what a modern woman would do. She'd have a strategy in mind. She'd win the day. She'd be poised, ready, in control. Harriet was trying to figure out exactly what the strategy should be but her mind kept drifting off along the mesmerising river. After breakfast, she spent forty-five minutes in the 'robe deciding what to wear. She ran out of time to finalise the strategy.

Ted had been feeling good, too. He was working his way through what Mattie had left him of their joint savings. Once a week, provided he felt up to it, he went to the casino with a thousand dollars in his pocket. He kept records, sometimes he even won, but on balance, he figured, it would all be gone in six months. He'd read somewhere that gamblers always talk about how much they win and never how much they lose, but the driving force in gambling isn't eros, the drive towards pleasure and life, but thanatos, the drive towards debt and death. It's losing that counts, and Ted knew that well. At nights he went home to his big empty house and drank quality scotch and listened to Willie Nelson. He didn't talk about winning or losing or gambling at all. He didn't talk. It was loss, that's what he'd have called it if he'd thought of a name, but a dreamy, easygoing kind of loss, almost comfortable. Sometimes he'd stop in the middle of a conversation, or while walking, and he'd have to lean on something. He'd pull over in the car, or stare out the window and an hour would pass, two. He had a sense that life had been happening, but at some small distance from the reach of his hand. He'd been slipping away inside. Then Harriet had arrived, and he'd thought he might have time. He'd been lucky last night. Seven hundred down. He was on a losing streak.

Ted's big red car smelled of fresh plastic and Harriet remarked that expensive cars never smelled old. On the Story Bridge, she pointed back towards Archangels and said it looked wonderful. As they merged onto the freeway south, Ted responded. 'I'll make a deal with you. I won't talk about Archangels if you don't call me a white-shoe developer. Just for today, let's you and I act like colleagues who enjoy each other's company out for a walk.' Marguerita had said not to trust him under any circumstances and Harriet knew enough about his tactics to maintain vigilance. We'll see, she thought.

They climbed to a ridge looking over lazy farms and a steel blue dam. Ted played country and western music and sang along, off-key on the higher notes, which made Harriet feel uncomfortable in that way she did when people were vulnerable. It had rained during the night, and she opened the window and breathed deeply the cool air. The sun was warm. Harriet agreed it was magic. Ted smiled across at her. His elbow rested on the console between them.

The national park followed a high ridge of the McPherson Ranges which had once been the rim of a massive volcano, quelled by the last ice age. In its wake, the ice had created a subtropical rainforest. Volcanic lava plugs jutted out of the valleys. One of these was Mount Warning, where the sun first touches Australia. Harriet read from the information panel at the park centre. 'The mountains were important places for the traditional owners of the land here. Early European settlers cleared their forests for timber. All that remains of this once majestic forest are this tiny national park and its cooking caves.'

The forest was cool and dark, and sunlight refracted through green to create a softness that illuminated what was normally hidden—a new red leaf on a tree, bright mustard fungi, a momentary flash of colour with wings. It reminded Harriet of the light in the chapel. Ted knew the names of all the trees. The most resourceful, he said, were the strangler figs. 'They seed in the top of another tree where there's plenty of sunlight, and stretch root fingers down towards earth. Until one day their strong roots choke the life out of their host and they replace it in the top of the canopy. They survive using its trunk for support and find a place in the light.' While everything else was struggling up, Ted said, the young strangler fig was starting where there was already plenty of light.

'That's dishonest.'

'Or clever. They get by when the others don't.'

A thought crossed Harriet's mind that if people were trees, Max Palethorpe would be a strangler fig. Ted's dark skin had a strange blueness here, more like a ghost gum. And Harriet, solid red and copper against green, was like a young rose mahogany making her way up to the canopy and light. She wanted to ask what stopped strangler figs.

Ted had brought a strange combination of food, an airline packet of water crackers and a large tin of baked beans, rendered pointless by the lack of a can opener. 'I always find valleys oppressive,' he said. 'I feel lighter all over, don't you?' They'd climbed to Wagawn peak from where they could see in outline the volcanic rim with the stark Mount Warning at its centre.

'They're just buildings,' he said after he'd eaten half of Harriet's lunch. 'Buildings people like you and me have replaced this forest with. You know something? We're destroying rainforests twice as quickly now as we were five years ago. The only difference is knowledge. Now we know what destroying rainforest does to the planet. But we're still doing it, even faster than before. Can you believe that?' His palm was flat on a rock. Here it comes, Harriet thought, the pitch for Archangels Chapel, just a building. He hadn't mentioned it all morning and she'd had to remind herself several times to be cautious. His eyes matched the algae on the rock. He got up. 'In Brisbane you can almost touch greenhouse. We're cooking the planet, and turning the heat up all the time, cooking it faster.' Harriet nodded. She felt simple despair and a vague sense of guilt when people talked about the environment. Ted didn't mention Archangels.

They watched two eagles gliding up and down the valley below them. 'You got a partner back in Melbourne?' At first she'd thought he meant the practice and started telling him about Richard Corsair and John Maple. 'No, I mean a partner partner.'

'I did have but it's finished. It was one reason I wanted to come to Brisbane.'

'Ah, running away from lost love?'

'Not exactly. I was twenty-one when we married, way too young. You know what I did when we split up?' She smiled. 'I got a tattoo.'

'You didn't.'

'I did, an iris, on my belly. It hurt, too.' She wondered whether to show him and decided no.

'I don't know if I could do something like that. Why?'

'I wanted to be different from who I'd been. I don't regret it.'

Ted looked as if he did. 'So what about the ring?' he said.

'This? I just wear it for the hell of it really.' She pulled at the gold band.

'It is your wedding ring?' She nodded. 'How long since you divorced?'

'Nearly two years.'

'That's a pretty long time just for the hell of it. You know the ring says stay away, don't you?'

'I guess.' Harriet wasn't sure whether he was offering advice or something else. 'What about you?'

'Separated, but I don't wear a ring.'

'Sam mentioned—'

'My wife Mattie.' He pointed to the eagles below. 'You know they're the only birds that fly for fun. Jonathan Livingston Seagull should have been an eagle. They soar for no good reason. If I were a bird, I'd soar for no reason, wouldn't you?' The larger eagle was poised at the top of the valley, wings trembling almost imperceptibly to stay perfectly still in the cold air, one gold eye looking down.

'How long ago did you separate?'

'Two years.'

'What happened?'

'She wrote a note.' Ted looked back towards her and smiled bitterly. 'She'd been unhappy with me for a long time.' He thrust his hands into his pockets and rocked from the balls of his feet to his heels. He was standing on the precipice and Harriet felt uneasy but said nothing. 'Tell me, Harriet, are you as trusting in your personal life as you are in your professional relationships?'

'What do you mean?'

'This thing with the chapel. You decided I burned it down, you decided I went behind your back, you decided I told Max to go ahead without giving you the week I promised, now you're not sure why I asked you walking today. It's a fair question. Do you ever trust anyone?'

'Max did go behind my back.'

'Yes he did, in a way.'

'And he also told me you'd given him the all-clear. So I don't trust Max, and I don't think he's on your side.' Ted looked at her sharply. 'Do you trust him?'

He considered this question. 'I know that as soon as you don't trust people they become untrustable.'

'Does that mean you're untrustable now?' Harriet asked.

'I guess it depends on whether you're going to take a risk.' He wiped his hands on his shorts and put them behind his back. 'When people meet new people, they say, look, here I am, this is me.' He held a hand out. 'Later they say well this isn't all of me, it's only one bit, what about this?' He brought the other hand from behind his back. 'But that's not all either. Underneath there are things.' He turned his hands over. 'And sometimes we can bear it, the strain of knowing each other, and sometimes we can't.' He walked over to her. 'Let's get back.'

It rained gently in the afternoon, and they smeared their legs with insect repellant to ward off leeches. A few suckered on to Harriet's shoes and started their ascent but none managed to penetrate the wall of cream. Ted took a black and white photograph of the two of them, holding the camera at arm's length. Later Harriet would put the photo on the pinboard in her office at home, just below the growing shrine to Mother Damian, replacing the shot of Mattie she'd bin that night. At the time, she'd wonder why she'd printed the Mattie shot at all.

He pulled up outside her apartment building. 'Will you be okay?'

She wanted to say no, she wouldn't be okay, she'd like him to come up, but instead she said, 'I'm fine. Feel like a coffee?'

'No, I'll keep going.' He turned off the engine and said he'd help her up with her stuff, one small knapsack but she didn't argue.

'I've had a wonderful day.'

'Good,' he said at her door. 'Tomorrow then.' He saw her inside. He wore her knapsack over one arm. They stood several feet apart in the hall, as if the magnetic poles pushing them apart might also draw them together. The door was open. She felt as if they were teenagers. 'I've had a wonderful day, too.' He moved forward and took her hand as if to shake it then held it in both of his. He stared at the hand as if he wasn't sure what to do next. She stood up on her toes and kissed him softly on the lips. She pulled back and looked at his face. He was smiling. She could feel blood running through her body to places it might be needed. He leaned down to her, they kissed again. They were holding each other's fore-arms, not touching anywhere else, not closing the door, Harriet fearing that if she stopped or went further one of them might call a halt. It was Ted finally who pulled back. He frowned and looked at the ceiling and said her name as a kind of sigh from his chest. She looked at his eyes, long lashes, the mess of his hair, the sandy stubble of his beard under the halogen light in the hall.

To Harriet, the idea of a winning strategy was a foreign language now. The important thing was sex. She wanted to slam up against Ted Dawes and know there was someone there. He was breathing fast from his mouth. She pushed out with her palms and backed him against the opposite wall and looked at him. 'We have to talk,' he said in a whisper she could kiss away. She did. He pulled away and took her arms from his shoulders. 'I mean we have to talk. There are things I have to tell you, about me, things I don't want you to hear from someone else.'

She felt clear in the head and relaxed. She wanted to say I've heard them all, it's all right, Sam told me, I understand everything. 'I want you to stay,' she said. Her voice was uneven.

'I want that, too,' he said. He dropped the knapsack and pushed closed the door. 'Let's start with that coffee.' She smiled and leaned in to kiss him again. But he held his hands up. 'Coffee? You remember coffee, the drink, to chat, wind down, think about our actions, reflect, get to know each other. I want to talk.'

Harriet made the coffee and worked on a temporary rationalisation that would get them as far as her bed. Ted called from the lounge that he needed to check his voicemail. There was no point pretending her objective was strategic. If Ted Dawes wanted to make her like him, he'd already succeeded and Harriet had already failed on Marguerita's terms. She did like him. She felt light in a way she hadn't felt for years, ever. She heard his voice talking into his mobile, deep and rich, and the sound made her want him. She put her head around the corner to look and make sure he was real. He couldn't be real. She couldn't stop herself feeling wonderful. As she poured coffee, she decided to make pancakes for their breakfast tomorrow, and she checked for raspberries in the freezer. She would not think beyond raspberries, to work, Neal, the chapel and the fact that Ted was vice-chancellor of the university that wanted to destroy it.

When she walked into the lounge, Ted was pulling on his boots which he'd only just taken off. He didn't respond when she asked a milk question. He didn't look up when she asked what was wrong. He got up from the couch and walked towards the door. 'I have to go.' He stared at her face as if he might hate her. 'Brisbane Man, Mother Damian,' he said. 'It's not a man, it's not Mother Damian, it's my wife, Mattie, they've found her.'

CHAPTER
TWENTY-THREE

By morning, even television was convinced that Mother Damian was Mattie Hamilton. Footage of the chapel in fading light ran behind a journalist who repeated the police announcement: 'The remains found at Archangels University last week are believed to be those of Professor Matilda Hamilton who disappeared two years ago without trace.' Next was living Mattie, in a long white lab coat with her hair tucked into a surgical cap. Her smile was the antithesis of Brisbane Man's macabre grin.

'That was the story on GIFT,' Sam said. 'I remember that story.' She was told to shush. They ran the clip in slow motion to fit the sound. Born in Sydney forty-two years ago, the obituary solemnly declared, Matilda Hamilton was the daughter of prominent Liberal MP and medico Dr Sir Alexander Hamilton. They had footage of her parents going somewhere. He was lean and fine in a black suit and she was blonde and perfectly thin. Their daughter was made a Member of the Order of Australia for her work to help infertile couples, and rumoured as a likely nomination for the Commission for the

Future. As if they'd suggested the nomination to Mattie herself, she threw back her head and laughed, with slow-mo sleepy eyes, to reveal a long lovely neck and sparkling teeth, her open mouth saying 'I love you' to the world. Behind her a large computer looked about as likely to produce babies as a test tube would have looked a few decades before.

They crossed back to the young journalist, with gaping-mouthed Ted on visual, arriving somewhere the night before in the clothes he'd worn bushwalking. 'There he is,' Sam said and was shushed again. His hair and shirt were a mess and he needed a shave. Harriet felt almost unbearably tender towards him. Jack Champion was close on Ted's left, with a bigger man on the right. Ted folded into them like a boy caught shoplifting. 'The police are treating Professor Hamilton's death as suspicious,' the journalist said.

Ted's staff and Harriet had gathered to share their shock around the television in his office. 'I just can't believe this,' Harriet said. 'How could they get it so wrong? It's Mother Damian.'

Sam looked at her. 'Seems you bombed out there, girl. They said suspicious, Marguerita. What do we do now?'

'We wait, Sam, like I said.'

'This is ridiculous anyway,' Harriet said. 'I told you, there was a blue rosary, Mother Damian had a blue rosary. I just need to go to the police and explain. Poor Ted.'

Harriet thought the police probably had ways to determine whether a missing person was dead. They didn't spend money or open bank accounts or file tax returns. Perhaps Mattie Hamilton was dead, just as they were saying. And they had ways of identifying whose skeleton was whose. But they were wrong there sometimes, too. Harriet had read a story about a skull found in a peat bog in the UK, originally believed to be that of a woman murdered in the fifties, that later was found to be sixteen hundred years old. Meantime, her husband confessed and was convicted. Still later, they decided it was the woman again. It made no sense that the skeleton in the chapel was Mattie Hamilton. It was Mother Damian. Why on earth would Mattie Hamilton be reaching for Mother Damian's rosary and pound note?

Sam turned to Kevin McAnelly, who'd been slouching on a chair in a corner staring at the screen. 'Have you talked to Ted?'

'He called before. Didn't say much. I'm picking him up from the police station.' He unfolded his arms to check his watch.

'Can you ask him what he wants to do for the memorial service? I think something formal, in the university, but not too serious, a celebration of her life rather than a morbid death thing.'

'Hang on, Sam,' Marguerita said. 'The last thing we need's a bloody party.'

Kevin said, 'I'm with Marguerita. Ted won't want a service after everything that's happened.'

Sam ignored him. 'I'll talk to Max about it.' She turned to Harriet. 'Isn't it horrible to think she's been down there all this time and we haven't known?' She breathed in sharply and covered her mouth with her hand. 'You don't suppose she never actually left, and that all this time he's been thinking she didn't love him anymore but really she's just been dead, murdered in the church.'

'That's inane,' Marguerita said. 'There was a letter.'

'Maybe Ted said that to save face. He was pretty messed up. I never saw any letter.'

'I did. She said she needed time, she needed to think through her life and where it was going, a little dull for Mattie Hamilton all things considered.'

Kevin stood up. 'The police inquiry concluded she left of her own free will. You know that as well as I do, Sam. There was never a suggestion of foul play.' He walked over to the door. 'Anyway, if Mattie Hamilton wanted to disappear, she could disappear, believe me. Good riddance far as I'm concerned.'

'Kevin, you mustn't talk ill of the dead,' Sam said.

He laughed bitterly. 'Mattie Hamilton dead? She'll never die.'

Marguerita said to Harriet, 'Kevin worked with Ted and Mattie when Ted was dean in Sydney. What was she like then?'

'Same only younger.'

'You didn't like her, did you?'

'She's like you, Marguerita, from the other side of the tracks. She liked me to stay in my place.' He paused. 'I'm with Harriet. I don't believe it's her, and let me assure you, I'll be checking that police evidence very carefully.' This was said with conviction, but he looked more like a boy repeating something he'd heard an adult say than a crime expert, and it didn't fill Harriet with confidence.

'The international policeman strikes again,' Sam said after Kevin had left. 'Sometimes I think he knows more than he lets on.' She lowered her voice. 'The police are saying suspicious. I heard she was shot in the head.' She let the words sink in. 'I'm thinking of a particular someone in her research centre, Marguerita. Someone the police were interested in when Mattie disappeared. Remember? I'm talking about a guy named Dugald Charmer, Harriet. He and Mattie were big enemies.'

Marguerita smiled. 'Wouldn't be the first time academic jealousy led to murder. But Dugald? Bit of a wuss, Sam.'

'I have to visit the centre this week to talk to them about a move to new premises,' Harriet said. It was a small project Max had given her. At the time, she'd been glad he wanted her involved. Now she realised he probably wanted to distract her from Old Archangels while he went his own sweet way.

'Weren't you doing some sort of review in the centre, Marguerita?' Sam said.

She nodded. 'Ted asked me to have a look at their books, so the audit team's paying them a visit. They've found some discrepancies, nothing major yet, but it's been impossible to get an accurate picture. They might be good at making babies but they're the accountants from hell.'

'Money missing?' Harriet said.

'No, just the opposite, we think, too much money.'

'That is strange.' Sam leaned in. 'You know, Marguerita, I wasn't surprised Mattie left. To be honest, I could never figure what she saw in Ted.'

'Integrity,' Marguerita said. 'We all want what we don't have.'

Sam looked puzzled. 'You said you saw the actual letter, didn't you?'

'Yes.'

'Was it handwritten?'

'It was hand-signed, Sam. Why? What are you implying?'

'Nothing, it's just talk, that's all. Oh pooh, I may as well say it. People are saying things about Ted, that he and Mattie . . .' Marguerita scowled. 'You remember what it was like last time.' Sam looked at Harriet. 'Of course, Ted just adored her, Harriet, I'm positively sure about that, we all did, but people read things in. Now they're saying there were problems.'

'From what I remember, the biggest problem was that you kept stirring the pot,' Marguerita said.

'She was a sexy woman, had this way,' Sam said to Harriet. 'I often wondered if there was someone else. Ted's a darling, but . . . They say the quiet ones are the worst. Maybe he was jealous and then, pow. Even Max talks about Mattie in hushed tones. She always liked Max, didn't she?' Marguerita rolled her eyes obviously. 'Well you know everything, don't you, Marguerita? You saw the letter, you talked to the police, you were with Ted through all of it. What do you think?'

Marguerita looked squarely at Sam. 'Ted with a gun? Max and Mattie? You've got to be kidding, Sam.'

'No,' Sam said, 'I've really got it now, a way we can come out on top, so to speak. Picture this. Devastated Ted left by Mattie for his deputy her lover Max Palethorpe. Archangels University in bizarre sex triangle. If we can't make Ted famous as a VC maybe we can make him the jilted husband.' The three women started to giggle like schoolgirls. 'Imagine the triangle. Ted, Egoboy, Mattie. And the denouement! Egoboy slays Mattie because she was leaving him!' Marguerita and Harriet were laughing and Sam could hardly speak. 'Or maybe, Ted slays Mattie because he's in love with Max. OOOooo! It's cabaret in Brisbane. I love Ted to death but he's lucky he's got me to run his image. I'll spice him up all right.' She broke up again. 'It would even keep the Board awake!' Just then Max Palethorpe and Sir Francis Lynch walked in, and the three women stopped laughing and looked towards them.

'What?' Max said. It occurred to Harriet that he looked more shocked to see them than they were to see him.

'Nothing,' Sam said. 'We were just chatting.'

'Sam and Marguerita, Frank and I need to talk to you, if you'll excuse us, Harriet.'

Kevin McAnelly was waiting at the bottom of the stairs. 'What were they saying?'

'We were just talking about what might have happened to Mattie.'

'I don't know what your game is, and I don't know what you're basing your claims on about this Mother Damian, but you should watch yourself.'

'What do you mean?'

'What were you doing in Max Palethorpe's office on Saturday?'

How did he know? Were his cameras everywhere? 'I was looking for some papers I'd left behind.'

He smiled nastily. 'And did you find them?'

'Yes, as a matter of fact, I did.'

'And do you mind telling me why you printed Mattie Hamilton's picture from our web page?' Had he been into her apartment?

'I was curious. Why, what's the problem?'

Kevin leaned over to her. 'Curiosity killed the cat,' he said.

Maybe he'd spoken to the librarian who'd given her the printed photograph, or maybe they knew how many hits they had on their web page. Either way, it felt creepy knowing that he was watching her. 'Just what are you trying to imply?' she said as firmly as she could.

'I'm not sure where it is you're coming from, Harriet. If you genuinely believe the skull is Mother Damian, then go to the police, and now. But if you're trying to make trouble for Ted over Mattie Hamilton . . .' Harriet's expression must have shown the fear she was feeling because Kevin's face softened and he looked young again. 'I'm sorry, I didn't mean to . . . You just don't want to know about her kind of people, believe me.' He put his hand on Harriet's shoulder, smiled weakly and turned and walked away.

CHAPTER
TWENTY-FOUR

Harriet saw Ted on television again, during the news coverage of Mattie Hamilton's Sydney memorial. It had been organised quickly by her family, who'd decreed there would be no Brisbane equivalent. The police had kept the bones so it was a coffinless service. Outside the cathedral, the Sydney medical establishment looked more like Melbourne, rich and rosy cheeked in overcoats and hats on a bright cold morning. Harriet saw a few seconds of Ted shaking hands and smiling hospitably at a national politician. Mattie's parents were a good distance away, scanning the forecourt as if they'd lost someone, but just for a moment. She was like both of them, they were like each other, and they were all beautiful. The police were still investigating, the report said. After panning to the large crowd, they re-ran the footage of Mattie in her research centre, beatified in front of steel machines.

None of what she'd heard or seen had suggested to Harriet that she might be wrong about Mother Damian. She had the rosary. All she needed to do was to keep looking and she'd find proof. But even as Harriet wound her way through her own logic, a question was niggling. If it wasn't Mattie Hamilton down in the chamber, how come the police and Ted and all those people at the service thought it was? She'd been sorting through material in the archives for over an hour when Neal appeared at the door. 'You promised you'd keep tidy,' he said.

Harriet felt as if she hadn't spoken to him for months, and she was relieved to see him. 'It's not as bad as it looks.'

'I bring the good news. Kevin McAnelly phoned this morning. The police let Tim into the chapel on the weekend. And guess what?' He was holding up a report. 'The crypt and chamber are linked. They've done the tests.'

Harriet jumped up and hugged him. 'Fantastic. I've been dying for something like this. It proves our point, wouldn't you say?'

He was blushing. 'Certainly does, HD. It's only a crawl space but it will do me.'

'But, Neal, you know what this means? Mother Damian must have been alive when they put her in the crypt.'

Neal slumped onto the steps. 'God, that's horrible. Surely not. We're being fanciful now.'

'I've heard of cases.'

'Eighteenth-century cases, not 1940s. Let's assume she was dead when she was placed in the chamber. The alternative doesn't even bear thinking about. Damian's death certificate gives heart failure as cause of death which isn't unusual; she was old. Normally I wouldn't think twice, but given we've found her in the wrong side of the church, I wondered . . .'

'Go on.'

'Well, what if the nuns didn't want her buried on the consecrated ground of the church?'

'If she died in mortal sin, you mean?'

'Whatever. I went back through newspaper fiche for the period. Damian's funeral doesn't rate a mention in the Catholic paper. Even *The Courier-Mail* ran a little obit, but the Catholic press was silent. So I wonder if there was some shame around her death they'd covered up. If she'd been found out, her affair with the bishop I mean, they'd ignore her, wouldn't they? That's what you Catholics do to sinners.'

'Why would the chamber be unconsecrated? It's part of the chapel.'

'Often a church has an adjoining hall or house which wouldn't be consecrated. If the chamber wasn't part of the church, or if they'd forgotten about it, it wouldn't be part of the consecrated space.'

'But they'd have known about the chamber when they first blessed the chapel.'

'We didn't.'

'I suppose not. I wonder why Canali chose not to put it on the plans. Why would he do that?' Harriet thought about what Neal had suggested. 'I see where you're headed. But frankly, I think it's even more fanciful than my suggestion that she wasn't dead. There was no tomb, she was just there on the ground reaching for the rosary. She must have either crawled there or been put there by someone who didn't want anyone else to know.' She looked up suddenly. 'Of course. She was murdered. The police say there are holes in the skull. How else did she get into a secret chamber, and in that position? You know as well as I do, Damian had enemies. She stepped on toes. Someone murdered her and hid her body in the chamber. And she's been there ever since.'

'There would be records in the press.'

'I'm talking about a cover-up, Neal. A convent is the one place you could cover a murder perfectly. She died in office, didn't she? So, who came after?'

'Vincent.'

'And Vincent's crazy. Maybe she killed her to take over.'

Neal rolled up his sleeves. 'This is all speculation, what we really need are facts. Let me go through what we've got and get some notes together.' He looked around. 'How can you work in this chaos?' While Neal sorted the letters into chronological order, Harriet went through other boxes in search of something new. They'd been going for several hours, sharing any information they discovered when Neal said, 'This is a hell of a long way from our original brief.' He was holding an unopened box of Damian's draft letters. 'Mind you, I'm enjoying what I'm doing, but I think investigations are out of our league.'

'Yes and no. We're investigators of a kind. It's just that mostly we focus on buildings rather than people. Mother Damian will be great in our report. It can only help to know as much as we can about her. And if we prove the police are wrong, it's more publicity for us and the chapel.'

'I guess so.' He opened the box and took out a small pile of letters. 'The nuns were incredible, weren't they? Damian nearly went broke, you know, more than once, but she always recovered. She relied on Providence and God provided. I admire that kind of blind faith.'

'I don't,' Harriet said emphatically. 'Faith didn't do much for the chapel last weekend. And it hasn't done much for it since.'

'But that's just it, we don't have faith. We don't believe in God or each other or anything.'

'You on faith? Hah. You've always been such a cynic. You laugh at me when I talk like that.'

'Maybe Damian's converting me. The Lord works in mysterious ways. You don't talk like that anymore.' Harriet didn't respond. 'You used to be like her, you know.'

'Damian?'

'Yeah, when we first started, you used to have that sort of faith.' Again she didn't respond, although what Neal said bothered her. As she continued to search, she thought about the old nun who'd managed to hold on to her faith for so long. 'Hey, listen to this,' Neal said. 'It's a letter to Damian, not a draft from her.' He read aloud.

'"My dear Reverend Mother, I write in respect of the matter we discussed on Sunday last. Your student has been moved from the infirmary back to her dormitory. Her arm is healing and she can look forward to returning to school next week. I must stress that my position has not changed. I am relieved you have at least relented with regard to your resolve that her parents remain ignorant of her injuries, and would wish that you also reconsider your position on the other matter. It is not our place to make decisions like these about your charges, and I must ensure a dependent child's parents know of any injury or harm which comes to that child. I am pleased you have telegraphed the girl's parents and look forward to speaking with them when they arrive. Mother, I shall respect your confidence on the cause of the girl's injuries, provided you can assure me that some action will be taken to make safe her classroom so that such injuries cannot occur again. This is not the first time we have come to debate on this matter. I disagree completely with your strict disciplinarian stance and I must say to you that unless you take some remedial action, I shall be forced to do so myself. I remain, yours sincerely, and with deepest respect. Harville Parker."'

'Harville sounds angry,' said Neal. 'Looks like my Saint Damian might have laid into one of the kids.'

'Not a chance.' Harriet grabbed the letter from him. 'Although Ted Dawes said something similar.' She read the letter. 'No, Neal, it's obvious. This letter is just a coded way of talking about Damian's love affair.' She smiled.

CHAPTER
TWENTY-FIVE

The woman was impossible, with no respect for Holy Office. First, she'd refused his order to reinstate appropriate discipline, then she'd contradicted him in front of a tradesman. Now this, demanding he do something about poor Sister Mary Vincent who, it seemed, had been a little zealous with the cane. Not at all a bad thing in His Grace the Most Reverend James Douglas' opinion, and not before time. Those girls of Damian's ran around that hill like scullery maids, in nowt but bloomers and blouses. She'd started democratic elections for a student representative council, for goodness sake, as if those slow-witted sluts could represent anything, and then she'd let them write their own rules, no less. He was the bishop, although the way she treated him, you wouldn't know it. He'd said to Gerard more than once, you let her get away with too much, but Gerard was weak, always smiled amiably and went his own sweet way like he did everything. And it hadn't really been his place to tell his bishop what to do. Well, now Gerard was gone. She was skating on thin ice, if she only knew.

And the money. She went on about money for her precious buildings as if his pot were unlimited. She told him she was building for the greater glory of Our Lord, but it was her glory she was building towards. She'd shown him the latest plans, to be completed by the end of the decade. She had the audacity to point out that he spent money on the boys up on the terrace but not on her girls. Surely his reasons were transparent, he'd replied. The boys were preparing themselves for careers. Were her girls? They were off and married soon enough. Most of them didn't pass scholarship. She wanted separate school rooms for different grades in the new buildings. How many developmental stages were there in learning to cook a cake? he wanted to ask.

She'd told him Vincent needed treatment. 'What do you mean?' he said.

'Vincent needs a rest, some help with communication,' she replied. 'I have a colleague who understands.' A psychiatrist, she didn't add.

'Rest, Mother? Last week you were complaining about too few hands. Now you're saying we'll send your best worker on holiday?'

'But, Your Grace.' He was certain now it was the education that was destroying her. She'd started at university in the city. When she'd put the idea of study to him, he'd told her to pray for guidance. She had, she said, and could see this as part of her mission. Last week, it had been evolution. Fine if you wanted to believe your grandfather was an ape. Communication indeed. He'd told her he'd talk with Vincent himself.

Poor fat Vincent walked into the parlour and passed wind. She was wrong if she thought His Grace was too deaf to hear it, and at any rate he could soon smell it. Vincent was nervous. She said she'd been teaching the scholarship class. 'Maria Goretti died a terrible death,' Vincent had told her

MARY-ROSE MacCOLL

young charges, 'for refusing to commit a sin of impurity with Alexander. He stabbed her fourteen times. She was your age, girls.' Alexander had visited Maria Goretti on her deathbed and had pleaded with her to forgive him, and Maria Goretti had told him that since God had forgiven him, she could do nothing else. Go in peace, she'd said. 'Girls, her last breath was offered in forgiveness and the love of Jesus. What does that say to us?'

Maria Di Maggio's hand had shot up, Vincent told the bishop. 'She's Mother's favourite,' she hissed.

'Sister Mary Vincent [Smevincent], what's a sin of impurity?' Maria said, all innocent black eyes.

'What?'

'The sin, what was the sin of impurity Alexander wanted Maria Goretti to commit, Sister [Sta]?' Vincent was no fool, she assured His Grace. She blushed as she told him she could see the smiles on the faces of those teenage girls. They knew, if only in vague terms, but probably more clearly than Vincent herself did, the sin into which Maria Goretti was tempted. The week before the same girl had asked, with a shameful smirk on her black face, what a virgin was. An unmarried woman, Vincent had replied cleverly.

'Maria, what in Heaven does it matter?' Vincent had said. 'He killed her and she forgave him.'

Maria said she needed to know the degree of forgiveness. Why was Alexander stabbing Maria Goretti in the first place? She asked this question.

'Maria, that's not what—'

'But, Sister—'

'Vincent,' His Grace said, adjusting the pink zucchetto which nearly slipped off the back of his head when her waving arms knocked it. 'Settle, dear Sister. You have acted rightly and in good conscience, just as I thought. Nothing wrong with a little discipline. It helps the girls become women. But I'd like you to do more for me.'

'Yes, Your Grace.' He was a thin beaked man with sharp, close eyes. Vincent liked him immensely.

'I'd like you to watch Damian.'

'Watch, Your Grace?'

'Something is wrong. I'm worried for her. I'm afraid she's slipping into temptation.'

'What sort of temptation?' Vincent had mad eyes, Mother was right in that respect.

'That's what I don't know, and why I need you to watch, my dear Sister.'

'Of course, Your Grace, His will be done.'

'Quite.' His Grace felt dirty afterwards, it was low, but at least he'd know what went on. They arranged to meet for confession and discussion once a fortnight.

His Grace assured Mother Damian that Vincent's communication skills were fine. That night, Mother let the girls have as much bread and jam as they wanted with tea. She said Sister Mary Vincent hadn't been well. But she'd seemed healthy enough when she'd slapped Maria's face over and over and punched and kicked her on the floor until one of the girls roused Mother. The war was on, Mother told them, and strange things were happening. Doctor had been called. When he asked, Maria told him she'd fallen just like Mother Damian said, and Mother told him there was nothing to be done about it. 'A mild concussion and three cracked ribs in a fall? I don't think so, Mother. You must tell her parents. And it mustn't happen again.'

'Of course,' Damian said. The bishop had made his decision.

After he left, Maria told Mother she forgave Sister Mary Vincent. 'Like the other Maria, Mother, Maria Goretti.' Damian stroked Maria's hair away from eyes.

'Of course, dear.' Her bottom lip quivered as she said it. The next week, Maria was moved to a new home class and Mother Damian was her teacher.

CHAPTER
TWENTY-SIX

'You're drawing a long bow there.' Neal reread the letter before placing it carefully on top of one of his piles. 'In fact, you're being bloody stupid.'

'It was a joke, Neal.' She sighed. 'We're not getting very far, are we?'

He looked at his watch. 'And we're going to be late.'

'What for?'

'I told you, the guy who was involved in the dig at Archangels in the seventies. We have to be there in twenty minutes.'

As they walked towards the city, Harriet asked, 'How do you figure Ted Dawes in all this?'

'He wore white shoes first time he met you.' In the end, Harriet had told Neal about the anonymous meeting. 'I thought that was funny.'

'But do you think we can trust him to do the right thing?'

'Oh ye of little faith. I read the speech you said he gave at the Trust conference. He was moderate but not pro-development. Maybe he's okay.'

'He might be our only hope,' Harriet said.

~

'My colleagues call me Bones,' Dr Jim Skelly said. 'You know, "Star Trek", Dr McCoy.' Harriet had never watched 'Star Trek' and thought a bone specialist named Skelly was funny enough, but Neal smiled encouragingly at the reference. 'Always loved bones, right from when I was a boy.' Dr Skelly was a sprightly pink specimen. He had glasses that might have been stolen from an eighteenth-century cadaver and red wine written in the lines of his nose. Harriet couldn't imagine he was ever a boy.

His office was nothing like the laboratory she'd expected; no body benches, stainless steel or hoses to take away remaining fluids. Perhaps there was an adjoining lab, she thought, or perhaps there were no fluids in his line of work because bones were dry like Dr Skelly himself. His room was more like Harriet's office, with papers and books and slide packs over every surface. One small grimy window was filled with a mildewed air conditioner that was doing little to chill the humid air.

'Hah,' he exclaimed. 'They thought they'd found another Aboriginal burial site. This was the seventies and we were all enraptured by Aboriginal burial sites. Of course now we're not even allowed near them.' Neal looked at Harriet with a raised eyebrow. 'Bones, they found bones, and the pathologist reached what I still think was a reasonable conclusion. A two hundred-year-old Aboriginal girl of twelve or so. They'd already dug up artefacts. It was an important site, you know. I wasn't even part of the team, although I should have been. Professional jealousy. Edgar Goldblum was in charge, the archaeologist. When they found these bones, they got themselves very worked up indeed. Then they decided to involve me, didn't they?

'They brought them to me here.' Neal looked around the room as if they might still be there. 'I was annoyed at the time, because I'd have liked to see the site intact. That always helps. Anyway, even before I saw their bones, I thought they'd probably found one of the good sisters rather than a native. I have a map somewhere.' He got up and started to hunt round the office. Harriet could imagine him finding bones in a similar way. He fossicked through a filing cabinet drawer labelled 'Forensics'. There was another labelled 'Bones' and one labelled 'Body parts'. Folders on the shelves were called things like 'Croc kills', 'Airlines', 'Burnings'. Harriet would have preferred a little more mystique. She didn't want to know what 'Airlines' was about.

'Here!' He showed them a dusty yellowed map of the Archangels site with fewer buildings and markers for what must have been the archaeological site. 'You see, they were digging near the cemetery. Of course a cemetery is going to have bones around it. Sometimes people get buried then forgotten, then they change the boundary and you have bones outside the new perimeter. I was sceptical from the start.

'I worked on Burleigh, you know, with Goldblum, I have a book.' Dr Skelly put the map down on his desk and wheeled his chair across the office. He stood on a footstool to reach the book and on his chair again, wheeled back to Harriet and Neal. 'Beautiful site, just beautiful. Look at these.' There were photographs and drawings of skeletons. 'See these bundled bones. What the Aborigines did was bury their dead then dig 'em up later.' They were looking at a photograph and sketch of a neatly tied package of long bones like a shaft of wheat topped with a human skull. Harriet felt they were looking at something private. 'Beautiful site, beautiful. Rich rich rich.'

'So, was it one of the nuns?' Neal wanted him to come to the point.

'My work can be crucial,' Dr Skelly said. 'I was in the west through the sixties. I aged a skeleton at thirteen years which would have been correct absolutely in our European culture. What I didn't know was that Aboriginals matured much more slowly than us. It was a serious mistake to have made because there was sex involved, consent or not. I have slides.' Harriet wondered if he was planning to show them. 'The buildings cover the site now, but I always thought it strange that there would be an Aboriginal burial site next to the nuns' graveyard. What are the chances of that?' He cackled.

'There are one or two mismatches,' Harriet said, 'where we have a record of death but no tombstone. Or where we've been told someone died, but there's no record of death. In particular, what we'd like confirmed, Doctor, is that there were no remains in Mother Damian Ryan's grave, plot thirty-seven I think.'

'Exactly. There weren't. Quite right. So I concluded, on the basis that there are no nuns in that grave, and they'd found some bones, that they'd found the bones of one of the nuns.'

Harriet said, 'Have you been consulted about the remains they found recently at the Archangels Chapel?'

'Ah yes, the holy bones, but Marcus Holt's your man there. Pathologist. Bit of a know-it-all to be honest, but a good lad. I gave him my report last week. Can't comment of course, the case is ongoing, police and all.' He smiled. 'But a surprise for everyone, isn't it?'

'Yes,' Harriet said. 'Can you at least confirm what the police are saying, that the remains are Mattie Hamilton's?'

'I'm not the pathologist,' Dr Skelly said. 'I don't decide whose bones we have. I just help with the detail. Check with Marc on the name. But yes, my report was crucial, even if I do say myself.'

'Can you at least tell us the cause of death?'

'Of course, matter of public record, and quite jolly obvious to boot. Brain crushed.' He tapped his head. 'I'm thinking a pickaxe, hammer, blunt, two blows. Wham wham, and she's gone. Quick. Kind really, in a way.'

Neal checked his notes. 'So the bones you found in the seventies,' he said. 'Was it one of the nuns?'

'Oh no.' Dr Skelly had been saving this punchline and wasn't going to waste it. 'It was a dog. They'd found the bones of a dead dog. A labrador as I remember, that one of the sisters had run down.'

CHAPTER
TWENTY-SEVEN

Vincent saw the dog before the dog saw Vincent. It was the one all right, the yellow labrador with milky cataracts over its eyes. From this angle, she could see his little thing dangling loosely below his solid middle. He'd been visiting the convent for some months. Vincent herself had started leaving scraps for him. He wasn't exactly the convent dog, that would have been an extravagance, but Mother Damian had told the novices they could feed him out of loving kindness as they would care for all God's creatures. 'Thank you, Mother,' Angelina had said and grabbed her face and kissed it so that Mother blushed.

When Vincent was a girl named Maryellen her mother left the family for an Italian fruit grower with greasy hair and skin that smelled of coconuts and made Maryellen sick. Later, when Vincent taught cooking, the smell of coconut could turn her stomach so much that decades of classes of fourteen-year-olds as middle-aged women never used coconut in their cooking despite a husband's or son's predilection for lamingtons or coconut ice.

Vincent hated anything Italian with all the passion she possessed in the Latin blood she'd always suspected ran through her veins. She was blonde and blue-eyed Irish like her mother but she knew she was probably sired by the ugly little Sicilian she first met that Tuesday afternoon after school as a taut bronze rump in the air in her mother's bedroom. She should have been sitting down to milk and freshly baked Anzac biscuits. Her poor father, God rest his soul, had no idea, and Vincent didn't know how to tell him until it was too late.

Mother was slipping into madness, His Grace was quite right. Cuckoo land, he'd said to Vincent at their last meeting. It was after she and Mother had visited the building site of the new primary school. Damian had worn a hard hat over her veil, and boots, and she'd giggled like a girl. 'Mr Stanley gave me these,' she'd told Vincent. 'He says I visit on-site so much I should have my own.' Vincent had wanted to push her down the stairwell.

'Imagine falling, Mother,' she'd said, too loudly, because Mother had stepped back from the chasm then and had looked at her.

Mother had allowed Maria to join the order. She's not right for the life, Vincent had said, but Mother had ignored her. Remember Maria Goretti, she'd said, and Mother had covered her mouth with her hand in a gesture that suggested she was shocked at the reference. And it was shocking, what that brazen hussy had said to Vincent. Now Maria was Angelina, and Angelina and the dog had become friends. First, she fed him scraps in accordance with Mother's direction. Then she gave him a bath which Mother failed to notice, on purpose in Vincent's view. Then the daily walks started along the river, Angelina and her dog, proud as all get-up, like any young girl with a new pet, not like a sister at all, no humility whatever. Vincent watched as Angelina again confirmed her slatternly ways.

Today Vincent would supervise the almonry at the front gate which provided for those who had nothing. Dirty men with port breath, home from the war with no jobs, their grimy faces lining up for her hot pea and ham soup and a steaming cup of sweet tea. She'd work with one or two younger sisters who always wore a pained expression as if they themselves were suffering the fate of these poor creatures. Lately Vincent had had the idea that she should release the men's souls. She imagined arsenic would do the trick, there was some in the rat killer. Vincent felt righteous anger at their suffering, anger at their shaking hands and the black under their fingernails, their endless hope and singing 'Nearer my God to Thee' while they waited each evening for succour. She'd bring them nearer my God to thee, that was for sure. The biggest problem would be getting the arsenic into their soup without also poisoning one of the young sisters who often dipped in without permission. Then again, she'd told them more than once the soup was for the poor.

Vincent had been out to the fruit and vegetable markets to buy oranges for the basketball games which were to be hosted by Archangels that weekend. Freckled girls in short skirts sucking orange quarters into their red faces like life itself. Vincent loved to watch basketball. She imagined taking off her hot habit, and donning a skirt and singlet. She'd run around the court with the freedom of a girl. On the back seat of the car were three boxes of oranges and one of apples, which had been cheap that morning. Vincent thought she might make stewed apple for dessert. And a pie, an A pie. She chuckled to herself, Who's for my A pie? They loved her apple pie, the poor souls at the gatehouse.

It was one of those moments in life when given a choice we do what we do, one of those events that foretell a future and outline a past as clear as mountains. When she saw the dog, there was just a moment to think and act before it moved out of the way. Vincent hardly hesitated before she put her foot down on the accelerator. The Austin hit the dog at thirty miles an hour. She cried when she felt the bump space bump of its ribs under the wheels of the car. 'Poor dog,' she said to Angelina's tears. They buried him up in the cemetery. His name was Michael.

CHAPTER
TWENTY-EIGHT

On the way back across the quad, they met Marguerita Standfast. It surprised Harriet to learn she shared Neal's keen interest in Archangels' history. 'Harriet's hopeless on this sort of stuff,' Neal was saying. 'I do it all for her, you know.' He was smiling widely, rocking from the balls of his feet to his heels, hands in pockets.

Marguerita was smiling, too. 'How charming, Harriet, how novel, a man who does the work.' Neal blushed under her gaze. 'Now, why don't you take me for a nice coffee and tell me exactly what you've found out about Mother Damian? Harriet hasn't given away a skerrick, and I bet you know more anyway.' Neal looked to Harriet, who shrugged amiably. If Marguerita was interested in Mother Damian, that was fine. She left them on the steps and headed back to her office to pick up papers for the next meeting.

Harriet had offered to shift her appointment with staff at Mattie Hamilton's research centre on the grounds that they would still be in shock. No, the Dean of Medicine, Professor John McIntyre, had said, we must get on. They walked across the quad together to the Australian Infertility Centre which was housed in Angel Square. 'This used to be the boarders' dining room,' Harriet told him.

'Those strapping young girls tucking into their stew and mash would be about as far from the centre's line of work as one could possibly be,' he chuckled.

It had been the first building for the postwar period. In spite of financial straits and tension Mother Damian wrote about in letters home, she had not spared any expense here. Now, suspended ceilings hid ducting, dirty linoleum and carpet covered the floors, and machinery and air conditioning hummed instead of hungry boarders. But under layers of paint and plasterboard were solid wood doors with brass knobs and carved architraves and cornices. Harriet had recommended that the centre be moved off-site, to something purpose built, and that John McIntyre and his administrative staff, who'd be gentle users, move back to the older building. She told him now that it wouldn't take much to replace the centre's clean bleach smell with wood polish.

'Next you'll be trying to turn it back into a dining room,' he said.

Harriet found it difficult to place Mattie Hamilton in the clean clinics and labs they toured. Mattie would be sipping an unoaked chardonnay at Noosa with successful sperm donors or preparing to fly to an exotic South American destination where a conference was about to begin because of her. Not here, managing the day to day realities of infertility. When they stopped for morning tea, the staff, mostly bearded bespectacled scientists and technicians, mulled around an urn and talked to one another or the floor instead of to Harriet. Mattie would have been the star here, the pin holding them together. Without her they were lost.

Mattie's deputy and now the acting director of the centre was Dugald Charmer and he was anything but charming. Harriet asked him about the proposal to move the centre to another site. He had few objections and little interest. He said he'd been at Archangels since the start, and had never liked the old building anyway. 'It was Mattie who insisted we move here,' he said. 'We were supposed to have a floor in the faculty building but she wanted history.' Harriet nodded.

'She never cared for anyone but herself, you know. And I don't care who hears me say it.' He spat words out and one or two of the staff around them looked up. 'They reckon someone hit her in the face with an axe.' He smiled.

'How do you know that?'

He ignored the question. 'Reckon it'd take more than that.' Other staff watched him now, some smiling. 'I'll believe it when I see the skull.' Mattie may have had many friends, thought Harriet, but her enemies hated her powerfully. 'Good riddance, ay lads?' One or two were nodding. Harriet ended the conversation quickly and arranged to send him a copy of her report on the relocation.

Harriet met with the centre administrator, Beryl Hanley, to discuss the move. After they finished, she asked about Dugald. Beryl grabbed at her neck nervously as she talked softly. 'Everyone here loved Prof Hamilton, even Dugald until they fell out. He shouldn't talk about her like that. Makes my blood boil.'

'How did they fall out?'

'He said she didn't give him credit for GIFT. He said she never did the real work.' She pursed her lips. 'It's true she wasn't all that interested in the details, mostly left that to the rest of us. Dugald has an international reputation in IVF. He was promised research money when he came from Strathclyde. Some people said he was promised the director's job as well, but I don't know about that. When Prof arrived, she wasn't as well known. People said she only got the job because Professor Dawes was appointed VC. Being a woman it was harder for her.

'Now people say they only gave Professor Dawes the job because they wanted Mattie. That's how I like to think of it.' She let out a nervous laugh. 'Prof was great. She set high standards and expected you to meet them. And as long as you did, she was fine. I loved working for her.

'She and Dugald worked together on everything. There was never any jealousy about whose idea was whose, not at first. But when Mattie wrote a conference paper on GIFT, Dugald said it was his research. Normally I think she always included him, but she said it was her paper and he wasn't an author. It was the key piece of work in the scientific community for GIFT II so it mattered a great deal to both of them.'

'Was it her work?'

Beryl shrugged. 'She was a woman scientist in a man's science world. That's always hard. After that, they fought, and I don't mean debating, I mean screaming battles, awful for the rest of us. He was so angry. Finally she offered to put his name on the paper. But he told her he didn't want it anymore. He said it was too late and she'd be sorry. I'm going to destroy you was what he said. Can you believe that? In a research centre. He said he knew about her and he'd break her. I told the police. I didn't care, I told them whatever I could to help.

'Mattie could make science accessible to people. It was her gift. If you ask me, Dugald got sick of the back room. I think it was pure jealousy. Mattie was aware of our clients as real people who can't conceive even though they desperately want to. She cared for them even though she didn't have kids herself. She used to say she had to keep some distance from the realities of conception for the clients' sake.' Beryl smiled.

'Sounds like you really admired her.'

'She was a treasure.' Beryl dabbed at her eye with a tissue. 'Now Dugald says she stole his ideas. Of course, she's not here to defend herself, is she?'

Harriet told Beryl she'd send her some space description forms. 'You'll have to complete them whether you're moving or staying,' she said. 'And I'll send you a copy of my report to Professor Palethorpe.'

John McIntyre emerged from an office to walk Harriet to the door. 'Must have been dreadful for the faculty losing Mattie Hamilton,' she said on the way out.

'Depends who you ask. Noticed Dugald bending your ear at tea.'

'He's very angry. What happened between them?'

'Can't blame him really. Feels he got shafted. Worst thing you can do to a scientist with a bit of flare.' He paused as if weighing up whether to go on. He didn't.

'What did she do to him?'

He looked at her. 'Ted and I go back a long way, and I don't want to criticise Mattie, but she could have been a bit more bloody mature when it came to Dugald. By the time I was involved, we'd almost lost him. She was so hell bent on being a bloody star. And really, they were both starry. She just needed to make him feel he was the important one.'

'Why should she do that if it was her work?' Harriet felt the colour rising in her face.

John McIntyre considered Harriet carefully. 'He's got a bit of an ego, old Dugald, and Mattie should have stroked it a bit more. She was the director.'

'Ted must have been devastated.'

'Well it was the not knowing, you see. We were all on hold. Even now, I don't like to suggest to Ted that we do something permanent in the centre, but time's getting on and it's not fair to Dugald, acting director two years. Ted's such a good man. I don't like to bring it up with him. But we'll have to do something soon.'

Outside, lorikeets screeched in the fig tree that dwarfed the tiny Angel Square. Harriet experienced a bitter chill that reminded her of opening the front door in Melbourne on winter mornings. She'd intended to go straight back to the archives and Neal. Instead she turned and went into the

183

Grotto for the Angels in Heaven under the fig. On the altar was a small alabaster sculpture, two stone angels entwined in one another's arms. Their feet and wingtips were light as air. Harriet sat at the little altar and looked at their blank white faces.

CHAPTER
TWENTY-NINE

From her stall in the front of the chapel, Angelina watched the lateral muscles holding Michael's arms lengthen and shorten under his shirt to prevent him flying away. Prayers droned on. 'Hail Mary full of grace, the Lord is with thee. Blessed art thou among women.' She thought of the first time she'd seen the sea, grey gulls and blue going on forever. 'And blessed is the fruit of thy womb, Jesus. Holy Mary Mother of God.' Angelina thought of Archangels and the many friends she'd lose if she didn't live here anymore. 'Pray for us sinners now and at the hour of our death.' She thought of Mother Damian, who looked away quickly when she looked over.

Michael hung from the ceiling on a trapeze. He was fitting the high stained-glass windows he held in his big safe hands. Angelina liked to watch him, his perfect arms and shoulders, his blue-black hair long in the style of Francis of Assisi. The darkness of boarded windows was becoming soft coloured light under those hands. Prayers floated through the chapel like bees around flowers, and the smell of burning incense after benediction made Angelina sleepy. It was a beautiful place to praise God and watch Michael. When he sang the 'Ave' it made her cry. He had a fine tenor voice that came out of his broad chest with joy.

Michael was promised to God the moment his mother breathed her first breath on him, as soon as she checked he had ten fingers and toes. This one's for the Lord, she'd said. She was Irish Catholic and laughed in a way that made people nervous. Michael had her eyes, darker blue, and he grew into a big strong boy with a clean big faith that was fed to him with breastmilk and potatoes. He wanted to make people happy. Michael had joined the life when he was twelve; he was just eighteen now. He loved the community, and he wanted to be with God and his brothers all the time. In his heart he was sure he was made for service.

When he saw Angelina for the first time, he was mute. He felt confined within his body. She was a vision, all he'd ever imagined the Virgin might have looked to men. He could see a square of face, dark and beautiful with sad brown eyes and a fine dark moustache. Under layers of black serge her body was full of grace. He couldn't stop looking at her. They were in the kitchen of the convent, a bright sunny room with breezes from large windows, the bustle of nuns and a faint smell of eggs. Some of the young ones were pretty, no doubt about that, and Michael knew it wasn't his place to look, but he couldn't keep his eyes off her. She didn't speak at first but her eyes met his squarely.

'Up on the roof after lunch,' Brother John said. 'Water coming through. Might be a few tiles need replacing.' As Angelina served their lunch, Michael became conscious of his sweaty work clothes. He couldn't speak to thank her. When she smiled it wasn't in that way nuns smiled where something is always held back. It was full and bright from her eyes. 'I'm too fat,' Brother John was still talking about the roof. He laughed and it came up out of him as if his body were hollow inside. He reminded Michael of the lacquered gaping-mouthed clowns he had fed balls into at the annual show. You never knew what you'd get. 'Do you think this poor old novice master should be the one on the roof, Sister?' he said.

'It's a good strong roof,' Angelina said. 'Slate.'

Brother John slapped his belly. 'But is it strong enough?'

'Only one way to find out,' she said. Her voice was deep and resonant, musical but not like a girl's, and she wasn't crushed quiet like other novices. 'Perhaps, Brother, if you skip today's dessert, you might—'

'And miss one of Vincent's pies. Not on your life. I'll send Michael up before I'll do that. What's it today?'

'Apple and rhubarb from our sisters in Stanthorpe.'

'Michael, get ready for the roof.' He didn't respond. 'You'll have to forgive our young friend, Sister. I think he's quite overcome by the roof. I don't think you've met.' He kicked Michael under the table. 'This is Brother Michael.' What was wrong with that boy? He kicked him again. Michael looked at him as if from a dream.

'I know, I've watched you working,' Angelina said, and smiled.

'I hope we haven't distracted you in prayer.'

'No, on the contrary, an inspiration.'

'Well, Michael, I'd say you're the inspiring one, eh?' He grabbed Michael's arm and held up his hand. 'These are the hands of a craftsman.' Michael's mother had wanted him to be a priest but the Lord gave him large hands and feet and something in him that said he didn't want responsibility for the sins of the world. He was a brother in Christ and humble in service as He was humble, serving the poor, his brothers, the community. Michael chose building because he liked the feel of wood. The idea of celebrating the Eucharist, of creating from bread and wine the body and blood of Our Lord Jesus Christ, filled him with trepidation. He watched over a flock of boys. He fed the hungry. He repaired a church. He saw his Angelina.

In chapel, Mother Damian watched Angelina watching the young brother, the girl's eyes shifting back periodically, as if she wasn't sure he'd still be there. He wasn't unaware, changing what he did, exaggerating his movements. Clearly they knew one another. But Vincent was making outrageous claims. Mother Damian knew she should do something, but what? As she watched her young sister, one part of her wished they'd simply fly away. The girl had experienced such sorrow in her short life, and she looked happy when she watched that boy. Damian opened her office, read the note again, 'I must see you, my love.' And the greatest of these is love. St Paul said that, or at least Mother thought it was St Paul. It certainly wasn't George Gershwin, whose name was the first to come to her mind. She closed her office.

After rosary, Sister Mary Vincent spied Angelina walking up the hill towards the quad instead of back to the convent for chores. 'Where you off to, Sister?' Slatternly, that's how you'd describe that girl, brazen and slatternly.

'Walking, Sister.' Walking Sta, Nothing Sta, Yesta, Nosta, Whatever you say Sta. Angelina wished a miracle would take Sister Mary Vincent up to Heaven, a blessed ascension. It would need to be blessed if it weren't going to collapse under the strain.

'Back for scullery.'

'Yesta.' Angelina walked past fruit trees and the fat white ducks Vincent would slaughter soon to celebrate the risen Lord Jesus. Come Lord Jesus, they'd sing, the night is dying. Michael was sitting inside the grotto. He held his head in his hands in whispering prayer. A candle burned. 'Who are you praying for?' she said.

'Won't work if I tell.'

'That's superstition.'

He laughed. 'And all this is not?' he gestured around the small cave. She didn't reply. 'Us,' he said. 'For us.'

She said it wouldn't work anyway. 'We're mortal sinners.' But when he kissed Angelina, Michael knew it wasn't wrong. He tasted her sweet young mouth, felt her fragile back shift against his frightened, respectful hands. Later, when her lips and warm breath were gone, he'd think of Brother John and what he might say. He'd think of the boys back at the school and what they'd think of their big dumb woodwork teacher. He'd think of his fat mother with stone blue eyes, lifting the covers and staring at his hand on his stiff dick. 'You're disgusting,' she'd said. 'How can you do this to me?'

When his lips met Angelina's, when he folded her tiny frame in his large chest and circled her in his angel's wings, he knew there was nothing wrong in the world. He kissed her. He looked at her tiny hands. He kissed her. This can't be wrong, this love. Come to me all you who thirst and I will give you to drink of the waters of eternal life. Come to me you who are weary and I will give you sleep in peace. Sleep, Angelina. Peace. Blessed be the name of God who is Yaweh who is good and whose mercy knows no end.

CHAPTER THIRTY

Ted had written the name Rowan Hannigan at the top of the blotter on his desk, but when he looked at it on the morning he returned to work, he couldn't remember who it was. It seemed like an age ago, before the police had told him they'd found Mattie. He'd written the name to remind himself he had to do something about someone named Rowan Hannigan. Max said, 'That's the Minister's son, isn't it? What's it about?'

'Thanks for reminding me.' Ted sighed heavily. 'He's applied for law. I think his father and Frank were in the brotherhood.' Ted put his right hand around his neck and over his left shoulder in a mock secret handshake.

'Did he get in?'

'I'm going to have a look.'

'If there's anything I can do to help at the moment, Ted, you know, while you get back on your feet.'

'Thanks, Max, I'm fine.'

'I mean, have you thought of taking a break, maybe a week or two, to give yourself time?'

'I'm fine, Max. I just want to get on. That's the way I handle things.' Max nodded and touched Ted's elbow, clumsily, and without looking at him.

When Ted found the time to phone the admissions director, he was told that Rowan Hannigan wasn't within reach of an offer in law. 'His score's way too low. He may not even meet the definition of life,' Bruce Martin said with a snicker.

Ted ignored the humour. 'Ah well, thanks for checking.'

Later in the week, he walked back to his office with Frank who was in a particularly good mood after an engineering firm promised to endow a chair in medical engineering. 'I checked on Bob Hannigan's boy for you, Frank,' Ted said.

'Yes, thanks for that, Ted, Bob's over the moon.'

'What do you mean?'

'He's delighted to get a place. Bob phoned me personally to say thanks.'

'But—'

'Mum's the word far as I'm concerned, Ted. What we do for this place, eh?'

Red faced and safe in his office, Ted picked up the telephone. 'What the hell do you think this is?' he said to Bruce Martin. But Bruce told him they'd forced the offer on instruction.

'Professor Palethorpe phoned me. He said to offer him a place. I'm sorry, Professor Dawes. I told him you'd called. I figured you'd instructed him to ring me.'

Ted strode into Max's office. 'What going on?' His voice was even.

'You said Frank knew him. I didn't think you'd have time to do anything after all that's happened so I called Bruce. I was only trying to help.'

'And Bruce told you I'd already phoned.'

'I didn't know about that.'

'At any rate, Max, the boy doesn't have a hope.'

'You don't know that. He's the Minister's son.'

'We don't do this stuff. Ever. Remember equity, ethics.'

Max shrugged his shoulders. 'I'm sorry, Ted. Frank was really pleased.'

'You told him?' Ted was furious now. He thumped the window with his closed fist. It made a dull thud and the glass cracked in one corner. 'Sorry,' he said. 'There must have been a weakness.' His hand hurt. 'When did you talk to Frank?' This was a bad sign, Max casually dropping into a conversation that Frank was pleased. Frank and Max, Max who helped Frank when Ted wouldn't help Frank. And Frank knew all this and hadn't said. A CEO must have the confidence of the Board at all times, avoid alliances developing between key Board members and others, first rule of governance, first thing they told Ted at Harvard. Kill any links between your exec and Board or they'll kill you. But Ted's grip was slipping. 'We have to be above reproach. We're a private university. They're all watching for stuff like this.'

'They pay fees to come here.'

'Well let's just open our doors to everyone then, shall we? Long as they've got a big fucking cheque book.' As he walked out of the office, Max's secretary looked up at him over her glasses. 'Sorry,' Ted said to her, blushing. 'I don't normally talk like that.'

'That's all right,' she said with a smile, 'I do.'

Suddenly Ted turned and went back to Max's office and closed the door behind him. He was breathing fast. 'Now they've found her,' he said, 'I want to go back to how we were, Max, when we first started. We were good, and we were a team. This investigation the police are doing might be bad for all of us, not just me, mate.' He stared hard at Max, who was frozen behind his desk. 'I've trusted you. I've given more latitude than most would in my position. You know that as well as I do. And in return, I expect loyalty. Understand?' Max didn't respond. 'I said, do you understand?'

'Of course. Absolutely, Ted. Goes without saying.'

CHAPTER
THIRTY-ONE

Brisbane was promising its hottest summer in fifty years and Harriet could feel the solid veil of humidity that dropped over the city from around mid morning. She hid under sunglasses, wide brimmed hats and greasy sunscreen, and scurried quickly from place to place to avoid headaches. From five in the morning until six in the evening now, her life was without subtlety. Love would be impossible in daytime Brisbane. Night came quickly like dawn, but it was full of noises and life, the low throbbing of insects getting ready for journeys, nocturnal people moving around their slightly cooler houses, bats chattering and screeching in the mango trees.

She'd met Marguerita and Sam at e'cco bistro. They drank a second bottle of wine and ordered coffee. Their conversation drifted back to Mattie Hamilton's disappearance. Sam fancied herself as a private dick, running through suspects. So far, she'd talked up Dugald Charmer as a killer, and Max Palethorpe, but she was stuck for a motive there, she said. Marguerita wouldn't let her talk about Ted. Sam leaned in close and pursed her lips. 'Okay, what about Kevin McAnelly?'

They both looked at her. 'He knew I'd printed a picture of Mattie from the web,' Harriet said, 'and told me to lay off.'

'There you go,' Sam said. She looked at Harriet. 'Why did you print a picture of Mattie?' Harriet said she didn't know, she just wanted to see her. Sam paused for a moment then nodded. 'Did you know our Kevin had a crush on Mattie?'

'Sam,' Marguerita said harshly.

'What's he gonna do? Sue me.'

'Probably.'

Sam ignored her. 'Yes, Harriet, as a boy back in Sydney, our Kevin was besotted by Mattie. He jumped her and tried for a kiss when what he was supposed to be doing was taking her to the airport. Only she didn't kiss back. She threw him out and caught a cab. She made a complaint. He was very nearly sacked for sexual harassment.'

'It wasn't harassment, Sam,' Marguerita said. 'There has to be unequal power.'

'There is, he's bigger.'

'No, I mean, he has to be able to withhold or grant some benefit.' It sounded as if Marguerita had explained this to Sam before.

'He was the driver. Maybe he refused to take her to the plane.' Sam said. 'That's a benefit.'

Marguerita rolled her eyes. 'You drive me to distraction, Sam. But I agree about Kevin. He didn't like Mattie one bit. And I could see him with a pickaxe. Those eyes.'

Harriet was about to go through her theory on Mother Damian again when Sam said, 'Even you must be able to understand why Ted's going ahead on the chapel now, Harriet. Imagine how he'll feel looking out his window every day and knowing that Mattie died there. Those spires like googly eyes looking up at him. And if Kevin, his best boy, did it. God.' She popped a chocolate into her mouth.

'What's going ahead?' Harriet said.

'Didn't he tell you? Whoops.'

'What are you saying?' Harriet looked squarely at Sam.

'When Ted came back to the office,' Marguerita said. 'He saw Max and me first thing. He said you'd had your week and come up with nothing much. We're going ahead.' She picked up the crumbs from her dessert plate with her index finger and put them in her mouth.

'Ted agreed to this?'

'Max has been pestering him, but yes, he said there was no choice.'

'They're not going to knock the chapel down, Harriet,' Sam said. 'They're just going to put an itty-bitty building next to it.'

'After everything I've done, he could just sign away the past like that. I don't believe it. And without telling me. The bastard, the absolute bastard.'

'They're all the same,' Marguerita said, but Harriet wasn't listening. She was thinking strategy. The Trust would have to move fast on a protest, surely the Commission would step in now. And they couldn't start building yet, not without planning approval. But if they already had approval, it was anyone's guess. Harriet needed to think, call Richard, tell him everything, get him up here. What if the new building did permanent damage and they couldn't retrieve the situation? That didn't bear thinking about either. Harriet only vaguely heard the ringing of a mobile phone.

'Kirk to *Enterprise*,' Sam said, fishing it out of her bag and smiling at the joke she used every time she answered. Her face fell and she blanched at what she heard on the other end. 'It's Ted,' she said without removing the phone. 'Max just told me the police have taken Ted away to question him about the murder of Mattie Hamilton.'

'What?' Harriet said.

'I knew it.' Marguerita looked at Sam then Harriet. 'They think he killed her.'

Sam was nodding. 'I told you Marguerita. It's the only thing that makes sense.'

CHAPTER
THIRTY-TWO

It made no sense whatsoever to Harriet Darling. This was going too far. It was one thing to drink a sweet young semillon and imagine who might have killed someone if they'd had a chance. Playing detective with Sam and Marguerita had been a way to relieve the tension they all felt. But arresting Ted for his wife's murder was impossible. The police didn't do things like that. He didn't kill her. How could he? It wasn't her down in the secret chamber.

Max was talking constantly as he marched from one side of Ted's office to the other. 'Sam, we need a media release, and I better call the chancellor.' He sifted through the in-tray on the desk as if there would be instructions while one shrugging shoulder nursed a phone. Sam stood with her arms folded and nodded agreement.

'We don't know anything yet.' Marguerita had sobered quickly.

'You weren't here!' Max shrieked. 'Ted came to my door with the police and said they wanted to interview him at the station. There was TV outside.' Sam drew her breath sharply.

'At the very least, I have to ring Frank. What do you think, Sam?'

'Absa-fuckin-lutely,' she said. 'At least! Believe me, we want control, and the press have the story already. This is the big time, Max!'

Marguerita stood apart from Sam. 'Don't you try your bullying on me, Max. It won't work. This is disgusting. We don't know if he's been charged.' She turned and walked towards the door. 'They reckon that within an hour of John Kennedy's death, Johnson made Bobbie, who'd just lost his big brother, fly out to Dallas so he could swear Johnson in as president. Difference here, Max, is you haven't even waited till Ted's dead. I should have known you'd do this.' She glared at Sam. 'But I expected more from you.'

Sam shrugged lamely. 'This isn't some loyalty thing, Marguerita. It's the real world. This is television, for godsake.' She looked over to Max and smiled weakly.

Harriet stood up. 'Marguerita's right. We don't even know what's happened.'

'I'm in charge, all right? I'll decide what happens,' Max said. 'The police called five minutes ago to say they want to talk to me. I couldn't get any more details about Ted, but we have to assume the worst. We need a contingency. I'm acting VC.' He looked at all three of them as if they were a team having a minor disagreement. His eyes stopped on Harriet. 'What the hell are you doing here anyway?'

'I should be involved in any meeting with the police, Max,' Marguerita said. 'And Harriet's a friend of Ted's.' The two women exchanged glances.

Max pointed at Marguerita. 'You just do what you're told.' He turned to Sam. 'You get started on that release.' He looked towards Harriet and was about to speak when the phone on his shoulder came to life. His grimace turned to a wide grin. 'Frank, it's me, great great, but I've got some terrible news.'

He motioned for them to leave the office and close the door behind them.

'You heard him,' Sam said. 'We have work to do.' She and Marguerita stormed off in opposite directions, leaving Harriet wondering what she should do next.

CHAPTER
THIRTY-THREE

Ted was alone. He should have asked for a lawyer immediately. That was unwise. He wasn't thinking straight. At their last retreat, his management team told him if he was an animal, he'd be a roaring lion. When he thought of himself as a lion, he thought of the cowardly lion in the *Wizard of Oz* who needed a heart to give him courage. Now the police were after him. Why were they so obsessed with time?

'In your statement, you say you left Lismore around three pm?' Detective Inspector Jack Champion sat on the other side of the laminated table. His partner, Bruno Otter, more like a grizzly bear, had squirmed his considerable bulk into a small chair. He glared at Ted from a blown-up face that suggested he was a long way from a healthy heart weight, with red-light ears on either side sounding the final alarm.

'We've been able to confirm that. And you got home?'

'Couple of hours later as I said. I can't remember the exact time.' They both had coffee in plastic cups. Neither offered one to Ted.

'Seven pm, that's the time you said in your first interview.'

'Sure, around six-thirty or seven, it's two years ago, Detective, and it was a distressing few weeks for me.'

'Lovely spot, Lismore,' Jack said. 'My kids love the beach down that way, Hastings Point, good fishing too. You got kids?' No, no kids. 'Anyone see you get home, Professor Dawes?'

'No.'

'Did you stop at all, talk to anyone?'

'No.'

'So you left at three?'

'Something like that.'

'It's about two and a half hours from here, Lismore, isn't it?'

'I don't remember.'

'So what did you do in that hour and a half between five-thirty and seven?'

'I don't know, Detective.'

'You're sure you couldn't have arrived home earlier, say five or five-thirty.'

'No, I'm not sure. As I said before, it was a long time ago.'

'Your office security system clocked you in at five-fifteen, so if you went straight home like you said, you'd have got there at what time?'

'Five-thirty I guess.'

'Just a couple more questions, sir.' Jack Champion consulted his notes. 'Now, you called us around ten. You waited so long because you thought your wife might have gone out. Would that be something she might do normally, go out without telling you?'

'My wife isn't someone who does many things habitually.'

Jack curled his lip when he smiled. 'Know the feeling. So what did you do when you got home?'

'I had some reading to do, I'd picked up my in-tray on the way through to the house. I guess I changed out of my suit, started work, maybe had some dinner, a few drinks. But it couldn't have been five-thirty, because I remember it was dark, so it had to be six-thirty or seven.' Bruno squirmed in his seat as if he wanted to say something. Jack gave him a slow look.

'Where do you work at home?' Jack said.

'At the table in the kitchen.'

'You notice if your wife left her things, bag and purse on the table?'

'Not at the time. It didn't occur to me to look.'

'See, that's what I'd notice. If my wife were missing, I'd check to see if she'd taken her bag. She hadn't, I'd figure she must be out in the garden. Did you look for your wife when you got home, Professor Dawes?'

'No, I already told you, the house and garage door were locked, there were no lights on, the security system was armed, I assumed she was out.'

'Tell me, Professor, you get on well with your wife?'

'Of course.'

'Ever fight?'

'Ever heard of a marriage where there are no fights?'

Jack smiled. 'Nah. But you and your wife, most of the time, pretty close?'

'I guess so. I don't have previous marriages to compare it to, my wife was my first serious relationship.'

'She wrote you a letter when she left, didn't she?'

'Yes she did.'

'So tell me why you called us? If she wrote you a letter, I mean.'

'I didn't find the letter straightaway. She left it in a book I was reading. I gave you a copy.'

'You still got the original?'

'No, I burned it, along with some other things.' Ted smiled bitterly. 'I was angry.'

'Pity.'

Bruno said suddenly, 'What about the phone?'

'What are you talking about?'

'We checked the phone records.' Bruno pressed an extended claw into Ted's chest before Jack grabbed his arm.

'You'll have to forgive Detective Otter, Professor Dawes. Sometimes he gets excited.' Jack Champion paused and gave Ted a long hard look. 'Ted, your wife's been found bashed to death under a church next to your house. How do you suppose she got there?'

'Are you suggesting?'

'Suggesting what?' he said quickly.

Ted sat back then. When he thought of Mattie now, he couldn't imagine her face, even when he looked at that last image they used on all the news programs, researcher Mattie, super Mattie, Mattie on the hunt for sperm in her white coat and hair net, looking more like a nun than a scientist. He'd known her twenty years, but he couldn't remember what she looked like, couldn't remember her face. A woman tossing her head back to laugh, Mattie's head going back, Mattie laughing, bringing her head slowly forward. Mattie's eyes, slow-blinking in that private reverie he never understood. It wasn't Mattie, that grab on the television, not really, it wasn't the essence of Mattie. The equipment wasn't even in the research centre, it wasn't even at Archangels, it was an engineering machine at another university as Ted recalled. Laughing happy eyes. Eyes that are laughing at Ted. Laughing as she says, 'You really think you'll have time, Ted?'

'I want my lawyer,' Ted said into their tape recorder.

At the door, Jack had turned around and smiled. 'Are you a gambling man, Professor Dawes?'

'Not really,' Ted said with a wry smile.

'Your wife insured?' Ted nodded. 'What was the policy worth?'

'I don't know the exact figure, maybe a million dollars.'

'Yeah, I read that somewhere. Little ray of sunshine in the clouds I expect.'

'No, not really,' said Ted. 'Not at all.'

CHAPTER
THIRTY-FOUR

In jeans and a Bob Marley T-shirt, Garrison Chandler was like a *Where are they now?* story about a sixties rock star. He was a criminal defence lawyer who talked at a million miles an hour and chain-smoked cowboy cigarettes as if they'd give him back his youth. When Harriet met him as arranged, all he could do for several minutes was repeat Ted's name. 'Ted Dawes. Holy moly. Ted? I been reading stuff in the paper, but Ted? I mean, Ted.' He was shaking his head. 'Any idea why he asked me to call you?'

'I know why, Mr Chandler. He thinks I'll help him.' He looked at Harriet, wanting her to say more. She didn't.

The police headquarters was a place of clean fluorescence over shiny scuffless floors, white walls and silver skirting boards. Harriet noticed her watch had stopped. She felt it should be night-time outside, even though she knew it was still afternoon. As she'd walked through the city earlier, clouds had hung low in the sky refusing to give and she wondered if it was raining now. Disinfectant mingled with the odour of cigarettes that permanently infused Garrison's yellow hair and beard. He was like a broken record to the desk clerk who was snug behind perspex. 'I need to speak with my client. And I don't wanna find out later you guys interviewed him without letting him know he's got a right to have me there. Cause we won't count a word without me there. Understand?' The clerk understood. 'So where is he?'

'I already said he's in processing.' His voice sounded metallic through the speaker. He had soft eyes. If he was scared of Garrison Chandler it didn't show.

'What's this processing? Where's your boss? I wanna talk to your boss.' This had been going on forever. The clerk nodded agreement with everything Garrison said and did nothing. 'Jesus, you listening? I'm his lawyer, you gotta let me see him. This isn't a nobody you've got in there. For Chrissake.' Finally the clerk got up and walked into a room beyond their view. Garrison turned around to Harriet and winked. 'It's all about the squeakiest wheel,' he said. 'Rule is we keep yelling, works every time.' The clerk returned to his desk without acknowledging them. 'Well?' Garrison said.

'You'll have to wait, sir, my supervisor's coming.'

Then it was the boss of the boss of the desk clerk. 'Waddaya mean he doesn't want counsel. You give him this card and tell him I'm waiting outside and all he's gotta do is ask me in. You do that or—'

Jack Champion emerged from the sealed door. 'Garrison, so nice to see you again. Understand your man's asked for you.' Harriet stood up behind Garrison. Jack took a moment to register. 'Harriet Darling, what are you doing here?'

'Helping me,' Garrison said. 'You're a bunch of idiots. Ted Dawes? Get out. What are you holding him on?'

'Suspicion of murder,' he said. 'How's a guy like Ted Dawes know a guy like you?'

'Never mind. How long's he been in here? You gotta let him go.'

Jack Champion leaned in and spoke quietly in Garrison's ear. 'He talked, Garrison, didn't even want counsel. Funny thing, you know, they always want to tell us.' Jack smiled. He was a different person here, Harriet thought, smaller and nastier. 'They really do.' He held the door open for them and called over to the duty clerk to show them to Ted.

'Garrison, what the hell is going on?' Ted was loosely gathered on a bench in a small holding cell with a dirty toilet bowl as its outstanding feature. His dark suit and shiny shoes were ridiculous here. He stood up and walked over to the other side of the bars. Harriet noticed his face was blue in search of a shave and his hair was a mess.

'You know as much as me about the facts, Teddy. But I can tell you about the process. It's like I said on the phone. They're questioning you on suspicion of murder. If they decide to lay charges at this stage, we're on to the magistrate where we'll plead not guilty, of course, and apply for bail. But I think if they were going to charge you, they'd have done it already. They're bluffing, holding you in a cell, trying to make us nervous. So right now, you and me need to sit down quietly and talk, you gotta take it easy, tell me everything you've told them. That Jack Champion, he's a girl.'

Ted looked at Harriet for the first time. He tilted his head as if he was trying to place her. 'They think I killed my wife.'

'So it seems,' she said coldly.

'You said the skull was Mother Damian.'

'The police don't agree.'

His face fell. 'Garris, they think I killed Mattie.'

'They don't know shit, Ted. We'll sort it out. Just tell me what you said to them. I need to have that clear in my mind. You didn't confess, did you?'

'What? No.'

'Yes, Ted,' Harriet said, ignoring Garrison. 'The police don't agree. But they're wrong. The skull in the chapel is Mother Damian just as I told you. She was put in that

chamber or crawled there over forty years ago.' Harriet felt
her voice sounded tinny.

'Slow down,' Garrison said. 'What are you talking about?'

'If we could get into the crypt, I know we could prove it.
That's where Damian and Bishop Gerard Ryan are supposed
to be. We have evidence that links Mother Damian to the
skull. I found some rosary beads.'

Ted said, 'You should listen to her, Garris. They're top
people.'

'They don't muck around with forensics. They'll have
checked all this out. Who's this Damian guy anyway?'

Harriet said, 'It's not your wife in the chapel Ted, it's just
an old nun.' Garrison looked from Harriet to Ted and back.
'Which means your plans can go ahead, can't they?'

'What?' Ted's fringe fell into his eyes. Harriet felt a pull
of tenderness.

'Marguerita Standfast told me you signed away the Archangels Chapel as soon as you got back. Didn't you even plan
to tell me?'

'I wrote to you before I went to Sydney. I couldn't get
you on the phone.'

'You urged moderation at the National Trust Conference.'

'So? I am moderate.' He looked bewildered.

'You betrayed me, Ted, I trusted you, and you betrayed
me.'

'What! I betrayed you? I've been straight about this right
from the start. I never betrayed anyone. You trusted me? What
a joke. You don't even trust yourself.' He looked at her. She
looked away. 'I can't believe we're having this conversation.
I'm about to be charged with the murder of my wife and you're
worried about a church?'

'Yes, I'm worried about a church. It's what I do. And
anyway, nothing's going to happen because I'll get into the
crypt and go to the police and tell them what I've found,' she
said matter-of-factly. 'They'll realise they've made a mistake

and forget about all this.' As the words came out, she started to doubt herself. She felt brittle inside, and she knew she'd crack in a second if she looked into his eyes. 'But I want something in return. I want your word that no matter what, you won't develop the chapel site.'

'We need the money.'

'That won't matter much from prison.'

'I don't believe this. How can you do this?'

'We have to separate the professional from the personal, you told me that. I have to be tough in my job, and I'm perfectly ready to do that. You need proof the skeleton was Damian. I need to save the chapel. We have a deal or we don't.'

Ted slumped back on the bench opposite the toilet bowl and ran his hands through his hair. 'All right, you've got a deal. You find the proof that it wasn't Mattie and I won't touch your church.'

'It's not my church, Ted. It belongs to Mother Damian.' She turned to walk away, came back and said, more softly, 'It belongs to all of us.'

Garrison called the guard to let him into Ted's cell. He walked over slowly, sat next to his old school mate and put his arm around his shoulders. 'That's some lady friend you've found, Teddy. Seems you and me gotta lot of catching up to do. Never thought I'd be defending a guy like you.' He offered him a cigarette. 'Must be what, ten years?'

CHAPTER
THIRTY-FIVE

Max Palethorpe had put on a dark suit over a white shirt and the Archangels tie, and he sat back in a chair at the coffee table in Ted's office with his legs loosely crossed. He'd showered and changed after his run. Chief executives had to make sure they put time aside for exercise every day, no matter what, he'd read that somewhere. Sharpening the saw, they called it, taking time to care for the body as well as the mind. His hair was combed back wet. He was relaxed but not careless. He was ready for whatever Jack Champion, who sat on his left, and Bruno Otter on his right might throw his way.

'As you appreciate, Inspector, we're in something of organisational shock over what's happened. First Professor Hamilton leaving, then her body discovered on our campus, and now this. Any breakthroughs?' Jack and Bruno had accepted Ted's coffee in Ted's cups.

'How long you worked for Professor Dawes?'

'Since the university started.'

'You been in the same job all that time?'

'Yes, I was recruited here as deputy vice-chancellor.'

'You get on well with him?'

Max smiled generously. 'Ted's been a great vice-chancellor, anyone here will vouch for that. I hold him in the highest regard.'

Jack nodded. 'He's pretty young to be in that job, isn't he?'

'We're a good team. I've got a few years in terms of administrative experience. He appreciates that. But he's the boss, and I know when to stop.'

'Would you say you have a close relationship with him?'

'Of course, and I have to say I find what's happened very distressing.' Max's voice trailed off as if he couldn't continue, then he did. 'Naturally Ted and I have had one or two points of disagreement, but I tow the line.' He smiled at Bruno. 'That's the job when you're Two-I-C. I can't believe you think—'

'Were you here the day Mattie Hamilton disappeared, Professor?'

'No, as a matter of fact I was in Perth all week at a conference. You can check if you like. My secretary has the itinerary.'

'So there's nothing you can tell us that might assist with our inquiries about Professor Dawes in that week, or other times.'

Max hesitated, and then said, 'No, not really. As I say, I wasn't here.'

'A couple of people have suggested Professor Dawes has a tendency to get angry sometimes.'

Max shrugged. 'I suppose so.'

'I mean, out of control angry.'

'Yes, now that you mention it, he does have a tendency to blow his gasket on occasion.' He smiled affectionately. 'Being a bit older, I tend to be a little more circumspect. But Ted can be hotheaded. He punched through the window in my office just the other day.' Max smiled as if they were sharing a small joke at the expense of a close colleague with a tiny flaw. 'Broke it. They're repairing it now, which is why we're meeting in here.'

'What was he angry about?'

'A misunderstanding. He thought I'd been disloyal, which I hadn't, and he's touchy about loyalty, especially now.'

'Why especially now?'

'I don't think it's any secret he's been nervous since the discovery. We all have. We knew Mattie disappeared. When the skull turned up, he must have wondered. I know I did.'

'So he'd be upset, but why do you think he'd be nervous?'

'Imagine if it were your wife down there, Inspector.'

'Tell me, did you know Professor Hamilton well?'

'Well enough. Mattie was a good fundraiser, and it wasn't always wise for her and Ted to do functions together. He was busy, and sometimes we'd want Mattie the centre director rather than Ted the VC as the star. Occasionally I accompanied her to avoid problems.'

'So you spent time alone together?'

Max nodded. 'I'd say I knew her as well as any deputy can know the wife of his boss.' Max smiled. Jack Champion didn't join him.

'Was Professor Hamilton happy here?'

Max thought about this. 'Do you mean at the university?'

'Whatever.'

'Mattie's research centre leads the country. That's a great achievement and its hers alone, whatever some of her staff might tell you. She built a great little team down there from nothing. I think she was very happy with what she was doing.'

'She have any close friends you know of, other people we should talk to?'

'Not really, not in the university. You have to remember that as well as being the centre director, she was also Ted's wife. It's a difficult role, spouse of a university vice-chancellor.

They entertained, of course, but I don't think she was particularly close to any one person.'

'Do you think she was happy in her personal life?'

'I don't know, I suppose so.' Max regarded Jack warily.

'Sounds like you're not too sure.'

Max took time to respond, long enough to suggest he experienced a twinge of conscience but not so long as to suggest it was more than a twinge. 'I'm not sure I should be saying this, but it will come out one way or another and you may as well know now. I had an idea Mattie was unhappy with Ted. I'm not saying it's anything to do with her murder, but I think she'd been planning to leave him for some time before she actually did.'

'She told you this?'

Max sighed heavily. 'Yes, in a manner of speaking. It was about a month before she disappeared. She and I had been to a drug company function and we were on a high because they'd promised to fund a scholarship. I dropped her at the house and she asked me in for a drink. She hadn't asked before, and I don't generally mix with colleagues outside work. Maybe I had a sense, too . . . She asked me again to come into the house and I refused again, and then she told me that she and Ted had been fighting in the morning, and she was afraid. I remember her words. She said, "He won't let me go, Max, and I'm so scared."

'Mattie was such a strong woman I couldn't imagine what would frighten her, so I asked what she was scared of. She wouldn't say.' Max swallowed. 'But I had the distinct impression that Ted had become violent with her. It was the way she talked about him, as if he could hurt her, physically I mean. I did go in then, of course, but Ted wasn't home. We shared a quick drink, I got her assurance that she'd call if she needed me again, and I left her and went home. She never mentioned it again and neither did I. But when they found her, it crossed my mind, what she'd said. I wondered if I should have done more.' He drank coffee and looked flatly at Jack Champion.

'How would you describe her mood the night she told you these things?'

'Frightened of course, but more than that. She was desperate, which was completely out of character. She said she felt trapped.' Max was about to continue when Marguerita Standfast burst through the door.

'Sorry I'm late, I didn't realise you were coming so soon.' She introduced herself breathlessly as the police stood up. 'I'm Archangels' counsel, please don't stand on my account.' She turned to Max. 'You forgot to mention the time, Max.' He glared at her. 'Thank goodness Ted's secretary called me.' She smiled over to him.

'We were just talking about Professor Dawes' relationship with his wife.' Max made a small headshaking movement to warn Jack Champion off, but Jack, unlike Marguerita, missed it.

'Were you, Max? I guess you'd be fine to talk about that.' Max said nothing but stared at Marguerita coldly. Jack looked from Max to Marguerita.

'Were you here the day Mattie Hamilton disappeared?' Jack Champion asked.

'I was,' Marguerita said. 'In fact, I saw her.'

'When was that?'

'Eight-thirty or nine that morning. She popped into Ted's office to pick up a guest list for a lunch. I was there.'

'How did she appear to you?'

'No different from how she always was. I hardly spoke to her. But she did make a big deal about Ted's return when she talked to the secretary. She looked in the diary and confirmed he was arriving that day. She said she thought it was the next day, and became very flustered when the secretary said he was coming back early because they'd finished the meeting. Mattie was not a person easily flustered, so I noticed that.'

'You think maybe she was worried about his return?' Jack looked at Max.

'No, I think she'd been planning to leave and needed the extra day to finish organising things. Certainly that's what I figured later, after she'd gone. She left a letter, you know?'

'Did you know Professor Dawes and Professor Hamilton well?'

'I know Ted,' Marguerita said. 'And I spent time with them both socially.'

'What would you have said about their relationship?'

'I'm not sure why you're asking. I'm here representing the university, as Max is, and I really don't think it's appropriate for us to give you information about Ted's relationship, at least not until you've let us know the nature of your inquiry. I can say it came as a great shock to everyone here that Mattie left. Personally, I thought they were one of the happiest couples I'd ever seen.' Jack looked towards Max but said nothing. 'I think you'll find the university community is very supportive of the vice-chancellor, and I simply cannot believe you are pursuing this line of inquiry which will lead nowhere.'

'And what line of inquiry would that be?' Jack Champion said.

'I understand you took Professor Dawes in for questioning,' Marguerita said. 'Has he been released?'

'He most certainly has,' Jack said. 'So are you representing him or the university?'

'I find it difficult to understand why you'd waste your time on Ted Dawes, who had no reason in the world to harm his wife, and ignore what I've been telling you about Mattie Hamilton's research centre where there are glaring discrepancies in funding.'

'What are you talking about?' Max said.

'Our audit investigation found problems in the centre's finances. They have too much money. We turned the results over to the police, but they ignored us. Dugald Charmer talks

215

openly about how much he hated Mattie. I don't suppose you've bothered to question him.'

'Matter of fact, we have Miss Standfast. We're pursuing a number of lines of inquiry. I can say that Dr Charmer has been ruled out as a suspect.'

'And why is that, if you don't mind me asking?'

'Not at all. He wasn't in Brisbane at any time in the month Mattie Hamilton disappeared. And we've verified his whereabouts. So if it's all the same to you, we'll continue our investigation the way we think it best serves our purpose.'

'It's been a very long day, Inspector,' Max said. 'I'm afraid we're all a little frayed by the turn of events. I'm sure you'll forgive me if I ask that we finish this at a later date.'

'Of course.' Jack Champion took out his card. 'Here's my numbers. Please call me, either of you, if you have more information you think might help us. We may need a statement from you at some stage, sir. And I'd like to talk to the secretary who saw Matilda on the day of her murder.'

After they'd gone, Marguerita turned to Max. 'What did you tell them?'

'Nothing but the truth. I certainly didn't tell them how to do their job. Anyway, they were on a fishing trip. I don't think they have any leads at all.'

'Don't lie to me, I saw the look you gave him. What did you say?'

'I told them Ted's a great guy. But I was honest, Marguerita, I didn't pretend he and Mattie were anything they weren't.'

'Did you tell them all the truth or just the parts that suited?' He didn't respond. 'I thought so. Ted could have done you in a long time ago, Max, and he chose not to. You owe him, and don't forget that. You owe him.'

CHAPTER
THIRTY-SIX

'They came here to the house, Garris.' Ted was standing at the french doors in the sitting room staring out towards the river. The Black Madonna's ruby mouth smiled down at him. 'A dozen guys in overalls, and they looked through my things. They took stuff. Can't you stop them?'

'Right now you're the number one suspect in a murder investigation. They can do whatever they have to.' Garrison was on the lounge and the material he'd gathered was on the coffee table in front of him. He'd knocked on the door for ten minutes before Ted answered. He'd walked past him and into the kitchen and had noticed the stack of dirty plates and cups in the sink and the faint smell of rotting food. He'd been trying to make Ted understand the seriousness of his situation. 'I have to be honest, I don't like the way Champion's talking. He's too confident.'

'Harriet Darling's convinced it's not Mattie.' Ted saw a jacaranda tree's waving lilacs just downriver at the edge of the campus. Every year he liked to see the first blooms, but this year he'd missed them. Already they were full and rich against the blue of the sky.

'If only that were true, Ted, but it's just not. How many times do I have to tell you. You might not want it to be Mattie, but it is. I got some contacts in the department, slipped me a copy of the path report. Pathologist's a guy named Marcus Holt. Young, good. It's conclusive, although God knows I wish it weren't, mate.' He sorted through the papers on the table until he came to the report. 'They've aged the bones as a young to mid-life woman, which fits with Mattie. They've found teeth around the site, no cavities. Mattie had perfect teeth.' Ted flinched at the mention. 'You want me to stop?' Ted shook his head. 'So does the skeleton. That's rare, and I very much doubt whether your old nun had any of her own teeth when she died, let only perfect ones. But the clincher's the femur. Mattie broke her leg five years ago, in a skiing accident.' Ted smiled remembering how impossible she was on crutches. Mattie had never been a good patient. 'Don't smile like that in court. Anyway, there's a break in the leg bone that matches. Of course, they didn't cross it with an X-ray, the records have been destroyed, but if you've got one, we could arrange our own tests.'

'I'll check round here.'

'Good. Let me tell you where I think they'll go with this. They reckon you came home from Lismore earlier than you say.' Garrison looked around the room. 'They've got this thing about times I don't like. We can't explain where you were between five-thirty and seven. You've told them you got home at seven, they say you picked up your stuff at five-fifteen. You have to work out where the time went.'

'It was years ago, Garris, and a time I'd prefer to forget.'

'They must have something so we've gotta keep working on it. Check with your office, your bank statements, phone records, everything you can to try to jog your memory.' Ted didn't respond. 'Back to their case. You get home, you and

Mattie fight, and it's not the first time either. But it's different. Maybe she tells you she's leaving you for someone else, someone you know about.' Garrison had walked over to the doors and was watching Ted carefully as he spoke, but the expression on Ted's face suggested he was listening to a story rather than the case against him. He was attentive but uninvolved. 'You're in a rage, you've got everything to lose if she leaves you, your reputation, prestige, the woman you love. Then she says something more, something about your manhood or work or just about the two of you. It tips you off the edge. You're unstoppable and you're a strong man. You go out to the garage, find a pickaxe. You go back to the house, you crack the pickaxe across her head. When you see what you've done, you look into her eyes and you crack her once more over the head. That's what they'll say, Ted. They'll build you into the sort of man who could do something like that.' If Garrison was hunting for a response, he didn't get one. Ted's face remained intent but unreadable, almost as if he were trying to nut out a difficult maths problem rather than think about murder.

'So what do we do?'

'For a start, we counter anything they bring up that suggests you and Mattie weren't happy. We build a picture of you as a fine, gentle man. You are a fine, gentle man so it won't be hard. We get your colleagues to talk, the ones who knew you and Mattie well.'

Ted smiled but not pleasantly. 'Things will come out, won't they?'

'Fraid so. Something you're worried about?'

'No, just that no one's private life is spotless.'

Garrison nodded slowly. 'The police have been to see your deputy, a Max Palethorpe. He loyal?'

'He's fine,' Ted said, rubbing his neck. He hadn't shaved for a couple of days. 'Needs a bit of looking after, you know, ego and all that, it's hard being second to a younger man. But when push comes to shove, I think Max will be there for me.'

'Does he know Mattie?'

'What do you mean?'

Garrison weighed up the question. 'You know, were Max and Mattie friends?'

'Yeah, they were friends, Garris. So?'

'Okay, Ted, but it's going to come up again. And we'll have to know how we're going to handle it. My investigator's had a look at him. She asked me the question. I'm asking you.'

'What do you mean, your investigator?'

'I've got a detective.' Ted started to object, but Garrison held up his hand. 'It's standard procedure for us, we need to pre-empt anything the police might find.' Garrison smiled. Ted didn't join him. 'It's not to find out what you know about yourself, you can tell us that, it's to find out what you don't know. I don't want the police springing any nasty surprises on us late in the piece. Whatever she digs up, you can be sure they'll dig up, too. She's on our side. It's the only way we can be sure. Unless there's something you want to tell me now.' Ted shook his head. 'Okay. I have one other thing for today.' He sighed and looked gingerly at his client. This was going to be a slow process and Ted was not making it easy. 'The casino.'

'What about it?'

'I hear a whisper you've been spending pretty big lately.' Ted nodded but didn't respond. 'That right?'

Ted sighed. 'How do I explain this? Yeah it's right. Mostly I lose.'

Garrison looked at his friend. 'Doesn't mean it's a problem, but money-wise, must be a bit of a stretch.'

'Mattie and I had savings. I've been using that. I'm not addicted.'

'Of course not.'

'No, I mean it, Garris. I don't know how to explain. After she left, I blamed myself. I was so angry. I wanted to hurt. It seemed a way to do that.'

Garrison nodded. To a jury, it would sound like guilt. 'Well, it's another thing we'll have to talk about. They'll paint a certain picture of you, and it would be a lot easier if you toned down your spending for a bit. Okay?' Ted agreed. 'What about the note Mattie left. Still got it?'

Ted smiled bitterly. 'I burned it, but the police have a copy.'

Garrison sighed. 'That's not much use to our side and a facsimile anyway. The court will want an original.'

Ted rubbed his face and walked out onto the verandah. With his back to Garrison, he said, 'I'm sorry about all this, being a scientist I should be better at it, but it's come up so quickly and I just feel trapped. This is not what I expected, at least not yet.' He looked down to the jacaranda tree. Through the low hanging blooms, he could see two teenagers on a bench curving round one another. He sighed again. Garrison had joined him. 'Mattie left me. Things weren't brilliant for us but we'd been together almost twenty years. Twenty years, Garrison. Last week I found out she'd been killed, on campus, where we lived and worked, right next door to our home. That was one hell of a shock. Now the police think I did that. It's so ridiculous it would be a comedy if this were a story.' He turned and looked at Garrison. 'That's why I hoped Harriet Darling might have something.'

'I know, Ted, I only wish she were right. But they've got some good evidence so far, and they're waiting for you to crack. We have to be careful right now. I'm sorry but that's the way it is.'

'Feel like I'm already in prison. Nothing will ever be the same for me.'

'Let's not give up before we've even started. They haven't got the weapon.'

Ted flinched. 'I didn't kill her, Garris.'

'No.' Garrison betrayed no emotion. He placed his arm firmly around his friend's shoulder. 'Tomorrow then. I might get someone to come and help you clean up round here, just in case the police are back to snoop around.' Ted nodded. 'Don't want them thinking they're getting to you, do you?'

CHAPTER
THIRTY-SEVEN

When Harriet told the cab driver to take her to Archangels University, he asked if she'd seen the news. 'Hear your dy-rector's been a bad lad.' She was still unaccustomed to the way strangers in Brisbane struck up conversations as if you were members of the same group. He checked her face in the rearview, and saw something there he read as encouragement. 'Wife disappeared a couple years ago. Now they're saying he's helping them with their inquiries. That always means they know he did it but haven't charged him yet. I thought he looked a bit shifty.' Dull black rosary beads were threaded around the rearview mirror, and the cross swung dangerously when he drove fast around corners.

As she was leaving the cab, she said, 'You're quite mistaken about the Archangels vice-chancellor. He didn't do anything at all, and God willing, I'm going to prove it.' The driver and his dangling rosary sped off down Princess Street.

Neal had sorted Damian's papers into years and sat at Harriet's desk at Archangels reading his notes and summarising on yellow cards. It made her think briefly of Max

Palethorpe, who'd sat in the same place and lost his temper with her. When Neal saw her, he tossed his pen down and stretched. There were dark halfmoons under his eyes. 'This is hopeless. You have to go to the police with the rosary beads. Ted Dawes is a suspect.'

'I know, I've seen him. If we can get into the crypt we can prove it's Mother Damian and save him and the chapel.'

'How do you figure that?'

'I made a deal, we save him, he saves Archangels. Simple.' As Harriet said the words, they sounded anything but simple.

'That's a bit rough. He's at one hell of a disadvantage.'

'I wondered about that.'

'I should hope so.' Neal stood up and walked over to her. 'That's as low as we've got, HD. You didn't really do that?'

Harriet nodded gingerly. 'He betrayed us, Neal. He went behind my back to engage Jamisons to do the work we were supposed to be doing. He didn't even tell me.'

'I didn't realise. Are you sure?'

'Yes, Sam told me.'

'And you're sure he didn't tell us?'

'He didn't tell me. Why?'

'I just remember something. Probably from before, when you were drawing the ultimate university casino for him. Did he write then?' She nodded. 'That must have been it. Even so, Harriet, don't you think you should go to the police and tell them what we've found?'

'Exactly what would I say? I withheld these because I didn't want to share them. Anyway, Jack Champion made it very clear at the start he wasn't interested in Mother Damian. No, we have to get into the crypt to prove Damian's not in there.'

'Not a chance right now. The police are in the chapel again, looking for more evidence.'

'Then we have to work on what happened to Mother Damian. We have no choice but to keep going. The chapel depends on us.' She frowned. 'Mother Damian depends on us. The very future of this place depends on us.' And Ted depends on us, she thought. She walked over to the desk and picked up a photocopy. 'Damian's will?'

'You'll find she left explicit instructions that she be buried with Gerard O'Hare.' Harriet brightened. 'Which is, I agree, a very healthy sign in favour of your love affair.'

She gestured to the pile of cards. 'So what else have you got?'

'Damian's letters.' He picked up a card from the stack. 'She was always in financial trouble, almost went belly up at least twice, in the first building period when she was bursar and again in the late forties, which is the period we're interested in.' He smiled. 'She liked crumbed whiting with a slice of lemon and abhorred roast chicken. She was worried about the novices and the influence the older nuns had on them, and started a satellite house down at New Farm to quote "give the postulants a chance to get off on their own now and then". She never wrote to her family as far as I can tell. She was close to the head of the order back in Ireland, who was a kind of mentor. She didn't tolerate fools well, and sacked three architects and two builders before she got what she wanted in the quad. She used to walk in New Farm Park and steal roses for her room until she was caught by a parks worker and nearly charged.' Neal paused.

'Is that it?'

'No, but I wanted you to appreciate how hard my job is.'

'Fine, you're wonderful. What have you actually found?'

'Might be something.' Neal put down the stack of cards and picked up a letter he'd brought from the archive. 'In the late forties, Damian was worried about Vincent, wrote back to Ireland suggesting they recall her for "treatment". It's all pretty veiled and careful but it could be important.' He read from a letter.

'"Mother, I do hope you can see your way to providing passage for Sister Mary Vincent who is unwell once again.

225

Her behaviour towards myself and some of the other sisters can only be understood in the context of illness, but the heat and life here will surely cause further deterioration. I would need her to be accompanied by one of our nursing sisters. I am frightened, Mother, that if we do not take action, our poor sister will do something we would all regret. Vincent needs care, and I know the Mother House, with its hospital and your support, is a safer place for her to find that care. His Grace is of the view that there is no cause for concern, and I would not be asking for your assistance if I did not believe the situation to be dire.'"

'Dire,' Harriet repeated.

'I've been thinking,' Neal said tentatively, 'that maybe we're looking in the wrong place.'

'What do you mean?'

'I'm working through the letters systematically, but Damian's never going to write what happened in a letter. For one thing, she might have been dead. And for another, the pound note and secret chamber and skeleton are so clandestine. Even if she were alive, she wouldn't write it down for a canny researcher like me to discover half a century later. The best we'll get is veiled mentions like this.'

'Maybe she'd want someone to know.'

'Maybe, but let's stick with the facts for a minute. You started out finding a set of rosary beads and a pound note next to some bones, so you made a reasonable assumption that the rosary and money belonged to the owner of the bones. We think Damian had some blue beads because Vincent told us she did. Vincent was executor of Damian's will and stood to gain if Damian died insofar as she was next in line for office. Here we've been madly reading Damian's letters, but I'm thinking maybe we've been trying to get to know the wrong nun. I reckon we go see Vincent.'

~

As they pulled onto the highway heading north, Harriet asked Neal about Archangels going broke. 'You said it happened twice. I wonder if it's related to her death.'

'If you can believe the letters, they were nearly shut down. The bishop, James Douglas, was conservative and tough, bought real estate like crazy and ploughed funds into education, for boys.'

'Typical,' Harriet said.

'Thought you'd like that. Damian's letters home are full of criticisms of him. In forty-eight, she started taking notes of their conversations, which is always a sign things are souring. But at the end of the day, he was the one with the power. She had the order behind her, but he had the cheque book and the order knew it. Damian went ahead with Angel Square with no money in the bank.'

'But they didn't close down.'

'No, and that's what I can't figure. They got out of trouble in forty-nine, finished the school and that's what we have now.'

'It's that year again, Neal.'

'You know, HD, I just wish I could go back there for a moment and watch and hear them talk. I'd know in a second, wouldn't I? We read all this stuff and after hours and hours we put together just a tiny fragment of the truth. Even that's so fragile. We never really know, do we, if we've got it right?'

'It's almost easier to make it up, Neal.' He smiled. 'No, I'm serious. What does it matter whether we find out what truly happened, or what might have happened.' He could get her to do it every time, the 'What is truth' routine. She was so predictable. He could tell what would come next. 'Either way, it's just a story.'

CHAPTER
THIRTY-EIGHT

The note sat on Damian's roll-top desk between the old nun and Angelina. Crushed rose petals had fallen on to it and stained the paper pink. It made Mother think of Jesus' blood. Next to it was a letter from the government. The Parliament had instructed the Minister for Education to commence inspections of the church schools and close those found wanting. The bishop had turned off the tap. The builders had delivered their ultimatum. The work would stop, the government would shut them down, and it would all be over, her whole life, her work, all those girls made into strong young women for nothing.

Damian hid her hands in her sleeves, which usually meant a conversation was finished. Angelina was getting up to go when the older woman said, 'Something else, child.'

'Yes, Mother.' She sat back down.

'The idea you spoke of a few weeks ago, the scholarship.' The girl's father had left her a large sum of cash and an insurance policy worth fifty thousand pounds. By rights Maria Di Maggio was an independent woman who could do what she liked, but once she took a vow of poverty as Sister Mary Angelina, all her worldly possessions would revert to the order. She wanted to use the money to endow a scholarship scheme for poor children in the local area. Of course, His Grace was opposed to it. He said parents wouldn't like the idea of these children studying beside their own blessed little ones, God love them. What's worse, he'd put the scholarships together with the building program simply because they both involved cash. 'Surely the money could be used to finish the square,' he'd said.

'Of course, Your Grace, if it were mine to use. But as it is, it belongs to Sister Mary Angelina who's a long way from final vows. We can't tell her how to spend her own money.'

'Mother, you have some influence with the girl. I've made my position known concerning these scholarships. We are not having barefoot children running around our premier girls' school.'

Mother hadn't pointed out that 'premier' meant first and that the good news had been that the first would be last and the last first. She'd never been strong on scripture anyway, raised as she was in the days when reading the Bible was something the others did because they had so little of the true faith. Catholics didn't need proof. She'd said, 'Our Lord mixed with prostitutes and tax collectors, Your Grace.'

'All of us are poor in the eyes of the Lord, Mother,' His Grace had said. 'And I will not have parents on my doorstep complaining that their daughters are at risk.'

Sometimes Mother felt as if the hill on which Archangels stood was a precipice and at any time her whole life's work could be washed into the river and out to the sea. Watching Angelina struggle, she didn't have the heart to say no. 'I think the idea is grand,' she said. 'I'll ask the bursar to draw up an arrangement. Did you want to use all the money for the scholarship?'

'I can't cash the insurance until I'm thirty. But the rest, Mother. Based on my calculations, I think we'll be able to pay fees and a little allowance for uniforms and books for twenty such students.'

Mother Damian found it hard to get used to the idea that her favourite charge had grown into a woman who could make adult choices. She'd changed so much and part of Damian wanted to go back to the smiling child with wonderful stories and a Black Madonna. She wanted to ask her if she still had it somewhere. They sat in silence for a few moments. 'Angelina, I need to ask you something now. Last night after truth-telling one of the sisters came to me privately and said she'd seen you alone with a young brother who is working on the chapel.' Truth-telling was one of the less sisterly aspects of convent life that Damian had been unable to eradicate after Mother Mary Joseph had died. Sisters confessed their sins in congregation, or worse, accused their sisters. While the weekly dob-in, as it was known among the postulants, elicited good intelligence, Mother Damian was ambivalent. She'd have preferred more camaraderie among her flock.

Angelina didn't offer Michael O'Fallon's name. 'There's nothing you need to tell me?'

'No, Mother.' Angelina looked out to the slick river.

'Well, child, I'm here if you want counsel.' Damian had her answer.

'Yes, Mother.'

'Are you sure about the scholarships? Sure you don't want to wait and see whether you might not use the money in another way?'

'Yes, Mother, I'm sure.'

'Good, child, off you go.' As Angelina left the room, Mother Damian couldn't help but feel she'd been fleeced somehow in making the deal.

CHAPTER
THIRTY-NINE

'I didn't know Sister Vinnie had anyone left alive.' Harriet and Neal were greeted by a bright nun whose pepper hair peeped out from her veil like a venial sin. She took them upstairs and down a long corridor past lounges full of men and women in pyjamas with the unmistakable smell of stale cigarettes and the sound of televisions no one watched. This was Damascus Brisbane, a home for alcoholic clergy and their quiet longing. 'If this is the alternative,' Harriet whispered to Neal, 'I reckon it's better to keep drinking.'

'Vincent,' their guide called out and knocked loudly. There was a grunt from within. 'Over to you.' She smiled kindly and left them.

Sister Mary Vincent was propped up by a pink wrap-around pillow in a mustard vinyl chair. She squinted at the visitors as she picked at the arms of the chair and continued to mutter. She was chewing, too, although it didn't seem possible that anything was in that sunken mouth. From a distance, her chatter sounded like a droned prayer or conversation, but up closer, it was nonsense, words and rhymes and non-words in a muddle. She had great white whiskers on her chin.

'I'm not deaf,' she said when Neal introduced himself loudly. She'd lost bulk judging by the skin flap that hung under her arm when she raised it. She still wore a polyester veil on the back of her head and a sleeveless nightgown. Harriet looked at her eyes, milky grey and wild.

'Sister Mary Vincent, we're from Archangels,' Neal tried again. But when she heard the name, she started a rendition of the school song. Her once soprano voice cracked on the high notes now.

Neal rolled his eyes at Harriet. 'Sister Mary Vincent, we want to ask some questions about Archangels and Mother Damian.'

'Where's Mother? Did you leave the gate open?' She chatted on for a while as if reciting a well-worn prayer. Occasionally her voice dropped and she became starkly lucid. She didn't want them to know what sort of home she was in. 'I've been unwell, dear, and the Sisters of the Adoration have taken me into their care, just till I'm back on my feet,' as if she might head home once recovered. 'She left the gate open. Slatternly.'

Neal asked about the financial problems Archangels experienced in the late forties, Damian's death, her relationship with Bishop O'Hare, the building program. Her eyes focused on Neal as he talked about the buildings. 'Yes I remember, the windows for the chapel, that's right, they're finally here. We've waited so long and they're so beautiful, Mother.' When Neal asked her about Damian, she lowered her voice even further. 'She never cared a whit for me.' A woman brought tea in a sucking cup and a giant lamington Vincent couldn't possibly fit in her mouth. 'Her daddy gave her that beautiful box at postulancy, a jewel box for his little nun, and a pound note she held on to, even after final vows. They had money, back in Ireland, the family, didn't they? We were poor as church mice but she wouldn't even see her da when he visited. I knew about her. Poverty, chastity, obedience. She broke them all. She hid nothing from me.' Vincent sniffed the air. Neal asked what Damian had tried to hide. Vincent sniffed again and wailed loudly. 'I can smell them, filthy filthy, take it out!' She screamed. 'Get out!' The desk sister rushed into the room, saw the morning tea, and whipped it out the door. When she came back in she stroked Vincent's brow. 'It's all right dear, it's gone now, we'll get something else.' She turned to Neal and Harriet. 'Coconut, she can't cope with the smell of coconut,' she whispered. 'Quite common with alcoholics, to find something they can't abide. You might say a little prayer with the visitors, Sister Vincent.' She turned to Harriet and Neal. 'It helps her settle.'

When the sister was gone, Harriet said quietly to Neal, 'I've got an idea. Desperate times call for desperate measures.' She replaced him in front of the old nun and said sharply, 'Vincent, it's me Damian, dear, I'm come back to you.'

'Mother?' Vincent said in a little girl's voice. 'Oh Mother, I prayed you'd come back.' Her face collapsed as if into tears but her eyes were dry.

'Yes, I'm back.' Harriet tried to sound Irish and authoritative, but it was a difficult mix. Neal laughed behind her and she had to elbow him hard to stop him.

'I love your visits, Mother. Let us pray. Our Father who art in Heaven, Forgive us our trespasses as we forgive those who trespass against us. Lead us not into temptation, lead us to Maria Goretti. Forgive me, Mother, as I forgive them who trespassed against me.'

'What did you do, Vincent, that I have to forgive you?'

'You know, Mother,' she said coyly.

'Tell me, Vincent, tell me what you did.'

'Oh Mother, you died and left me. I've been so sorry. You were good to me, the only good one I ever knew. But I didn't know. He told me lies, terrible lies, and I stole your last sweet breath. I took your life, Mother. I shouldn't have done what I have done in the name of Jesus the Lord and the Holy Spirit.' Harriet looked at Neal.

'You killed me because you found me out?'

'It was the bishop, Mother. It was him, not you, he was the beast, not you, not at all.' Her chin shook with emotion but her eyes remained dry. 'Bless me, Mother, for I have sinned.' Then she stared blankly and started to sing. '*One day at a time, sweet Jesus, that's all I'm asking of you. Just give me the strength to do what I can one day at a tiiime.*' Then, she called in a loud voice. 'Forgive me, Mother?'

Harriet placed her warm young hand on the old nun's scaly forehead and leaned over. She could smell sweet milk. 'I forgive you, Vincent,' she said gently, 'and God forgives you.'

The old nun leaned back and closed her eyes. 'Rest in peace, Vincent, rest in peace, Mother. Peace. Sleep. Eternal rest grant to them, O Lord, and may perpetual light shine upon them.'

CHAPTER FORTY

'That's one bit of history I'll happily let go of.' Neal sighed as they headed down the stairs and out onto the burning asphalt. They'd left Vincent snoring and the desk sister berating the tea woman.

'But she told us, Neal, she killed Damian.'

'Did she? She's pretty crazy, Harriet. I don't know what she told us.' He pulled out of the carpark and back onto the highway.

'Can't you see? She was talking about the affair, that it was the bishop's fault not Damian's. Maybe the order covered it up. Or maybe Vincent buried her in the chamber without telling anyone. I'm glad you were with me to hear it.'

Neal reached across and squeezed her hand. 'Me too, HD.' Harriet smiled and pulled her hand away to pick up her notebook.

'So, we're talking about murder, Neal. It's time to call the police.' She picked up his mobile. 'What do I do?'

'Luddite.' He grabbed the phone and pressed a button. 'Dial.'

Jack Champion was unavailable. 'Tell the Inspector to contact me as a matter of urgency,' she told the operator. The bored response didn't leave her hopeful.

'Wouldn't it be funny if we were right and the police were wrong?' Neal said. 'Here they are chasing Ted Dawes and his wife probably isn't even dead. I'd really like to see the love letter and prayer book.'

En route to the university, they pulled into the loading zone in front of Harriet's apartment building and ran upstairs. Harriet took down the saucepan and tea caddy. Neal watched but made no comment. 'I'm paranoid,' she said. 'I keep thinking someone's seeing all this.'

'Well, it's her office all right,' Neal said after he'd looked through the prayer book. 'It's got her name in it, Sister Mary Damian Ryan, in her hand. Not sure about this letter though. It's different from the draft letters, different paper, and if it's Damian's handwriting, it's neat. I want to compare them with the archives.' He placed the prayer and love note side by side on the coffee table. 'These two aren't quite the same either.'

Harriet leaned over and looked at them. 'Now that you put it like that, I know what you mean, but one's printed and with a different pen, so it's hard to be sure. I guess it could be a note to her from Gerard. Do we have something in his handwriting?'

'Let me check them against the others first.'

Back at Archangels, Harriet left Neal at the archives and went to her office to collect his notes for him. Inside, she thought she could smell cinnamon or nutmeg. Her voicemail blinked, half a dozen messages, including three from Max Palethorpe's secretary who said the acting vice-chancellor wanted Harriet in his office, 'As soon as possible', then 'Immediately', and finally 'Urgently'. He could wait five minutes.

Harriet was leaving another message for Jack Champion when Jack himself emerged from behind the open office door. She jumped and called out.

'I wanted to wait so that I wouldn't scare you', he said. 'Then I did scare you. Sorry.' He held up his pager. 'If you'd have left that message, they'd have rung this again, and then you'd have thought I was a bomb behind the door.' He smiled.

Harriet didn't join him. 'What are you doing in my office?'

'Waiting for you. You've been trying to get me.'

They sat down and she told him what she knew. His chair was lower than Harriet's and he had his hands joined on the desk, which made him look kindly. She said she hadn't set out to deceive. 'I should have told you earlier, but I wanted to be sure.'

'You're telling me that because you found some rosary beads in a chapel, they must belong to Mattie Hamilton?'

Harriet was surprised he hadn't been listening. She'd expected him to shake his head in amazement and tell her how smart she was. 'No, Detective, I'm saying the skeleton in the chapel isn't Mattie Hamilton. I'm almost sure it's Mother Damian Ryan. We have reason to believe she was involved with a priest at Archangels in the forties, which would have been scandalous. We think another nun found out about the affair and killed her. The other nun, Sister Mary Vincent, has confessed to the murder.' The sun stretched into the window and onto the back wall of the office like a bar heater. The room was still and steamy.

'Harriet, we know who we found down there in that chapel. It's Professor Matilda Hamilton. We got everything—motive, physical evidence, forensics. We found Mother Damian's remains, kid. She's in the crypt.'

'What?'

'The burial crypt, the one you told me about. I got forensics to go through there. It's got this Mother Damian and a priest. Probably the one she was dating, eh?'

He'd unsealed the crypt. How dare he? He had no right. He'd been in that private space with Damian and Gerard. 'Bishop Gerard O'Hare,' she said as evenly as she could.

'Yeah that's it. When you mentioned the crypt and Mother Damian, I decided to check it out.' Harriet's face must have shown her feelings because he spoke more gently. 'I know you want it to be someone other than Ted's wife, but facts are facts. Now I gotta check a few things with you. And I'm going to have to take the beads and stuff as evidence.' He looked around the office as if he'd find them there.

Her mind was racing. He said he'd found Mother Damian in the crypt. If he had, the skull wasn't Mother Damian. And if it wasn't Mother Damian, it must be someone else, but who? What was someone else doing with Damian's rosary? 'I don't have them. I sent them to our Melbourne office for tests,' she lied. 'I'll get them back.' She thought of Neal in the archives and hoped he had the sense to keep them hidden in case the police raided him.

'Good girl.' He wasn't like Stan at all, Harriet decided. He couldn't look at her when he talked about the skeleton. He was lying about something or at least he was less sure than he made out. Stan would have wanted the truth. He asked how long she'd known Ted Dawes. At the watch-house Ted's soft hands and long eyelashes had earned him the nickname, the Teddy Killer. Jack wasn't in the habit of using nicknames. He wasn't the nickname type.

'A few weeks, since I've been at Archangels. I've said that before.'

'Where were you before that?'

'Melbourne, that's where my firm is. I've told you that before, too.'

He smiled but not unkindly. 'People say you and Ted are good friends.'

'That's not something I need worry about, is it?'

'Couple of people here say he's a friend of a particular sort.'

'I'm not sure what you're implying, but I do know it's none of your business.'

'That's dead right,' he said. 'It's none of my business. You have a relationship with someone, that's up to you.'

'Who said we were close?'

'Tell me something, has Ted Dawes ever mentioned anything to you that might make you think he and his wife didn't get on?'

'No, from what I can tell he was very much in love with her.'

Jack weighed up whether to speak again. 'We think Ted and Matilda weren't so close. That's why I was kind of wondering if you'd known him for a long time.'

'If you're trying to construct some sort of woman-in-the-background for Ted Dawes and thinking I might do, forget it. He and I have a friendship. So what? Look, Inspector, I don't know what you want from me but I don't think I want to keep talking to you.'

He stood up. 'Harriet, Matilda Hamilton was murdered, and we have a suspect. It was brutal, honey, what happened to her. When she first disappeared I had a hunch, but they closed the case further up the line because of insufficient evidence. It's hard to do murder without a body. But too much didn't add up for me. You ought to think about yourself here.' Jack smiled and looked at her with soft eyes. 'You got family back in Melbourne?' She nodded. 'Maybe go visit. Maybe now would be a good time,' he said, and put a friendly hand on her shoulder.

She pulled away and stared at him. 'You know something, Inspector? Even if it were Mattie Hamilton down there in that chapel, and it's not, but even if it were, you'd have the wrong guy. There were at least ten people standing in line to do Mattie harm. Ted wasn't one of them.'

'Maybe, but I reckon we checked out the other nine. We're not here to make enemies.'

He gave her a card with his work and mobile numbers, just in case she needed him, he said. 'He's the killer, Harriet.' He took the time to write his home phone number on the back of the card. 'Call me any time.'

After he'd gone, Harriet walked back over to her desk. She noticed her hand was shaking as she went to pick up her notebook. He'd said Mother Damian was in the crypt. She reached into her pocket and worried at the rosary beads there. It was all she had, these beads, a prayer book, a love letter and Vincent's confession, and Neal was right about Vincent. She was crazy, and while she'd as good as told them she killed Mother Damian, she was also terrified by lamingtons. For the first time, it occurred to Harriet that she might have been wrong all along. Jack Champion said the bones were Mattie Hamilton. And if the bones were Mattie Hamilton, did that mean Ted had killed her, just as the police were saying? Harriet felt weak and sat down.

But Jack Champion wasn't sure of everything he said. There were lies in there somewhere or enough doubt that he'd checked the burial crypt and had listened to Harriet. She was on the right track, she decided, but had taken a bad turn somewhere. She stood under the dim light in the stairwell of the building staring at Jack Champion's card. Then she walked out into the quad, threw the card into one of the recycling bins that pocked the lawn and headed for the acting vice-chancellor's office.

CHAPTER
FORTY-ONE

Max was sitting at his new desk wondering whether to use the word 'acting' with his vice-chancellor title. Marguerita had told him it was mandatory. He'd already removed the paintings he'd never liked from Ted's office, he'd rearranged the furniture and he'd circulated an email to staff telling them Ted had been detained for questioning in relation to his wife's murder and was on leave until further notice.

The Board had met in an emergency session first thing. It was touch and go for a while as Ted had some unexpected friends. The student rep said no charges had been laid and they should support him. Sister Mary Cecilia said he was a good man and they should be ashamed of themselves. But Frank said that while it wasn't what any of them would want, the university needed leadership, certainty. Surely they all agreed on that. 'We must get on,' Frank said, 'prevent further damage to our reputation.' The deputy chancellor backed him. 'We're a private university, reputation is money.' In the end, it was a commercial decision. Mother Damian's portrait looked over as the Board, with a healthy if not overwhelming majority, voted Ted out, suspended on pay, and Max in, acting vice-chancellor until further notice.

Max had called the senior management group together after the Board meeting, but he didn't quite know what to do once they'd gathered so he talked at them. They were different without Ted, half a dozen deans and pro-vice-chancellors quietly leaning away from one another so that as the meeting progressed they came to look like bowling pins following a partial strike. Marguerita was the only woman in the room. No one said much except Max, who talked about a hard future once they'd dealt with the problem. The problem was Ted. 'We're managing the situation,' Max said. 'Ted Dawes has been suspended, and the Board has left on the table a decision to remove him from office altogether.' Marguerita tried to interrupt but he continued. 'Like all of you I wouldn't wish this situation on anyone, least of all Ted. But we have to think of the university here, not just individuals. The Board had to take a position in the best interests of the institution.' This was Max's moment, his time, a calling to resolve a situation, to manage a crisis, to arrive. He was going to be found worthy.

'He's been suspended, Max,' Marguerita said afterwards. 'They haven't sacked him.'

'Your legal models don't apply at his level, Marguerita. How can anyone have confidence in him again? Even if he didn't . . . do what they're saying, he's finished. And by the way, so are you. You backed the wrong horse.' He called to the secretary outside. 'Did you manage to get Harriet Darling?'

'Has it occurred to you that people are going to think you might have more than a modicum of self-interest in this?' Marguerita said.

He swallowed hard. 'I can't believe you're saying that. How do you think I've felt through all this?' He turned back to Sam. 'Let's get to work on the press strategy.'

The secretary came to the door and told Max that Harriet Darling was waiting outside. 'I went to your office first, Max,' Harriet said when he came out. 'I didn't realise you'd moved in here.'

After Sam and Marguerita left, Max sat down behind the desk and smiled generously. 'We haven't always seen eye to eye but I want you to know you have my blessing. This,' he held up her report, 'is a good piece of preliminary work. When Jamison comes on board, I'll make sure he gets a copy.'

'Ted's not here anymore, Harriet. I am. Don't get me wrong, I think your work's very good. But you lack experience, I'm sure you'd be the first to admit that. As it is, we're months behind. We have commitments next year.' Harriet had a mental picture of old Archangels crying out as Max and Martin moved in with a wrecking ball. 'I'm more than happy for you to stay on and work with the Faculty of Medicine on their move.' He tilted his head. 'Frankly, I like some of your suggestions.' He smiled. 'No hard feelings. But given your strong personal views, I don't think it's appropriate for you to be involved in the Old Archangels project.'

'You can't do this.'

'Of course I can. As soon as we've signed up, we'll start work. Martin Jamison's plans are well underway. I don't think we'll have trouble with state government approval.' He smiled remembering the Minister's son, soon to be an Archangels law student. 'And Martin's well connected federally, almost as blue-ribbon as Corsair Maple. I believe he knows you, too.' He sat forward. 'I've a lot to do. Thanks for coming in. Back to work.' It was a victory speech, and one Harriet wouldn't have known how to oppose even if she'd felt up to it. As she was leaving, she turned to him.

'Max, tell me something. Did Ted know you'd engaged Jamisons while he was abroad?'

He looked at her quizzically. 'I took executive action after the panel decided to put you on and you made it clear you weren't going to do what I needed. He hadn't even met you. Why?' Harriet turned and walked away without answering.

Marguerita Standfast knocked at the door of Harriet's office. 'Can you let Ted know I'm around?' she said. 'It's not my line, Garrison Chandler's a criminal specialist, but if I can help in any way, I'd like to. And it would seem I'm going to be indisposed, sooner or later.'

'Looks like we're both out.' Harriet sighed. 'I can't believe it's happened. Any of it. What will you do?'

'I don't know, take leave, wait for the payout, go back to teaching, that's what I liked.'

Harriet told Marguerita about Jack Champion's visit. 'I was so sure I was right,' she said. 'I just can't believe. I know it's not finished yet.' She breathed in deeply.

'I like Ted, always have,' Marguerita said. 'He can bend, which is rare. He appointed me, you know. I'd left my last job after a fight with management. Ted took me on trust. I've never forgotten that.

'When Mattie first disappeared, I'd walk into his office and find him at the desk, or at the windows, just staring. He wouldn't even notice me. I'd have a sense he'd been there for hours. At the time, I thought he ought to be out looking for her.' She smiled weakly. 'It was like he already knew what had happened. I suppose I made up my mind. And when you dragged up that skeleton . . . I've dreaded this, Max and Ted and the police. I still like Ted, whatever he's done.' She crouched down beside Harriet, who was packing her books into a box. 'Did you two ever go for your walk?'

'We did. You'd think less of me if I told you what happened.'

'Try me.'

'I failed the cause, fell for him in a big way, almost begged him to sleep over.' She was blushing. 'He's the one who called a halt. I didn't believe he was trying to manipulate me at all.'

'Maybe he wasn't.'

'But you said.'

'I've turned fifty, sweetie, I've seen things you'd be horrified by. It's my stock-in-trade response. I'd always hoped your generation would be smarter than mine, you'd learn from our mistakes, you wouldn't just roll over every time a powerful man looked at your tits. But you're just the same as we were.' Harriet went to say something then breathed a sigh. 'There I go preaching again. Ted's a good guy, I think. In principle, of course he's part of the patriarchy. But sometimes you can have universal principles and individual cases, and they're different.' She smiled. 'Otherwise we'd never get any sex.'

'I've blown it with Ted anyway now. I told him he betrayed me about the chapel. I'm not sure he did, and I was awful.'

'Good for you. Now you say you're sorry.'

'What if he doesn't do sorry?'

'What have you lost? I'm sure he could do with a few friends right now.' It was a good point.

After Marguerita left, Harriet sat on the sill and looked out to the quad. She didn't think about the work she'd done for Archangels and what a waste it was, how Max was tossing her careful plans in the trash on his way to a concrete tower and a lifelong friendship with her ex-husband. She didn't think about her next strategy, who she'd talk to, what she'd do to save the chapel, how she'd rectify what was wrong. She didn't even think about Ted and how he and she could never again be the two people who kissed sweetly, how dreadful she felt about her behaviour towards him, how wrong she might be about Damian and what that would mean. She sat on the ledge and drew pictures of hands and feet. For the first time in her life, Harriet Darling felt emptied of hope.

CHAPTER
FORTY-TWO

The last line of orange light was gone from the office wall before she got down from the sill. Neal's research still covered the desk, but she didn't bother flicking through his cards. They were hopeless detectives and they couldn't save Archangels. They should be protesting development, not scratching round for clues. She looked at the in-tray Neal had left for her from New Farm. His note said, 'DO THIS NOW HARRIET!' It seemed like days since she'd gone through it. At the top was a letter from a Brisbane-based architect inviting them to work jointly on a heritage project. No doubt the offer would be withdrawn as soon as people knew what had happened. Richard was right; it would destroy her reputation to be associated with a job like this. Harriet continued to flick through the tray, expenditure requests from the New Farm office, an order for an ergonomic chair for the assistant and a stack of reading. She scooped up the lot and tipped it into her satchel to take home.

When she turned over the empty tray to replace it on the desk, she noticed a memo whose edge had caught on the bottom lip of the tray. It was from Ted. 'I am writing further to our meeting concerning the Archangels Chapel. I have instructed the deputy vice-chancellor to contact Jamison and Jamison on their detailed plans for the proposed building as per our discussion. I know this is not your preferred option, but I hope you'll be able to work with Max and the other architects to create something special in the riverside area. I know we can do that, Harriet, and I look forward to your continued support.'

Harriet winced. He'd been telling the truth when he said he'd written to her. He might have done what she didn't want him to do, but he hadn't betrayed her at all. She stared at his big confident signature and thought of his large hands hanging between his knees in the prison cell, the lock of brown hair that fell between his eyes, the eyes she couldn't look at. Harriet felt giddy and steadied herself on the corner of the desk.

From the start, she'd been watching and waiting for Ted Dawes to let her down, but he hadn't. She'd been wrong on every occasion. The chapel fire was an accident. He didn't know that Max had engaged Jamisons, and he'd told Max to work with her, just as he'd said. Now she found that he'd written just as he'd said.

Just then, she longed more than anything to be back in her father's lap, waiting to land somewhere like Hong Kong. She sat down on the floor in the middle of the room and pulled her knees up. 'There's always guides to land by, love,' Stan would lean down and say into her ear, 'even here where the runway's so short the approach has to start on the tops of skyscrapers. See, see, there are the red lights now, on the roofs of those buildings, to guide our big white ship into port. You just follow your instincts, love,' he'd say. 'That's what you do in Hong Kong, because there's always lights.' The lights for Harriet were weak and hard to see right now, but they were leading her to Ted Dawes, and little else mattered.

CHAPTER
FORTY-THREE

Kevin McAnelly slipped into the Archangels chapel from the riverbank under the cover of night. In a black polo and black slacks with black on his face, he looked like a burglar or secret agent and a dashing one in either case. He slipped down into the crypt silently and walked to the far corner behind Gerard Ryan's tomb. There he lifted a trap door you'd need to know about to find and reached down into the storage area under the floor to pick up the one thing that would make the police case against Ted Dawes solid. He stretched down further until his hand hit the earth. The bag was gone.

He rushed up the narrow steps back to the nave and was about to leave through the side door when he heard voices. He flattened himself against a pillar and held his breath. Harriet's powerful flashlight played on the walls and ceiling like a searchlight around him. 'I don't like it,' Neal grumbled as he climbed in behind her. Walking down the hill, they'd heard flying foxes in the figs and gulls fighting in the lights of the Story Bridge. 'It's spooky, not to mention illegal.'

'It's only the dark,' Harriet replied. 'And it's a church. We've every right to be here.' But Harriet felt dwarfed in the burned-out chapel, too, and she put her hand on Neal's arm.

'The police can't just make things up,' he said. 'If he says Mother Damian's in the crypt, she can't be in the chamber as well. They've found her remains. What more can we do?'

'You're the one who told me to have faith. This is faith, all right?'

Harriet heard a noise. She swung the torch around and started to walk towards the back of the chapel when Neal called out. 'Hey, it's already open.' They knew the crypt entry had been forced by the police but the crime scene tape had been snapped and now hung on either side of the stair-well. The heavy trapdoor was open. 'If the police keep up this muscle work, we'll have no chapel at all by the time Palethorpe moves in,' Neal said dryly.

They descended the stone steps. 'It smells the same as the chamber,' Harriet said. 'Lemons?'

A long narrow corridor led to a large low-ceilinged room. 'Looks like we were right. They're both burial crypts, this one for the new church, the other for the first chapel. Canali designed them to mirror each other.'

'Doesn't explain why it wasn't on the plans.'

Harriet ran her torch around the edge of the room. The walls were finished with plaster and painted white and the floor tiles formed a blue night-sky pattern with gold stars. A pair of matching marble ossuaries, shoulder height and without ornament, leaned towards each other from opposite walls. On the inside edges were identical gold plaques: 'Mother Damian Nora Ryan, 1870 Dublin–1949 Brisbane', 'Gerard O'Hare 1860–1943'. On top of Gerard's tomb were carved the first two lines of the prayer in Mother Damian's prayer book, 'Lead kindly Light, amid the encircling gloom, lead Thou me on,' and on Mother Damian's tomb were carved the next two, 'The night is dark and I am far from home, lead Thou me on.' It was cool inside the crypt and there was a sweet dry smell of earth. Harriet leaned on Mother Damian's tomb. 'It's the prayer, Neal, we were right about these two.'

'Fine, but that's the point, Harriet, this is Damian, here, not over the other side. Satisfied?'

'Would the police have checked the caskets?'

'I have no idea, Harriet, but we're not going to check any caskets. What are you suggesting? Mother Damian got out of her tomb, crawled through the drain under the floor, and then lay down and died on the other side?'

'No, I just—'

'What?'

'I just don't think we were so wrong.' Her voice disappeared into the night around them.

'Well we were. Face it, Harriet. The police were right. It was Mattie Hamilton in the chamber and by coincidence she was near Mother Damian's rosary beads which got there, I don't know how. The police say Ted Dawes killed his wife. Maybe he did.'

'What about Vincent?'

'Vincent's crazy.'

'What about the love affair?'

'The writing doesn't even match. I compared her letters with the love letter and prayer. And neither was written by Damian. We were wrong.'

'Maybe it was a letter from him to her. If it wasn't a love letter, what was it doing hidden in her prayer book?'

Harriet heard a scraping noise in the chapel above them, heavy footsteps on the marble, a crash, the trapdoor slamming. Neal cried out and stumbled over Harriet to get to the corridor and up the steps. He pushed at the trapdoor which didn't move. 'Jesus wept!' he yelled. 'They've locked us in.'

Harriet rushed up behind him. 'Let me try.' She pushed at the door. It opened with ease.

Back in the nave, Neal was gulping air. 'I thought we were trapped.' Harriet shone her torch around the walls. She couldn't see anyone. Neal caught his breath. 'Thank God they didn't bolt the bloody door,' he said. 'Who the hell was that?'

'You know, Neal, I think you're right. Damian is here, isn't she? She's in the crypt, just as you say. And that was her, wasn't it, running through the chapel, warning us. I heard her feet on the marble, unresolved, you could feel she was with us. She wanted us to stay down there, to keep searching for the truth.' Neal looked at her sceptically and said he wasn't going anywhere near the trapdoor again. Kevin McAnelly melted into the night outside. 'She's here, Neal. I just know it, and she's not at peace. Something happened at Archangels, something to do with the place that won't let Mother Damian rest.'

CHAPTER
FORTY-FOUR

The moon was a spotlit yolk behind Damian's shoulder. To Angelina, it looked like a second head on Mother, nodding keenly as if it wanted to add something to her conversation. The old nun folded her rosary into the girl's tiny hand. Angelina was thin. 'These are for you, child. The brothers have finished their work,' Mother told her. 'We must talk.' They were on a swingseat under the fig. Long underwear and white singlets danced on the lines in the convent yard.

Brother John would be talking to Brother Michael by now, Damian hoped, although in truth Damian wasn't sure what Brother John was doing. He seemed dumb in relation to the matter. At first Damian thought perhaps he was acting so as not to have to face knowing. She'd seen plenty of that sort of behaviour in her time, had recourse to it herself. He'd said, 'Yes, Mother, Michael and I do so love to work here. He's a good boy, Mother. Closer to one than any others? I haven't noticed anything along those lines. His work, Mother, so fine.' But Brother John was stupid after all, Mother Damian had decided, and she could only say so much without becoming more explicit than custom would allow.

They'd met in Damian's office over tea. Mother Damian worried at her rosary deep in the pocket of her habit. 'His work is very good. It's not his work. He's very warm with the sisters.'

Brother John nodded. 'He's that sort of boy. One so young, he came to us at twelve you know. Promised to God like Abraham's son.'

'Abraham's son very nearly had his throat cut on Mount Sinai.'

'Ah yes, Mother, but his throat wasn't cut.'

'That hardly seems the point. Brother Michael as I say is friendly with the sisters. And perhaps you've noticed his affection for one sister in particular.'

'Sister Vincent, Mother, I think it's the pies.' He smiled a knowing smile.

Damian wondered then whether he had any idea what she was talking about. 'Let me speak plainly, Brother,' which Damian had not been able to do since she was a girl. 'Your Brother Michael is especially friendly with my Sister Mary Angelina, if you understand my meaning.'

'Of course, Mother, they are of similar age and interests. They're both from the country as you know. And young. We often see Mary Angelina in the kitchen. She has the fire of the life in her, that one.'

'Indeed so young, and we being older are charged with responsibility for their spiritual wellbeing. I don't think your Brother Michael should visit us again on account of his friendship with my Angelina, which puts them at risk.'

Brother John, who'd never experienced desire for a woman in his life, smiled then. 'Surely, Mother, you're not saying their friendship is in some way harmful to your young sister?'

'Sister Mary Angelina is unsettled.' The bishop was closing in on Damian, and Vincent told him everything. Damian was sure he knew about Angelina. He'd use it against her without a second thought.

'Well, Mother, perhaps she'd be unsettled whoever was working on the ceiling.'

'I doubt that, Brother.'

'You're saying a young brother about to embark on holy vows can't even speak to a postulant.'

'I could speak to the bishop if you'd prefer.' Damian could no more speak to the bishop than fly to the moon. He'd thrown her out of his office and told her, in a raised nasal voice, that the building work had stopped because of her, she had no one to blame but herself and this wouldn't be the last she'd hear of it. They hadn't spoken since.

'No, Mother, as you wish, I'll speak to the boy. But he'll be disappointed.' In Brother John's mind it was simpler than Mother Damian imagined. Not that he regretted his own life in service, he wouldn't have changed a moment. But watching them now, watching young love emerge and try out wings, he wanted to help if he could. In that moment of insight, he knew that all old Damian's intervention would do was fan a flame that might otherwise have extinguished itself with the effluxion of time and a place to smoulder. Imprisoned and cut down like this, he was sure it would burn and burn.

CHAPTER
FORTY-FIVE

The gates hung open into the night like an unfinished story. She found him sitting on the verandah steps behind the house where a fat moon hung over the river. 'I was wrong about you,' she said from the lawn. She stood with her hands in the pockets of her jeans.

'Were you?'

'You'd written to me about the chapel like you said. I'm sorry.'

He leaned forward into the light. 'Are you crying, Harriet Darling?'

'Not exactly. I wanted to save you.' She took a handkerchief from her pocket and blew her nose.

'Well, it appears I could use some saving. But why don't you come up here instead of prowling round down there in the night? Quick, before you set off one of Kevin's alarms.' He gave her a hand up from the grass and she sat down beside him on the top step. He turned her hand over in his and ran his thumb across the bridge of her fingers. 'Little hands,' he said. He'd been sipping from a glass of what looked like scotch. She declined the offer of a drink. 'Now let me get this right. You weren't sure I could be trusted before.' She nodded. 'But now you think I can be.' She said that was right. 'You thought I lied about Max engaging a new architect. Then you thought I went behind your back to start work on the chapel. But I didn't do those things, so you've decided to trust me.'

'Yes.'

'Very sensible, too. But now of course I've been accused of killing my wife.' He said it without emotion. 'I just wonder if that's a little worse.'

'It must be awful. I'm sorry I was such a jerk.' She told him about their visit to Vincent and the love letter. 'Your wife didn't own a blue rosary, did she?'

He let out a short sharp laugh. 'Mattie? No, rosaries weren't her thing.' He looked at her closely. 'It's not Mother Damian in the chamber, is it?'

'No, it doesn't appear to be,' she said. 'She's on the other side of the church from here. The police are confident it's your wife.'

He nodded. 'I've seen the pathologist's report.'

They sat together in silence. She could hear the leaves of the fig sigh with the breeze and she could smell, even at this distance, the charred wood of the chapel. Ted nursed his drink. 'I was going to call you after that night at your flat. It wasn't you, I mean, about us. I wanted to tell you about Mattie before . . .' He took a long pull on the scotch. 'Now it's out in the open, I almost feel better. What I mean is, if you're still interested in that coffee some time, I'd like it. I know I don't have much to offer right now, but things will be better and maybe we can . . .' He sighed heavily. 'What are the chances of this working?'

He stood up and walked over to the corner of the veran-dah from where he could see the fig. 'I used to be able to name over a hundred species of eucalypt,' he said. 'When I finished school, I wanted to do forestry. But I was a bright kid on a scholarship, and the teachers wanted me to do other things. I felt I owed them, I guess. But watching that moon out there tonight, the fig, I reckon I'll find out some more about trees.' He came and sat down beside her again. 'You're a funny little soul, Harriet Darling,' he said.

'Why?'

'When I saw you that first day in the chapel, I had that feeling you get sometimes, as if I'd known you before. A click in here.' He tapped his chest. 'You know that feeling?' She nodded. 'But I didn't know the way in here.' He touched her chest lightly and pulled away. 'All that mistrust over little things. Did I know about Max, did I sign the agreement, did I give away the chapel. And now, something really big comes along, and you just assume I'm innocent. Does that make sense to you?' She didn't answer. 'I mean, it's one thing for us to sit here together now, but if I'm charged with murder and found guilty, then what will you think?'

She leaned over and kissed him full on the mouth. His face scratched and his lips were soft and warm. They kissed for a long moment and when they broke apart, he held on to her. 'I love you, Harriet, that's the problem.' Their mouths met again. She could feel herself falling, the sure waves of a ferry wash lapping the shore in the rhythm of desire.

A loud knock on the front door made her jump and pull away. They were both breathing heavily. 'Timing,' he said and shrugged. 'Probably Kevin. I'll get rid of him.' He stepped into his shoes at the bottom of the stairs and pulled on a sweatshirt. And it was this image—his long arms reaching down, his back curved over the steps to pull on his runners, and then his smiling face emerging from the sweatshirt—that remained with Harriet long after he was gone.

She waited in the dim front hall and watched silently as Jack Champion took Ted Dawes away from her under the glare of television cameras. He tried to look around as they

257

folded him into a dark car. On the lawn, security floodlights, which had come to life with the disturbance, revealed a shadowy army of cane toads that formed a silent guard of honour under the auto-sprinkler system.

CHAPTER
FORTY-SIX

'Can you tell us what you were doing that night, Professor Dawes, between five-thirty and seven?' They were different now, openly aggressive. Garrison told him not to answer. They'd charged him with murder, Mattie's murder, and now they were moving in. Ted felt light in his chest, as if he didn't really take up space the way he was supposed to anymore.

'I don't remember.'

'You were seen in a boat between your house and Archangels Chapel. What were you doing?'

'You don't have to answer that, Ted.'

'Of course,' Ted said. 'I went for a walk. I came home from Lismore, all jammed up, and I went for a walk along the river. I didn't take the boat out, but I was on the riverbank. Of course I was seen. So I have an alibi.' He smiled but even Garrison could see how hopeless this was.

'You stopped at the chapel,' Jack Champion said.

'No,' Ted said. 'I walked up to New Farm.'

'Anyone see you? You meet anyone?'

They showed Ted photographs of the battered skull, they asked him where he'd put the axe. 'You want a break?' Garrison said kindly. Ted shook his head. He made himself think of Harriet. Before she'd arrived that night, he'd lain on his bed with the window open wide. The security lights on the lawn had flowed through onto the wall like bars in a cell. Max had phoned to tell him the Board had suspended him but he could stay in the house, for a few days, until he'd had a chance to think about what to do next. Garrison had phoned in the afternoon and said they were going to arrest him soon. Garrison had said to wear a good suit.

A month before, students had painted footprints from the marble feet of Mary the Virgin Mother of God to the toilets and back. 'Who could do this?' Ted had written in an email to staff and students. 'We're not just defacing a religious icon. We are destroying the great history of this place.' The two boys who confessed had been drunk, they said. Ted made them work with the team of grounds staff that sanded and cleaned the paint off the statue and asphalt. They slouched miserably around the clean-up operation. Ted visited every day for a week before he told them they'd repaired the damage. Afterwards, alone in his office, he felt despair.

Ted had made an early life decision that he'd never have simple happiness the way his sister Genevieve did, married with three bright kids now. At nights he wished he could see them, wished he could be part of them, one of Genevieve's kids, or a picture on their wall, Uncle Ted. Simple happiness was just too obvious and easy for Uncle Ted. He'd gone for the complex life, the fathomless wealthy important weary Mattie Hamilton life. What a joke.

Then he'd found Harriet, lovely little redheaded Harriet, dancing in the chapel, nose screwed up with concentration, and that freckle-filled smile. He'd been worried when she said she had a tattoo, as if it was something that mattered. He was going to be charged with the murder of his wife and he'd worried what his Board might think if they knew his new girlfriend had a tattoo. Today, he'd thrown away his suits, taken them down to the St Vincent de Paul shop where the staff had eyed him suspiciously until he'd said he didn't want money.

When Ted thought of Harriet he couldn't help feeling warm. He hankered now for the smell of her hair. Like almonds. He wondered if he'd remember that in prison and guessed he would. He wondered if she'd visit him and guessed she wouldn't. Mattie would have visited him though, with picnic food and a camera to take snaps of her jailbird. But, of course, Mattie couldn't visit him, since he'd be in prison for her murder. Mattie had got bored with Ted. That was for sure. Now the police were in front of him, and they were asking him about someone's voice on a tape.

Apparently, it was a message recorded on Alexander Hamilton's machine. 'Daddy, it's me. I'm sorry, Daddy. I'm so sorry. It's Ted, Daddy.' Soft crying or laughing. 'Ted?'

'That your wife's voice, Ted?'

He didn't respond. He hadn't heard Mattie's voice for such a long time, and it was a strange sensation to know so much about someone and find their voice could still surprise. Mattie's was a voice that could spin stories and make people do things they didn't want to do. On the tape, it sounded slow. In another context, it would have sounded sleepy and sexy, a message left for a lover not a father. Mattie's voice was an asset worth all her research. It had magic in it just like her laughing eyes and glistening teeth.

'So what?' Garrison said. 'She says "Daddy".'

'This call was made from the house at six-thirty on the night of Matilda Hamilton's murder, after Professor Dawes returned home and before he called us. In other words, it was after the victim supposedly disappeared.'

'Stop.' Ted looked at Jack Champion sharply. 'I want to talk to Garrison.' When they were alone, Ted said, 'They're right about the time, Garrison. But I didn't know she'd made a call.'

'What do you mean?'

'Mattie was there when I got home from Lismore.'

'Jesus, Ted, what are you talking about? We went over this.'

Ted ignored him. 'It was around five. I'd stopped in at the office, just as I said. My secretary said Mattie had been in that morning. She'd cancelled a few lunches we'd scheduled. She used to do that, go into the office and order the staff around. I hated it. By the time I got to the house, I was already feeling annoyed. I just wanted to go out for a walk, you know? Lismore was a pretty difficult meeting, the national vice-chancellors, and I just wanted peace.

'Before I even got through the door, she started on me. She had this way of getting me going, I can't explain.' Garrison watched Ted's hand, which closed into a fist. 'You know Mattie, you know what she can be like.' Ted smiled bitterly. 'That day, Garris, I just couldn't take it on top of everything else. So I went upstairs, got changed, and went out. By the time I got back, she was gone.'

'Why didn't you say this in the first place?'

'I didn't want the police to know we'd fought. How would that look to people? In my job, I can't afford to be anything but perfect. The VC and his wife don't fight. I didn't know then that . . . She must have gone out and met up with someone. And they . . .' Ted rubbed his chin. 'I couldn't help but think later, when I went over it, that she'd picked that fight with me. Something about it didn't ring true. It was like a setup, like she'd planned the whole thing.'

'Okay,' Garrison said nervously. 'I agree it's unwise to volunteer this information, especially now. At least until I've had a chance to work out what we do. Just answer their questions as honestly as you can. Okay?' Garrison stopped to gather himself before he opened the door.

'Do you recognise this bag?' Jack Champion explained to the tape recorder that he was showing the suspect a green canvas bag, item fourteen.

'No,' Ted said.

'What about this?' Jack Champion was holding a Waterman Diamante pen in a plastic ziplock bag.

'That's Mattie's pen,' he said. 'She took it with her.'

'And these?' Diamond and gold rings.

He swallowed. 'Hers.'

'And what about this, Professor Dawes?' Bruno was holding an X-ray film.

'Never seen it before,' Ted said.

'This is an X-ray of your wife's leg following a break five years ago. It's a unique identifier and the only copy left. How do you suppose these things got into this bag we found in the crypt under Archangels Chapel?'

'I have no idea,' Ted said. 'None whatsoever.'

CHAPTER
FORTY-SEVEN

In the magistrate's court, the charges were read and the police prosecutor didn't waste words. Ted Dawes came home from Lismore, bludgeoned his wife to death with a small pickaxe, struck her twice here and here as he pointed to the front left side of a white skull picture against a black display board. Then he rowed her body around the river to the chapel in a dinghy and put it in the chamber. He went home and bleached blood out of the floorboards, burned her clothes and waited four hours before phoning the police. They had witnesses, motive and scientific evidence to prove Ted Dawes killed Mattie Hamilton.

Harriet knew she needed to think clearly but her head was filled with images. Check for stress fractures, that's what her father would say, tiny cracks, that's what matters. Tiny cracks lead to big cracks, and big cracks lead to disasters. Two hundred and seventy-four passengers and crew who never reached Guam. What was Mattie Hamilton's story? And if Harriet found the story, could she believe it? If Ted was tried and found guilty, what would she do? If he was found not guilty, would she always wonder? Would she have some part of herself that could never believe he didn't kill his wife?

Jack Champion was sure they'd found Mattie Hamilton's skull. Everyone believed him, Marguerita, Ted, even Neal. They hadn't seen the hand reaching for the beads, but if they had, Harriet sensed, it wouldn't have made a difference. They posted bail, ten thousand dollars, and no one objected. It would come from Mattie's savings, a magnanimous gesture given that the charge was her murder. Ted smiled bitterly as he signed himself away to his solicitor's care. When Harriet looked over towards him, for just a moment she couldn't place him. She could only see the back of his head, thinning hair and hunched shoulders, and she wasn't sure who he was. She'd sat where he couldn't see her. A pickaxe, Ted. Did you hear what they said? That you struck her in the forehead, two blows with force, and she was facing you, you brought the axe up above your head and down hard on Mattie's broad intelligent forehead. For the second time in as many weeks, Harriet wished she'd listened to her yoga teacher on mind control, so that she could focus on the undulating pattern of the ceiling, on the grey linoleum floor, on the nature of shoes, instead of on pickaxes.

Ted looked towards Harriet as he walked from the court as if he'd always known she was there. 'Next step's the trial,' Garrison said to him. 'Let's hope we have a nice jury.'

Outside Brisbane blistered and yearned for a storm.

CHAPTER
FORTY-EIGHT

W hen Michael kissed his Maria he thought of sweet strawberries and swimming in the sea. He felt healed inside and cared nothing for the future. 'Marry me, Maria,' he said. He'd taken to using her given name because the name Angelina reminded him too much of the life that was making him sick to his soul. Michael's fingers bent slightly like the Lord Jesus blessing his flock. She wound the beautiful blue rosary round both their wrists. Blessed are the poor in spirit, blessed are the meek, blessed are ye that hunger and thirst for justice, blessed are the poor for they shall inherit, the poor shall inherit. 'When I think of God now, it's you. I want us to be together,' he said. 'Forever.'

'We'd have to die,' she said.

'The longest day of my life,' Ted said. He looked at Harriet and looked away quickly, burying his face in his hands. 'I'm sorry we didn't have more time.' They were side by side on the lounge in the sitting room at Archangels House. A sudden gust of cool air off the river brought what relief it could to the still steamy night.

'It's not over yet,' Harriet said. She took his hands from his face, and held them in both her own. He moved to pull away but didn't.

'Garris says it will go to trial,' he said, without looking at her face. 'He's not confident. He thinks I killed Mattie.'

'Did you?'

He looked at her. 'You need to ask?' She didn't respond. 'No. Mattie and I were unhappy, and I did some ugly things. But I didn't . . . do what they're saying.'

'I believe you,' she said.

A shock of white lightning followed fast by loud thunder scudded the sky. They leaned into one another under the smiling Black Madonna and kissed. 'Will you stay with me?' he said. She nodded and took him in her arms. 'You sure?' She was.

The green sky cracked open with lightning and thunder, followed by hail that turned the lawn below them white. They left a trail of clothes up the stairs like clues while the heavens heaved, and angels whipped trees, frightened small animals and shifted the house with wind and ice. Harriet could smell the steamy rain on the roof but she hardly noticed the storm. She felt as if she were sunburned when Ted touched the bare skin of her belly. And again when he entered her she experienced a shudder, fear and desire, as if this was the first and last time. They made desperate love, thrusting hard against one another, as if they both needed to confirm they were right. As if eros, the great drive for life, could somehow obliterate thanatos, just under the surface of their lives.

Harriet woke to heavy rain on the roof and they made love again, turning to each other in the dark without speaking. She had a sensation of diving into relieving water, waves and salt enmeshed as part of her sex. Afterwards she was lulled into sleep by a pair of storm birds who wept just before the sun appeared.

They'd left the french doors to the sitting room open, and they banged back against their frames calling Harriet to come and close them. The room smelled like a rainforest. The walls and bookshelves were surprisingly dry, but the floor was covered in wet fig leaves that must have blown in during the storm. The Black Madonna had fallen to the floor. Her head had snapped off cleanly at the neck and lay at Harriet's feet on the carpet of leaves. She stared at the Black Virgin, who smiled upside down from the rainforest floor. What a shame she'd broken, Harriet thought. She picked up the two pieces and looked at them. Suddenly, she was stopped, like Saul on the road to Damascus. In a moment, she was back in time, remembering everything that had ever happened in the place that was Archangels. The original owners murdered, the first settlers, the bishops, Mother Damian and Angelina. Angelina. Of course, there was no one in Mother Damian's grave. The archaeology report had said so, and Dr Skelly had said so. No one, not Damian, and not Angelina who was supposed to be buried with Damian. Damian was in the crypt. And Angelina was in the secret chamber. Harriet breathed deeply, and knew.

Ted hadn't moved in his sleep, although his frown let her know his dreams were full of fear. He opened his eyes and looked at her.

'I have to go,' was all she said. He rolled over and covered his head with a pillow. He did not see in the brightening sky outside his window, as Harriet did, the lone star that was calling the young lovers home.

CHAPTER
FORTY-NINE

S he phoned the homes of four Skellys from a booth before
she found his brother, who gave her his number. Then
she ran three red lights on slippery tar to meet him at
his office.

'They ignored my report,' Dr Skelly said. 'I told you that.'
What Harriet remembered was that he'd all but told her the
skull was Mattie Hamilton's. 'No,' he said now, 'I said pathol-
ogists don't know everything, and I said my report was
crucial.' Harriet wanted him to get to the point. Instead he
told a story from the annals of osteological history. 'Once a
pathologist laid out bones for me that he said were those of
a twelve-year-old child who'd gone missing, but anyone could
see it was a dog. Anyone with my training that is. The
pathologist was embarrassed, as you can imagine.' Harriet
didn't say she'd heard it before, albeit with a different beginning. She wanted him to get to the point.

'Mattie Hamilton,' she said. 'Why did you think it was her?'
'I didn't. I prepared a report disputing the pathologist, but
they didn't use it. They don't have to, you know. I said to

Marcus,' Marcus the pathologist, '"Marc, if that's a forty-year-old woman in that church, I'm a babe in arms, son." Marc doesn't like those sorts of comments from his seniors and he wants to please the police. He's the boss. I'm just a consultant, aren't I?'

'What do you mean about the forty-year-old woman?'

'The skeleton is not the skeleton of Matilda Hamilton. Or at least I don't think it is. I think it's a much younger woman. I told them all this. My estimation is we're dealing with a woman of between fifteen and twenty-five years.'

'How do you know?'

'They'd ruined the site, completely, by the time I got there. They'd thrown the bones into a pile and trampled everything. Most unprofessional.' Harriet was not going to get the short story. 'I collected what fragments I could, including a piece of the hip joint.' He went to a box in the corner of the room and sorted through bones like toys. 'See.' Harriet wondered if this was supposed to be a piece of Mattie Hamilton. 'Here's the hip section of a woman who's forty. Notice we have fusion here and here. This occurs at between twenty and twenty-five years.

'And here we have no such fusion.' He had another bone. 'What does that say to you? It's a solid piece of detective work, even if I do say so myself. But not irrefutable. The problem was the teeth and that blasted femur. They recovered some teeth, molars, no cavities. Consistent with Matilda Hamilton. Rare enough for the pathologist to question my finding.

'Then, what I claimed was damage to the femur post-burial, the pathologist saw as evidence of a break. Matilda Hamilton broke her femur skiing some five years ago. Written on the bones forever, that sort of thing. I'd have wanted an X-ray to be sure but there wasn't one. The coincidences were enough for the pathologist. But not enough for me.

'Airline disasters are like this, you know, where you have a list of names and histories and a collection of charred bones.

I'm good at airline disasters. Loved puzzles when I was a kid too.' He asked Harriet if she'd been to Guam. 'It was the combination. Broken bone. Teeth without cavities. The dentist said excellent nutrition, probably fluoride. Matilda had no trouble with her teeth and the X-ray of that femur had been destroyed. Terrible coincidence. The pathologist has drawn what some would call a logical conclusion. But he's wrong.

'Down in that church was a young girl, perhaps twenty, perhaps not even. Possibly European extraction, and probably there a long time. I had more trouble with the time of death, and the fire didn't help. We don't always know what a body will do in response to various conditions. We can make educated guesses, but there are still errors.'

'Peat Bog Woman.'

'Exactly. Out by a millennium. But I think it's more than two years for that skeleton in your church. I think we may have been dealing with adipocere.' Harriet asked. 'It's a waxy coating that forms on a body and preserves it, sometimes perfectly. More often in women where there are more pockets of fat.' He grabbed at Harriet's hip before she could express surprise and then grabbed his own. 'Feel this. Even a fit woman will have at least twenty per cent fat in her body. I have eight.'

'In certain conditions, a body can be preserved for thousands of years with soft tissue intact. In that area, we're dealing with wet, alkaline soil, ideal for mummies. I think before the fire we had a well-preserved body which would have looked to an amateur as if it had been there for only a very short time. I think the time was much longer in fact, more like twenty years than two, and the fire just added to the confusion.

'They didn't finish digging the site either. I found a bone that didn't fit. I mean, it belonged to someone else.' Harriet was already on the way out the door.

~

It was nine am. There were messages from Neal on her machine telling her to meet him at New Farm at eight-thirty. He was waiting for her outside. She told him breathlessly about her visit to Skelly. 'This fits, it fits,' he said. 'That's one of the reasons I've been trying to get you. But the other, Harriet. You gotta do something. Max Palethorpe. Archangels. They're going to start work. Martin Jamison already had all the approvals. You were right, they were doing us over all the time. I don't know when they're going to start, but it can't be long.'

'Call the Trust, tell them what's going on. We need a storm down at the site, a public demonstration, banners. And get on to the ABC. The "Seven-Thirty Report" was interested. Talk to the producer. Her name's on my desk. We only need to stall them and once Ted's back he'll stop them forever.' Harriet's mind was racing. 'What fits with Angelina?'

Like Harriet, Neal had worked out Angelina was the missing link. 'When we were sure it was Damian in the crypt, I decided to go back over the report of that dig in the seventies and make sure everyone else was where they were supposed to be. I guess your doubting Thomas routine inspired me. We knew Angelina and Damian shared a plot. The report said there was no remains in the plot. As in not Angelina either. Supposedly, she died of pneumonia in 1949 and had to be buried quickly. They had a bug that killed a few of them at the time. But why not bury her in the cemetery? I knew there had to be more. Looking at the press around that time, there's a young brother who went missing, a Michael O'Fallon, and he—' Harriet interrupted.

'The X-ray!' she screamed. 'I bet they never checked the X-ray.' She told Neal to call Garrison Chandler. 'Tell him to arrange a meeting with the police in an hour.'

She left Neal and sped to Archangels. She walked into Ted's now Max Palethorpe's office above the protests of the new secretary. Max and Martin were sitting either side of the desk sipping what smelled like peppermint tea. 'We're in a meeting,' Max said. 'Is it urgent?'

'Is it urgent?' Harriet said. She turned to her ex-partner. 'What are you doing, Martin? You should be ashamed of yourself. Max doesn't know any better, but you start mucking about with that chapel and you'll be sorry.'

Max wasn't smiling. 'I told you your contract's finished, Harriet. I think you should leave.'

'This doesn't look so good for you, sweetie,' Martin said softly. 'Maybe we can talk later?' He was wearing a cream suit and a matching panama hat lay on the table.

Harriet looked at him. 'Doesn't look good for me? I'm going to stop you, Martin, you watch. You're wicked.' Max got up and started walking around his desk to her. 'Don't you come near me,' she said. 'Ted's coming back. You hear me? I've found out the truth. Ted's coming back. And you know what, Max? I reckon he'll put you over his knee.' Max stopped. Harriet held her index finger in the air to keep him there.

'And Martin,' she was still watching Max, 'it's you who's sleeping with the enemy not me.' As she turned to walk out the door, she said, 'The suit's overdone. They always were.'

She ran into the foyer of Garrison's building and was still trying to get him on Neal's mobile when she saw him heading out of the lift. 'Garrison!' she yelled.

CHAPTER FIFTY

After the choirs of angels had sung His praises, God Himself had come down from Heaven to thank Vincent for completing the mission. She knocked with the authority of the truly righteous on Mother Damian's door. It was past midnight. She wore no veil and her long yellow hair hung loosely round her face. Her quilted lavender dressing gown was spattered with blood, and there was blood on her hands, spectacles and in her hair. 'I've dealt with the matter, Mother,' she said. 'It's finished now.' She giggled nervously, the axeblade glinting as it hung limply at her left side.

Mother Damian knew the blood that covered Vincent in the middle of this night had not come from the ducks she was due to kill the next morning for Easter lunch. Mother had been woken from a dream by the knock at her door, and now she vaguely remembered a ship, steering a ship, rough seas. Vincent was talking loud and fast. She'd heard the voice of the Lord God, she said, just like Mother. The Lord came to Vincent, praise His holy name and Alleluia, and under instruction, Vincent had gone downstairs and out into the yard. It was a cool night with a full moon the colour of that labrador. 'I walked first up the hill to the Blessed Virgin, Mother, and from there my shadow pointed the way to the new square. The grotto glowed as a beacon in the night. The path across the terraces shimmered as if it had been raining, even though the night is quite dry.' Vincent's body was dry, too, and felt as if it had been talcumed. She'd found them in the grotto together. She'd been able to act quickly because she had the axe ready. 'I wanted to take off their heads but it didn't work as well as I thought it might. I'm not as strong as I once was, Mother.' She smiled nostalgically. She'd laid them out. 'I'll make my confession in the morning, if it's all the same, Mother.'

Vincent was silent then because, for the very last time, she saw in her mind's eye that Sicilian rump in the air from her childhood. The rump that had come all that way through time and space to await her in the Grotto for the Angels in Heaven. She couldn't say why she'd picked up the axe on the way to the grotto and Damian didn't think to ask. From the time of Vincent's knock on her door, it all took on a horrible kind of relentlessness.

The moon had disappeared and the night was black. Damian walked in silence with Vincent across to the square by the light of a kerosene lamp. She told herself they were going to find slaughtered ducks or chickens or geese in the square which, while serious, would be recoverable. She got as far as imagining a mess of feathers, like a bloody lusty pillow burst all over the floor. But what she saw as they approached the tiny grotto in the lamplight changed forever the landscape of Archangels. It was shocking, horrible, and presented a moral choice of a stark nature. Damian acted with characteristic speed to save Vincent and Archangels without a thought to Angelina and Michael, whose bloody battered bodies lay across the altar entwined together like a pair of *pietà* Christs.

Tears streamed down Brother John's face as he carried sweet Michael to the chamber under the chapel. 'They'll never find them here,' Damian said matter-of-factly. 'This was a wine cellar for John Ambleton.' When Brother John failed to respond, she added, 'He was bishop when the chapel was built. A bit of tippler, I understand. No one else knows about it.' John took Michael's hand for the last time and kissed it tenderly. 'We can't afford to be sentimental,' Damian said. 'We'll say he's disappeared. Or we won't say anything and his disappearance will speak for itself.'

'His mother,' Brother John said.

'Yes, yes, well what would you prefer, Brother? We send Vincent off to prison. She's mad, John, mad as a cut snake.' They looked over to smiling Vincent. Vincent didn't feel mad, she felt as clear as a bell, pure oxygen filling her lungs with a clean feeling she hadn't had since she was a girl. There was no longer the smell of coconuts to make her sick. She was ready for high office.

Mother Damian and Brother John conducted a small priestless ceremony over the makeshift graves in the crypt. 'They should have a proper burial,' John said, 'or they'll never join the choirs of angels.'

'Nonsense,' Damian said. 'I'll arrange it.' It was then she saw the sprig of lemon myrtle in the corner of the sacristy. She went over and picked it up. She turned to the wall, away from the others, and crushed the flowers in her fist as her face fractured into tears.

CHAPTER
FIFTY-ONE

He was humouring her, she could tell. 'They never get that stuff wrong, Harriet. They musta had dental records.' Garrison looked at his watch.

She moved away from him. 'Mattie had no dental X-rays. She had perfect teeth. Same as a Sister Mary Angelina who died at Archangels in 1940. The official story is that Angelina died of pneumonia and they buried her quick in the cemetery. But she's not there, there are no remains for her, and they never mention her again. I don't know what happened to her yet. My researcher's working on it. But we're sure they hid her body under the church. It's not the bones of Mattie Hamilton in the police morgue, Garrison. I'm right.'

He sighed heavily. 'Hang on, I'll get the path report.' He walked over to his desk. 'Here it is. Dr Marcus Holt was the forensic pathologist. Let's see broken femur above the blah blah, teeth four adult female, age between twenty-five and forty-five years. Hey.' He was walking towards Harriet. 'Where's the osteologist's report? They haven't dated the bloody skull,' he said. 'They always do that, but the bone guy's report isn't here.'

'I just told you that, Dr Skelly's report, that's the one we want.'

'And look here, says on the balance of probabilities and despite some small indications to the contrary, it's Mattie Hamilton. So who's this Angelina?'

Garrison called Dr Skelly and managed to get a copy of his report. He arranged the meeting. 'You guys charged him before all the forensics were in,' he told Jack Champion.

'We don't need forensics, Chandler,' Bruno said. 'We got everything we need.'

'But it's not her, it's not his wife they got down in the morgue.'

'What do you mean?'

'Read this, man. And get someone to check the X-ray you so carefully dug up. Then tell me you got the best case in the world.' He thrust Skelly's report into Bruno's chest, and turned to the pathologist.

Dr Marcus Holt looked nervously from Jack Champion to Garrison. 'You have to understand we make assumptions. Aging a skeleton is a delicate task even in ideal conditions. And these were far from ideal. There was much circumstantial evidence to take into account. It was all so obvious,' he said, blinking frequently and fiddling his spectacles like a radio dial. Jack was glaring at him.

'So exactly how did you arrive at your conclusion, Dr Holt, that this was Mattie Hamilton?' Garrison said.

'We have a number of tests. But at the end of the day, we have to be guided by circumstance. Matilda Hamilton was missing. We found bones from a female.' He went through the perfect teeth, the femur, the placement of the bones. When Garrison asked him about the Skelly report, he said you couldn't always take osteologists at face value. 'Dr Skelly is a highly competent scientist,' he said. 'But once he picked a dog's skeleton as that of a twelve-year-old boy.' He was smiling. No one else was. Garrison read from Skelly's report then went through Neal's and Harriet's evidence about missing Angelina.

'What you seem to be saying, Dr Holt, is that while you suspected many things, you really didn't know any of them for sure.'

'Yes, that's correct, and that's what my report reflects.'

'Your report says it was Mattie Hamilton in the crypt.' Dr Holt went into a lengthy explanation of the differences between basic science and applied work and the way balance of probabilities was taken into account. 'Surely you accept now though, Doctor, that on this occasion you were wrong?' Holt didn't respond. 'The hip bone found at the site could not have come from a woman in her forties. You accept that.'

'Yes.'

'The bones could have been there fifty years as easily as two.' He responded yes again. 'And a broken femur could be post-mortem damage.' Yes again. Garrison spoke softly, without cruelty. 'And it would have been useful to check the X-ray of Mattie Hamilton's broken femur with the X-ray of the skeleton found in the chapel.' Dr Holt nodded and said yes, so quietly he had to repeat it.

'So, I'm wondering, Dr Holt, how we can possibly think it's Mattie Hamilton in the crypt.'

'Yes, it's quite probably not Professor Hamilton, when you put it that way.'

The charges were dropped. Jack Champion was on his way to let Ted know. He caught Harriet on the steps. 'Dugald Charmer died last night in hospital. Heart attack coupla days ago.'

'Maybe we'll never know what happened to her,' Harriet said.

'I know what happened,' he said. 'We mighta had the wrong skeleton but we didn't have the wrong defendant. Ted

Dawes killed his wife, Harriet. She hasn't used a bank account or credit card for two years. And her bag of stuff was in that church. I'm going to come after your guy one way or another.'

'You're wrong, Jack,' Harriet said. But in truth, she didn't know what had happened to Mattie Hamilton. Admittedly, Ted hadn't jumped for joy at the news of the outcome. Garrison told her that when he'd phoned, Ted had said he needed time to think. Perhaps he was in shock, Garrison suggested, or wondering now, if it wasn't Mattie Hamilton down in the crypt, where Mattie was.

CHAPTER
FIFTY-TWO

Just at the moment Harriet wished she knew where Mattie
Hamilton was, Mattie herself was deciding to come
home. It had been a sobering experience, life-changing,
to watch her memorial service via satellite, attended by so
many of her friends and her family. And now the news that
Ted had killed her. It was preposterous, little Ted a killer, but
there you are. On the net, she'd logged into the centre to
learn that Dugald Charmer was dying so there was no risk of
discovery. And Mattie had realised that what she wanted more
than anything in life was Ted.

Behind the wheel of the truck, a somewhat slimmer
Mattie Hamilton looked more like a commando on the way
to a manoeuvre than a scientist. She smiled to expose perfect
white teeth that contrasted with her tanned face and close
fitting jungle greens. 'It's up to you,' she said to her passenger.

'What you do is wrong,' Esperance said. 'Taking our
babies.' Just then she had a contraction and told Mattie to
hurry up.

Mattie's eyes were bluer than they'd been before she'd left,
her vision clearer, and she glowed with the stinking heat and

her mission. She'd found her own kind of heaven here, where she could play her own kind of god. 'Esperance, darling, we've talked about this. You want your baby, you keep your baby, I don't want it. But I know a couple in Australia who long for a child, a father who cried in my office and paid thousands a pop for pipettes of sperm and eggs that did nothing. His poor wife spat them out of herself as quick as we could put them in. Thousands of dollars, Esperance, enough to print the paper for another year without help, enough to go away with Jean if that's what you want.' Jean was the father of Esperance's baby, a French citizen caught in another nation's troubles. Mattie rested her cigar in the truck ashtray as she pulled hard to turn a corner.

It was maths to Mattie. There were women here who were having babies they didn't want. Women in the resistance, women with large families, young girls. There were couples back in Australia whose loving hearts were broken by Mattie's inability to help them. She was a broker, a messenger, an angel bringing the good news. 'I think we have child for you,' she told the Australian agent. 'A beautiful little South American French girl. Exotic and healthy.' With Dugald Charmer dead, no one could pin anything on her. Selling children was illegal in Australia. God knows why. It was a service to all concerned. Not that it mattered, the truly righteous were above the law, she'd always believed that.

'Sweet girl,' Mattie said. 'But you must decide. It takes time to set these things up. I have a family ready for your little one.' Mattie put her about two centimetres dilated, plenty of time to get to the hospital.

'Oh! Should I see her, Mattie?'

'Up to you. I wouldn't. I'd go in there and give birth and walk away and never look back.' When Esperance left the hospital the next day Mattie said again, 'and never look back', as if the strength of her saying it would be enough. Esperance was betrayed by Jean and escaped to Australia to live with her mother and said she looked at her little girl every day and thanked the angels she'd changed her mind at the last minute.

As for Mattie, she was on the next plane home, winging her way back to Brisbane, and Archangels, and Ted.

CHAPTER
FIFTY-THREE

'I helped her get out,' Kevin McAnelly told Harriet and Marguerita. 'She had to go when Dugald Charmer threatened to expose the baby business. I arranged false papers. I never thought I'd see her again.' He smiled. 'She even made me hide her things so no one would recognise her if something happened. She had it all planned out. She was like that.'

'Why didn't she just take them with her?' Marguerita asked.

'She said if she died over there, she wanted to be anonymous.'

Out the window in the quad it was raining softly. When Harriet had seen Ted after his release, he'd been quiet, in shock she supposed, and then Mattie had called. As he was leaving, Ted had taken her hands in his. 'This doesn't change us,' he'd said, 'but I have to talk to her. Give me a few days.'

'Of course,' she'd said.

It had been three days and the quad was dull puddles. The rain hadn't stopped since she'd arrived. Harriet had seen them together. They walked a few metres apart with separate umbrellas. 'You must be Harriet,' Mattie had said as she grabbed Ted's arm. 'Ted's told me so much about you. You must come over for dinner. I'd love to talk to you.' Her voice made flesh was more mellow and rich than Harriet expected, experienced. 'Ted has always loved architecture.'

'Let's go, Mattie,' Ted said wearily. He looked helpless.

'Ted has always loved architecture,' Harriet said to herself after they'd gone.

'So she feeds the money into the research centre,' Harriet said to Marguerita now.

'That's right,' Marguerita said. 'Explaining their funny finances. And Frank, it seems, is willing to turn a blind eye so long as the money keeps coming in. Now Dugald's out of the way Mattie comes back.'

'Isn't it illegal?'

'Not in South America where she's working. The money's supposed to be to cover costs. It's a lot more than costs of course, but everyone wins, except the mothers and the babies, I guess. It's illegal here in Australia, thank God, and she'd be charged if she brought babies here.'

'Why didn't you say something to the police?' Harriet asked Kevin.

'What could I say? I come forward and say Mattie Hamilton is alive but I don't where she is. They'd laugh. I thought she'd see it on the news and come home. I never expected it to go so far, and the further it went, the less I could do.'

'Did Ted know Mattie was alive?' Harriet asked.

'No,' Kevin said.

'What about you and Mattie?' Marguerita asked him.

He hadn't tried to kiss Mattie Hamilton at all, he said. 'It was a misunderstanding.' Marguerita raised an eyebrow. He didn't bother telling them the truth. There was never any use defending himself against someone like Mattie Hamilton.

That day in Sydney, he'd gone to the house to collect her. She'd offered him a drink, which he'd declined. 'You think you're better than me, don't you?' she'd said.

'No, I just don't want a drink.'

She'd asked him to kiss her and he'd said no to that, too. 'Don't you like me?' she'd said. He'd told her that wasn't the point. 'I don't like you,' she'd said. 'Not a bit. You're sneaky and I don't trust you.' When Ted got home she'd cancelled her trip, she was in tears because, she said, Kevin had made advances. Ted had nodded in his quiet way. The next time they were alone, he told Kevin he wasn't to kiss Mattie. Kevin said he didn't kiss Mattie. Ted said that was good, and to make sure he didn't in future.

For weeks, Mattie had heckled Ted. 'Aren't you going to do something? Do you want me to put in a formal complaint?'

'No, I don't. I just want you to stop going on about it. Okay, so he tried to kiss you. I'm sorry, that's not my fault. He's a good driver.'

'He's a good driver. Ted, you're unbelievable,' Mattie said. And Ted guessed this was probably true, he was unbelievable, but by then he didn't know where he ended and the rest of the world started. He was on his way to becoming a vice-chancellor. He was unsure of everything.

'I won't pretend I'm glad she's back,' Kevin said to Harriet. 'I hate Mattie Hamilton, always have. I told her I wished she was dead.'

Harriet knew it would take Ted some time to sort things out. And she had to go back to Melbourne anyway for the weekend, to see Richard Corsair who wanted an explanation of the turn of events at Old Archangels.

CHAPTER
FIFTY-FOUR

'What I'm doing now, Ted, it makes me feel alive.'
'I nearly went to prison.'
'I didn't know, darling. And how could I come home? What would that have done to us?'

'To you, Mattie, it's what it would have done to you. I don't think my reputation could have suffered much more than it did. I've lost my job, everything.'

'All that can be fixed, Ted. And I can keep the business running, from here. You can't wear that with the brogues, darling.'

'I don't know if I want it fixed.'

'What do you mean?'

'I never thought I'd be able to live without all that stuff—the job, the status, those bloody suits. It's become so much a part of me, I thought it was me.'

'I don't understand.'

'No, I don't suppose you do.'

She laughed lightly. 'Don't worry, darling, it won't last.'

'And the parents of these babies you're selling?'

'Giving, darling, finding a home for, not selling. They don't want them. Most of them have seven or eight other kids already. They need the money. And my share goes straight back into our research. No one need know. We can go on as before, only I'll be in South America instead of Sydney. I need you, Ted, that's what I realised. And now Dugald's gone, I'm back in business.'

'When will we see each other?'

'I'll come home once a month. It's no different from how we used to be when we commuted Brisbane Sydney.'

'You've been gone two years. Don't you remember? We weren't doing that well when you left.'

'But it's different now, Ted.'

'What about Max?'

'What about him? That was nothing, I needed to reach out to someone. He started it.' Ted winced at her easy admission. Mattie threw her arms around his neck. 'But don't you see, darling? I've changed. It's changed me, watching these people. I've realised you're the one for me. I just know we can make a go of it. I want your baby, Ted.'

Mattie was staying at Ted's house, their house. He felt jammed in and couldn't catch his breath. Things were confused. Frank visited and he and Ted walked out on the verandah and watched the river. 'After everything that's happened, Ted, the Board would like to offer you your job back.'

'Well that's great, Frank. I don't know what to say.'

'I always had faith in you, Ted, I want you to know that. Max talked us all into the suspension. We can get rid of him if you like.'

'Yeah, I think that's a good idea. I don't want to see him.' He glared at Frank. 'At all.'

'Won't be cheap, but leave it with me. Mattie looks great, Ted. She and I talked. I want you to know it's all right with me.' So Mattie had told Frank.

'Well that's great, Frank. You know, Mattie and I have been apart for a long time.'

'I know that.'

'I'm just not sure how things will be between us now. And frankly, I really didn't expect her back.'

'No, I imagine you didn't.'

'Fact is, there's someone else in my life now.'

'We all have flings, Ted. But you're a powerful man with a highly successful future. With us. Mattie's your wife.'

'I know. You can't imagine how difficult this is. Just let me get this straight, Frank. Are you saying I don't get the job back unless I'm with Mattie?'

'Won't come to that, old boy. She loves you.' Ted didn't say anything. He didn't know anymore if Mattie loved him. Before she'd gone away she was bored with him. He wasn't strong enough, he was too quiet and in himself too much, he didn't warm enough to people. She could trot out her litany of complaints, and he agreed with everything she said, but that only made things worse because then she'd say he wasn't strong enough to stand up and disagree with her. Ted felt like his body was covered in a blanket and if he could only gather up enough strength to lift it off, things might be different. For a while he'd try to be more like she wanted, to think of things to tell her, things that would make her see he was open and able to change, and then she'd look at him as if she didn't know he existed. 'Hmm, darling,' she'd say. 'Oh that's nice.' It was true, since she'd been back, she'd been different. She'd smiled at him again like when they were young. She said she'd found what she wanted in life. And it was Ted, she said. And kids, Ted thought, his own kids.

CHAPTER
FIFTY-FIVE

Until she'd broken with Martin, Harriet had always loved to fly. As a girl her father took her on trips and she remembered late nights listening to pilots and engineers tell their stories, falling asleep with her head in Stan's lap in the haze of cigarettes and alcohol in airport lounges, him overexcited and animated by the stories he told, her wishing she could stay awake until they finished talking.

Harriet stopped travelling with her father when she started at St Pat's at the insistence of her mother's mother, who said she was getting too old for flitting around the country. On her last trip, they took a charter back to Sydney from country New South Wales. Harriet was thirteen. There was only one door into the plane and her father's group filled the small suffocating cabin, so she was allowed to sit up with the pilot, a Slavic boy who spoke English with precision. Both their faces were tinged green by the control deck lights and from the front they had an almost one-eighty degree view. The moon rose opaque through gunmetal clouds and left Harriet speechless for several minutes while the boy held her hand. Sydney wheeled into view and it seemed as if they were still and perfect up there in the sky while the city and its lights flew around beneath them. It was a significant moment of Harriet's youth in which she felt merged with everything, the pilot, the plane, the sky and the world.

As they fell from the sky to Brisbane, Harriet saw the diamond lights of the south bank moving fast in the blackness, the orange Story Bridge across the river, the tiny city centre, and felt, for the first time, she was coming home. She was not nervous as she listened for the big wheels that would cushion their drop to earth. The lights on the wing slowblinked out her window. They hit the tarmac easy.

Ted met the flight. 'They've offered me my old job back,' he told her.

'That's great.'

'Yeah, I can hardly believe it.'

'I've got some good news too. We just got a big contract here which means I can stay a while.' She threw her arms around his shoulders and stood on her toes to kiss his lips. He took her arms down and held her two hands in front of him.

'Well that's great.'

Harriet was no fool. She'd been here before. She could make it easy for Ted. She could say, 'So Ted, I get the impression you want to tell me something.' But she was sick of making things easy for people like Ted.

'Harriet, I really want us to stay friends,' he said across the coffee table in her apartment after their silent journey in his big car. She nodded but said nothing. She looked at his eyes, which were watching seconds go by on his watch. 'Mattie wants to get back together.' His eyes lifted towards her face and dropped again before they met hers. 'And the Board's giving me my job back is conditional.'

'I see.'

'And I want.' He stopped. 'I think it's for the best.'

'Of course,' Harriet said. 'She's your wife after all.'

'I need some time to work things out.'

'Sure, Ted,' she said. 'Don't fret, I'm not the sort who'll make trouble for you. I have no claim on you, not that I ever felt I did. I have no reason to want to, to want anything, anything at all. I think it's great. I'm happy for you.' She stopped looking at him because she no longer trusted herself. Instead she watched her hands on the table, they were clenched and white. Tears ran down her face but she remained otherwise composed as he left her.

CHAPTER
FIFTY-SIX

Harriet arrived at Archangels early the next morning prepared for the worst. Ted might be back, but Max and Martin were still running Old Archangels. She dragged her feet to the top of the hill and looked down towards the chapel, expecting it to be no more. Instead she saw hundreds of candles like stars flickering in the dawn breeze. She could see the shapes of bodies emerging from inside the chapel. The spirits of the Redemption sisters had returned to protect their sacred site. They were singing.

She heard Neal's voice behind her. 'Ho, HD, the National Trust's come through. Must be a hundred protestors down there. The "Seven-Thirty Report", too. They want to interview you.' Behind him, Marguerita Standfast looked as if she hadn't been long out of bed. Harriet looked from Neal to Marguerita and back. On the way down the hill she said to Marguerita quietly, 'Fuck the lawyer and get away with anything?'

'Where do I sign?' Marguerita said.

Outside the chapel Trust members had set up cake stalls and a coffee urn. Inside, a small group of them sang softly to guitar accompaniment. 'Kumbaya My Lord'. 'Five Hundred Miles'. 'Country Roads'. This was day three, Neal said. They'd stopped the work. 'Now Ted Dawes is back, maybe he'll stop them for good.'

'Don't bank on it,' Harriet said. She faced the interviewer. I can do this, she told herself. 'This is nothing short of a criminal act,' she told the camera. 'We have here the oldest church in Brisbane that's still standing. And it is standing, steady as a rock. We have a great history of Queensland women who carved out a life for themselves in a new settlement and transformed the education of women. And we have this precious place to remind us all that we're here for such a short time. We must not destroy these buildings with some horrible casino.' The singers came out of the chapel, and the hundred or so picketers linked arms and sang 'Be Not Afraid' for television. Sam D'Allessandro was among them.

'What are you doing here?' Harriet said.

'I don't have to agree with them in my spare time,' Sam said. 'I sort of like the old place.'

On a similar dawn almost fifty years before, Mother Damian ascended to Heaven beckoned by Our Lady the Virgin Mother of God. It was as fine a day as could be had in Brisbane summer. The lemon myrtle blossomed, and Damian went out to pray as she did every morning. She was sure the Virgin had changed this morning, imperceptibly for others perhaps but Damian's keen eyes had been watching for close on a century. To Damian, Our Lady was as different as the silky oak and bougainvillea on the drive. Deirdre Nolan wasn't the only one with visions.

Mother knew well enough to keep her visions to herself by then. When she'd tried to explain that Angelina had become part of the choirs of angels and was reunited with Michael in death as she'd never been in life, her sisters looked away. She tried to say that God was more just and merciful than she Damian could be. But they didn't understand.

On her last day on earth, Mother Damian sat under the rose trellis and watched as the hands of the Virgin Mother of God moved towards her to welcome her home. At first the old nun wanted to stay. The Education Department had very nearly closed the school. The bishop had remained obstinate. It was only the fact that Damian had been left an inheritance of sixty thousand pounds by Maria Di Maggio that they'd survived. There was still fifty thousand left and Damian knew she should use some of it to endow the scholarships for poor students Angelina wanted. She'd always meant to. But another block in Angel Square was a temptation. And now, to be called, when the best work was just beginning. It seemed unfair. The money sat in the ivory-inlaid document box she'd brought from Ireland. Her will had made clear what was to happen. Surely the new reverend mother would ensure it did.

The Virgin said, 'Be not afraid. One who comes after you will right what is wrong, exalt your name and the name of God who is goodness. In the name of the Father, the Son and the Holy Ghost.' On her left and right were Michael and Angelina, angels in the celestial hierarchy who decades later would do their very best for Ted and Harriet and their own souls. They walked down the hill to the river together and watched choirs of angels rejoice through the long day. And Mother Damian ascended to Heaven with Gerard at her side.

CHAPTER
FIFTY-SEVEN

A week later, Harriet sat under the rose trellis on the green garden seat where Mother Damian had sat on her last day at Archangels. There was flesh on the bones of the story now. Mother Damian, who'd given her whole life to something good, ended up doing something for which she probably felt shame. 'What I've done,' Damian wrote in a letter home that was never sent. 'What I've done. I made a decision today that will haunt me for the rest of my days.'

What she'd done was bury her little Angelina in an unconsecrated space without anointment. By now Harriet and Neil had contrived their story for what had happened at Archangels when Sister Mary Angelina died suddenly one night and Brother Michael O'Fallon disappeared. Harriet had been back in touch with Dr Skelly and they'd done a proper dig around the chamber and crypt. They'd found more bones and worked with Sister Mary Cecilia and Vincent to piece together the missing parts of the story.

Angelina's inheritance had finished the last of the new buildings and had meant the school stayed open and Mother

Damian never had cause again to fear the bishop. Damian created an edifice to the glory of God, and she covered up a crime. She lied and used bloody money to finish off her edifice. Harriet wondered at the goodness and badness of women.

Damian's rosary beads had been given to Angelina, her favourite novice, and this was confirmed by Sister Mary Cecilia. Vincent had confirmed that Damian had bought a pound note with her from her father in Ireland and had failed to surrender it to the order. It must have been hidden in the rosary purse. Harriet and Neal decided that in their final report, they'd say the love note was from Michael to Angelina or vice versa although they had no sample of either's handwriting. Who else could have written it? They told Sam D'Allessandro that the uncanny resemblance to the handwriting of Gerard O'Hare was just that, uncanny. Facts, Harriet had said, that's what we're after.

Later, Neal would find the rest of Angelina's fortune, fifty thousand pounds, locked in the ivory box Vincent had coveted, the box Harriet had seen in the convent archives on her first visit. The old pound notes together were now worth over five million dollars, and their rightful owners were the Sisters of the Blessed Redemption, who would be more than happy to buy back Archangels Chapel from the university and see it restored. The university for its part would remain open, put up its business building, and establish a scholarship scheme for needy students which Marguerita Standfast would take on with a vengeance.

When Harriet was sure Jack Champion had the last remains of the two lovers, she and Kevin McAnelly would arrange for them to come home and be buried in a new grave in the old Archangels graveyard. The small ceremony, midsummer, would be attended by a young Catholic priest who was the university chaplain, Neal, Harriet, Kevin McAnelly and Mrs O'Fallon, close to ninety and relieved to learn finally what had happened to her son. Their bones would be anointed and laid to rest. Their tombstone would read: 'Michael and Maria. And the greatest of these is love.'

Harriet was joined on the garden seat by the Virgin Mother of God who, with considerable decorum, had climbed down from her pedestal step by step and walked over, her stone robes rustling like fresh washed linen on a breezy day.

'I meant to get that fixed,' Harriet said, pointing to the Virgin Mother's left index finger which had been snapped off by one of the boys who'd taken Mary to the toilets and back some months before.

'Gives me character,' Our Lady said.

'There is that,' said Harriet.

'Aren't you wondering why I'm here?'

'I know why you're here. Mother Damian put you here. Mother Damian put us all here.'

'I mean here on the seat with you.'

'No, not really. Not much could surprise me now. I guess you know about Mattie.'

'Tell me anyway.'

'She was supposed to be down there in the church, and it's great she wasn't, because it meant Ted didn't kill her which would have been awful.' Harriet had read *Rebecca* when she was at uni. She wondered afterwards what to make of a story where the heroine's new husband had shot his first wife. She was sure there was something incorrect about liking *Rebecca*. But she'd liked it all the same. 'It was one thing in 1938 to stand by your man,' she said to the Virgin Mother of God. 'But now nothing's so clear.'

Anyway, thought Harriet, Jack Champion wouldn't have given Ted the chance to run off to the Continent if he really had killed Mattie. Jack had visited Harriet at New Farm after Ted was freed. 'Looks like I owe you an apology,' he'd said.

'Ted, not me,' she'd replied.

'Don't worry, I'm never frightened to admit I'm wrong,' Jack said. But he only admitted he was wrong because the evidence to the contrary, a living breathing Mattie Hamilton, was irrefutable. 'I've already seen him and apologised. He was gracious.'

'You should have been looking at the facts instead of making up stories,' Harriet said, rather hypocritically she thought only later.

'If you're hanging round a while,' Jack said, 'you could maybe come over our place for dinner or something. The wife's a great cook and my daughter's your age. She could show you round Brisbane.'

'I'd love to,' Harriet lied.

Back on the hill with the Virgin, Harriet said, 'Why do you always stand on top of a snake?'

'Evil. Stamping out evil.'

'I thought it was sex.'

'That's repressive,' Our Lady said.

'I'm not the virgin in child,' Harriet said in an attempt at humour. 'They say mine's the nihilistic generation, the generation lost between the baby boomers and the X-ers or something, we don't care about anyone but ourselves. We've lost the faith. We have no morality, believe in nothing, blame others. Well, if we do, it's all their fault.' When Our Lady didn't laugh, Harriet said, 'Get it, we're the blaming generation, but it's all their fault. That's blaming.' She smiled weakly. 'My grandmother says the only thing I can do better than her is hug people. It's not much, is it? Ted's gone back to Mattie. I'm going back to Melbourne. Archangels is going back to its future. At least the buildings will be safe now. I do think I should have got your hand fixed. That sort of thing isn't very professional. Typical of my generation.'

Mary smiled and put her damaged hand on Harriet's head. 'I like it this way,' she said. 'Blessed be you Harriet Darling, whose faith has been strong and whose heart is full to the brim with love. And blessed be God in Heaven, whose life is eternal and whose fuse is short.' Our Lady winked. 'I've told him to look after you,' she said.

He was standing in the alcove outside Harriet's door when she arrived home. 'I've been waiting for you a long time,' he said.

'What do you want?'

'Can I come in?'

'Did they sack you?' He shrugged.

A storm broke. The night was soft and cool. Afterwards, they slept like angels.

NO SAFE PLACE
Mary-Rose MacColl

Shortlisted for the *Australian*/Vogel Literary Award

' . . . an excellent achievement . . . a polished stone of enduring value.'

Australian Book Review

Adele Lanois is Registrar of Walters University and chief investigator in a sexual misconduct case. A lone woman in a powerful institution, Adele is unsure of herself, unsure of her colleagues and increasingly unsure that anything in her life is quite as it seems.

A novel about sex, power and personal responsibility, *No safe place* is a contemporary thriller with the unexpected at every turn.

1 86448 174 9